Also by Owen Mullen

PI Charlie Cameron Books:

Games People Play
Old Friends and New Enemies
Before the Devil Knows You're Dead
And So it Begins
In Harm's Way

Praise For Owen Mullen

Clever book with great character development." **Janice Lombardo – reviewer**

"Wow! Atmospheric dark gripping and brilliant." **Sarah Hodgson – reviewer**

"an excellent novel, part cop thriller and part study of human relationships." **Chris Nolan – reviewer**

"If you like a good detective thriller you'll love this one." **Annie Belford – reviewer**

"A truly believable story of misconceptions and being alone even when you are with your loved ones." **Breakaway Reviewers**

A dark, gritty and suspenseful thriller that tickles the taste buds to the max and another cracking read from Owen Mullen! Keep up the good work. **– David's Book Blurg**

The plot is dark and Mackenzie's ordeal is terrifying, the scenes are graphic, written very realistically. **– Between the Lines Book Blog**

…an intriguing and dark read which once again proves that Owen Mullen is an author who is always on the lookout for new directions to take with his characters, his plots and his novels. **– Chapter in my Life**

Out Of The Silence

Owen Mullen

'A man first loves his son, then his camel, and then his wife.'
Arab proverb

To Devon and Harrison Carney

1998
National Press Awards,
The Dorchester, Mayfair

A rainy evening in London: from the window, Hyde Park is grey and forbidding in the fading light, as unwelcoming as the sweltering heat of the subcontinent the day I stepped off the plane, hungover and fortunate to still have a job.

This city used to be my home. Tonight I feel like a stranger – worse – an imposter; a teller of half-truths.

But they asked me, so I came.

Not long ago, I would have relished an occasion like this and the ballyhoo that goes with it. I see it differently now. Soon, we'll go downstairs, have dinner with colleagues, listen to speeches from the great and the good of the newspaper world, and applaud in the right places. Towards the end, I'll be called on to say a few words and accept an award for something I rejected until a pretty face persuaded me to take a second look.

In my wildest dreams I couldn't have imagined the reaction the piece would provoke, or the praise it would receive. Some have called me courageous for putting my name to it. That makes me smile. There was courage, certainly, but it wasn't mine. Nothing changed because of me: I was the one who was changed.

The truth about what really happened will always be a mystery. I have my own ideas, of course: Jameel and Gulzar; Doctor Simone Jasnin; Ali and Idris; and the irredeemable Dilawar Hussein family, all carried a part of it.

I never knew Afra, yet she spoke to me. She speaks to me still. I owe her my life.

It began in a Punjab village, a dusty settlement miles from the road, and ended in the city of Lahore. Not the story that brought me here, this story – the one I didn't write.

Rural Punjab
One year earlier

Nurse Idris Phadkar's shift had been uneventful. Now it was almost over. Out here the air was warm and heavy, the monsoon was coming. She walked as far as a giant jacaranda standing guard at the edge of the hospital compound and gazed at the stars, enjoying the time alone. Idris was twenty-four, petite, unmarried, and at a crossroads in her life.

At first, she thought what she'd heard was an animal, a rat perhaps. The Punjab was full of rats and everything above and below them in the food chain. She heard it again, closer than before. The nurse panicked and ran for the hospital lights. In the darkness, she tripped and crashed to the ground, winded and shaking. A sound nearby rekindled her fear. She stifled a scream, afraid to move, and waited for her breath to return. Idris felt something against her feet. She screwed up her courage and let her fingers search the grass.

It wasn't an animal; it was a woman.

***

Doctor Simone Jasnin marked the shredded clothing, the dust and the blood, and heard the tortured sounds escaping the lips. It was essential to establish how bad the woman's injuries were but her position made it difficult; a salwar and a kamiz covered her torso.

'Easy. You're safe now. Easy.'

The nurses stood by the door. She caught them looking at each other. Had they injured this patient bringing her in? That better not be the case. The doctor moved to the other side of the bed and immediately understood why they were subdued.

She bent, reluctant to believe what she was seeing. One side of the face was almost without feature, livid and white. An eye was missing, leaving a covering of bloodied film in its place. Some of the nose definition had been lost too, and part of her lips had melted together. Where the hairline should have been, a scorched raw mass extended into the scalp. At the edges, singed strands of hair fell over the vanished skin. The pain must be beyond imagining.

An acid attack.

She'd seen several, never as bad as this. Acid attacks on women were not uncommon in rural areas where wives were considered the property of their husbands without rights of any kind. Reports of these atrocities were on the increase.

'Morphine! Now! Now!'

The doctor completed her diagnosis. On the woman's wrist she noticed six carved rounds of dark wood. They'd survived the attack better than their owner. The poor creature lying scarred and broken had been the subject of a prolonged and vicious assault: raped and beaten. The extent of internal damage was as yet unknown and her throat was bruised.

After all she'd gone through someone had tried to strangle her. It was a miracle she was alive, though it was impossible to say for how much longer. What could anyone have done to deserve this?

In the following days, the woman was kept sedated. The doctor thought of her often. Who was she? Where was she from? What had happened to her? And how had she managed to get to the hospital?

The local police were called and didn't respond. They weren't interested.

***

Simone lifted the telephone on its first shrill ring.

'She's regaining consciousness, Doctor.'

'I'll come at once.'

She replaced the receiver and pinched the sides of her nose. Good news in other times. This time no, not good news at all.

She hadn't ever wanted someone to die. Even when there was no hope she did what she could; efficient, effective, detached. But for the last four nights the woman in her had won over the medic and she'd wished, hard and often, that this one would slip away. Simone was shocked by the effect the case was having on her. Her professional disinterest was little more than a veneer, and a doctor who shared their patient's pain needed to find another line of work.

The light from the lamp on her desk more than filled the book-lined box. It was cramped, yet she liked it. Just as well, half her working life was spent here.

She had arrived at the hospital to find neither desk nor office, not even a cupboard with her name on it. Simone hadn't been discouraged. She knew the way of it. She was a woman in a man's world: a woman in Pakistan.

At thirty-two, the only child of a French mother and a Pakistani father, she had her mother's high cheekbones, her father's deep brown eyes and the intellect of both. Long black hair and perfect teeth, skin lightly coloured and unblemished; Simone Jasnin was a beautiful woman, fluent in French, English and Punjabi. Her first seventeen years were spent in Lahore, the thousand-year-old capital of the Punjab, where Shah Jahan, creator of the Taj Mahal, built the Shalimar Gardens. The young Simone had often walked with her father in its marble pavilions, through its terraces, past the many cool fountains, listening while he told the history of the Mogul emperors as if it had been yesterday and he'd known them personally.

How she'd devoured the glories of the past, determined to keep pace with his longer stride, her small hand lost in his, while he explained the architectural legacy from a time when reverence for art and beauty was at its height.

The memory made her sad. Because, like her father, that civilisation was gone.

She took her white coat from its door-peg hanger and shrugged it on, dreading what would come next.

she's regaining consciousness, Doctor

Simone sat on the edge of her desk. She wouldn't leave yet. She wasn't ready. Another minute would make no difference. Her gaze fell on the picture in a simple wooden frame, a tall man and a smiling girl. The adult curved a protective arm round the child's shoulders. She leaned in, accepting the safety. Simone looked at her father – if only she could speak to him now. His deep confident voice would coax her to find the courage she lacked, to recognise herself, and be the person on the nametag: Doctor Simone Jasnin.

When he died, her mother struggled to cope with things that had been of little consequence to her before – the heat, the culture, and, of course, the loneliness. They arrived together one day, and from then on life in her husband's country was no longer bearable. Going back to a world she understood had been an easy decision. The French capital was familiar, and to her teenage daughter, it was the beginning of a dream. The aesthetic brilliance of the Shalimar Gardens was no match for the clubs and discos near the Rue Saint-Germain.

It had been wonderful and soon her life in Asia might have been something Simone had been told, by her father maybe, on one of their walks. Memory faded, but it didn't die, and sometimes in August when the city sweltered, the tree-lined boulevards reminded her of Lahore. If she closed her eyes, she could smell roses mingled with jasmine, and hear the childlike cry of wild peacocks.

Four years after she qualified, her mother died. Then the city seemed to her as Lahore had once seemed to her mother – dirty and vexatious; no longer home. She took the traditional route through grief, burying herself in her work, though its point had been blunted. The return to where she'd lived as a child was a return to purpose.

And here she was, sitting on the edge of a rickety desk at 3am, in a cramped excuse for a medical resource in the Punjab, struggling to function. Simone chastised herself. 'Do your job, stupid. Give help don't need it.'

She crossed the courtyard separating the administration offices from the ward. Lightning flashed in the distance, a dog barked, and miles away, another answered. Dogs bark at night. In Pakistan dogs barked all night. She entered the low whitewashed building where the corrugated roof made sleep impossible during the rainy season, keeping as quiet as possible. A few patients stirred. How strange, the incessant barking disturbed no one yet a muffled footstep – hardly a sound at all – brought some to the edge of consciousness. At the end, past the last beds, were two rooms. Doctor Simone drew a heavy breath and opened the door on the left. Two people were inside, a nurse – the one who had telephoned – and the tiny figure in the bed.

Simone said, 'When did she start to come round?'

'About two-forty she moved and spoke. A few minutes ago, she spoke again and tried to turn.'

The nurse offered the clipboard progress chart. Simone dismissed it with a shake of her head. It was a prop. A useless piece of hospital procedure.

'What did she say, did you hear?'

'Yes, she called out a name. Jameel.'

***

The woman was on her back under the crisp white clothes, a tangle of wires running from her body to the monitors at the side of the bed. The left side of her face was hidden by a dressing but she was awake. The doctor smiled a reassurance she didn't feel. 'Don't try to move. Everything's all right. You're safe here.'

The single eye stared.

'You've had an accident. We'll take care of you.'

It sounded lame. Jasnin was embarrassed by it. The woman said nothing.

'Lie still, I'm here.'

'Please, I have to tell you.'

'I think it would be better – '

'Please.' Her voice was a whisper. 'If you want to help me, listen.'

This might be her last wish.

'Listen, and write down what I say. Please, Doctor.'

Simone was going to do whatever her patient wanted. She turned to the nurse. 'Go to my office. Bring paper.'

'How much?'

'Just bring it. Quickly.'

The patient stared at the wall. Simone felt uncomfortable with the silence, though not as uncomfortable as hearing herself spew obvious untruths, all starting or ending with "everything's all right". The sister returned with a box and set it on the floor.

'You can go. I'll take it from here.'

She pulled up the only chair and took out a pen.

'How long before the pain becomes too much?'

'Fifty minutes, an hour – it's hard to say. Is that enough?'

'It will have to be. My family have to know what happened to me. Send what you write to my village. To my mother, to Fatimah and little Shafi.'

'Jameel?'

The half-face showed no surprise. 'No, not Jameel. He must never know.'

Outside a dog barked and in the room, Simone readied herself.

'I'll tell you about my life. How I came to this. I am *kari*: black woman. In Lahore they will say I dishonoured them. It wasn't so. When my family thinks of me they must remember that once everything was good.'

The doctor poised to begin. She looked at the pitiable figure in the bed and the tear rolling down the destroyed face.

The woman said, 'My name was Afra.'

Simone began to write.

***

On the porch outside her office watching the sun come up, the doctor had never needed a cigarette so badly. A drink would be even better. The story she'd just heard shocked her. Afra had finally succumbed to the pain. The drugs would give her release, for a while.

But what release for Simone Jasnin? Where was that to be found?

Her beliefs had altered forever. As she wrote, her father's vision – the epic tales of the past, even ideas about her fellow-man – were swept away. She'd been a fool to believe them.

What good was ancient splendour set against present misery? What good were rulers who allowed injustice to go unpunished?

She was sad, sad for herself. Her world was not as it had seemed and never would be again. Sad for Afra, who would probably die, and soon if there was mercy. And sad for the country, disgraced by cowardice masquerading as honour.

The woman might live – anything was possible – but what kind of life could she have? Simone threw the last of the cigarette into the dark. Soon a new day would speak its name but who would speak for this poor woman? Who would care? Who would cry?

Who would avenge her?

Part One
The Road to Lahore

Chapter 1

Mundhi village, Southern Punjab
Eleven years earlier

The evening sun was warm as it began its descent into night over the lands to the east of the Indus River, a place rich in history passed on in songs, epic tales and romances. Seventy million people lived between the North West Frontier, the foothills of the Himalayas, and the northern edge of the Thar Desert and Rajasthan in India.

Jameel Akhtar was one of them.

The boy neither knew nor cared about the Punjab's glorious past. His thoughts were with the girl walking beside him. By day, he was obsessed with her, and at night, she dominated his dreams. To him she was the world. The most beautiful girl in Mundhi village. He planned to marry her.

Her name was Afra and she held her head high, scanning the darkening horizon where slashes of blue and grey, orange and red, overlapped in fantastic competition. Every evening, the same procession of men and women returning from tending the sugar and rice crops could be seen throughout the region. The couple strolled, yards apart, Jameel kicking stones in lieu of conversation. Talking to a girl wasn't easy, they were so different.

Afra did nothing to release him from his awkwardness. She was amused by it, and, though no words were spoken, she knew what was going on with her handsome companion.

Jameel glanced at her face, amazed by its contours and the texture of her skin, warmed by the light that seemed to radiate from within. When she looked at him her eyes were deep and wise and kind. Jameel loved her the way a teenage boy anywhere loves his girl. Except she wasn't his. Life didn't work like that here.

She smiled. His heart soared.

Ahead lay the outline of the compact settlement, the domed roof of the mosque in the centre of the village, more distinct than the houses, marking the focus of life in Mundhi. Soon they'd pass under the arched gateway and go their separate ways – Jameel to the house left to him by his mother, Afra to her family.

He kicked at another stone. A cloud of dust rose and fell to the red earth path. Afra knew he'd speak and say the same thing he said every evening. She waited for the familiar question, ready with the well-worn reply.

Jameel pretended to be interested in the stone and followed its progress through the short grass. He shuffled, tense, prepared for rejection. Afra frowned, bemused by his performance. How long had this been going on? How many times had they walked home in a group, laughing and joking, or together in the straggling line of weary villagers? The answer was since they were children. And it would continue like this maybe all their lives.

'Will I see you tomorrow?'

His anxiety perplexed her. They lived in Mundhi, where each day was like the one before, no different from the one after.

'Jameel, why do you ask? Yes, of course. What other answer is there?'

Her voice was sharper than she intended; she sounded cross. Inside, the boy died a little. Could she really not know? Did she really not understand?

The exchange made them strangers. And the girl did understand; she understood too well, that was the problem. Jameel was certain, she was less sure. Of course she was fond of him. He protected her even when there was no danger and made her laugh at his silly jokes, but he was Jameel, just a village boy. Anyway, she had no choice. When the time came her mother would decide, and her ideas, reinforced by centuries of tradition, were mindless of notions of love.

***

Afra's words lay between them as they passed under the arch, leaving the flat verdant plain, broken by trees, and the glint of fading sunlight on irrigation channels behind. 'Tomorrow then?'

'Tomorrow,' she replied, and took the farming tools from him. He hesitated, reluctant to part, then relaxed his grip on the rusty implements and allowed her to have them. She strode to the other side of the compound, clasping the tools, wondering why she felt low.

Her family lived in a house similar to the other houses in Mundhi. Behind a door was a courtyard where their animals were tethered. Two rooms ran off it – a bedroom and a main room where they ate and talked, and where her mother slept on a covered wooden seat converted into a bed each night. The door was ajar. She opened it and her jaw fell in a silent scream.

Shafi stood against the wall, a pool of water gathering on the floor at his feet. Eight-year-old Fatimah was between her brother and a dog. Afra had seen the animal outside the compound, purposeless and lost, wobbling on shaky legs. She knew the dogs in the village; this was a stranger. The mongrel would have been unmemorable in other circumstances, the Punjab had tens of thousands just like it, except not quite.

This one was rabid.

White foam balled at its mouth. It staggered and bared its teeth. Eventually it would strike. Bite and keep on biting. Afra had heard that victims drifted in and out of consciousness, violent and deranged, until death released them. But worse, in brief moments of lucidness they realised what was happening.

Her family would die in this room.

Her fingers scrabbled for the door and found its rough surface. She drew it open and screamed as she'd never screamed, long and loud.

'Jameeeeeeeelll!'

The dog looked through a bloodshot glaze. Its teeth ground together as a deep growl came from its throat. The stand-off was drawing to a close. Another scream would send it into frenzied attack. Suddenly, the door jarred her hand and cracked against the wall. Out of the corner of her eye she saw him.

Jameel hadn't walked away. When Afra went inside, his eyes followed her. Even then he didn't go, he stayed, wondering the way every man at some time did, why one small show of impatience could leave him ruined. He was searching for the answer when he heard the cry.

The fever in the canine's brain made it unpredictable. And indecisive. It didn't strike. The crazed head moved from side to side. Shafi whimpered; he wouldn't hold on much longer. Jameel pulled the cloth from the bed and threw it over the animal, scooped it off the floor and ran out the door, across the yard and through the arch, hauling the snarling material behind him to the old well a hundred yards from Mundhi. In the past, it had supplied water for the village. No one used it now.

Jameel swung the insane parcel away from his body, letting its momentum carry it clear of the stone wall around the waterhole. The cover fell into the darkness and disappeared.

In the house the scene had changed. The siblings huddled together, holding each other, crying. Then they threw their arms around Jameel. Little Shafi held on to his leg. So this was what it was like to be a hero.

Later, when everyone had calmed, he went outside. Afra went with him to where they'd parted bad friends. He saw her tear-stained face. 'Tomorrow then?'

'Tomorrow,' she said and watched him go. Jameel: just a village boy. Only now she felt the way her mother had when her father was alive. Was it possible she'd been blind to his worth all this time, and it had taken a mangy dog to make her see.

***

She stood in the yard to the front of the house, dipping her hand into a brown cloth bag slung round her waist, bringing out seeds and scattering them over the low wire fence and across the flattened earth. As always, the hens ran clucking and scratching after the tiny pieces.

In a corner, tethered to the wall, Uncu – the family donkey – witnessed the commotion without interest. At the hottest part of the day, he lay in the shade, out of the glare.

Afra spoke to the clamouring birds. 'Easy, easy. I've enough for all of you. Don't worry. No need to fight. You! Let the others have their turn. See, there's more.'

The hens preferred to squabble. Afra's mother stayed inside the door. Not the mother her daughter recalled, who had encouraged her children and inspired their interest through a thousand examples and explanations as she taught them about the world.

That mother had gone. Without her the family, like Uncu, lived life out of the sun.

A tired, careworn woman, older than her years, was in her place, her mind always on something she didn't share.

They weren't poor. Their house was comfortable, with a ceiling-fan for the hot summers, a refrigerator and a television. The source of her anxiety was fundamental: they lacked a man.

She remembered them carrying his body from the fields, the unlined face showing no trace of pain. The night before they'd made love, quietly so the children wouldn't hear. In the morning, they'd laughed, not knowing it was their last time together.

Since then, she'd lived with more than loneliness. It would be years before Shafi could take his father's place. And the girls, what of them? She and Tahir had married in love, chosen each other and been happy. Her parents may have picked Tahir for her anyway because he was the right choice. Now she was alone. Her daughters dreamed of a man to fall in love with. Well, that would never be.

They'd be married by arrangement, and the bride price – first with Afra, and later with Fatimah – would keep the terrible fate so many women in her situation endured, at bay.

She was sad for them. But life was sometimes sad. Who knew that better than her?

Chapter 2

Three years later

The hens chased the last fistful of seeds and each other, squawking and bickering. Afra shook her head. Stupid birds. No matter how often food was brought they learned nothing, preferring to fight, never at peace and always wanting more.

In the village compound, Fatimah and Shafi were playing with Jameel. He'd become their older brother; they trusted him and loved him, just like her. She heard Fatimah and Shafi giggling, trying to catch him and failing – Jameel was too fast and strong. Shafi was ten now and small for his age. He fell.

Afra shouted. 'Careful, Shafi.' Nobody heard. The frantic chase ended when Jameel tumbled under arms and legs and laughter. 'Enough! Enough!'

'We win!' Shafi raised his arms in victory. 'Told you! Told you!'

Jameel sat on the ground, grinning. Sweat ran down his face. He clapped clouds of dust from his trousers. Afra said, 'They'll kill you, you're too old.'

The children went off on a new game, one with no rules, a lot of running about and screaming. Afra chastised them. 'You'll hurt yourselves then we'll have tears.'

'You're wrong, I'm not old, not yet, though time won't wait for me.'

Fatimah whispered in her brother's ear, her eyes blazing with excitement. 'Okay? Ready? One. Two. Three. Afra and Jameel! Afra and Jameel! Afra and Jameel!'

Afra pretended to start after them. They ran away, giggling. 'Those rascals. Sorry about that.'

'But they're right. Our names are on people's lips, even children's. I don't want to go on as we are.'

'What do you mean?'

'I'll speak with your mother if that's what we want. Is it?' His eyes filled with hope. 'If it isn't, tell me.'

The youngsters reached new heights of hysteria, Afra made a mental note to bring the horseplay to a close; they'd had their fun. 'I want what you want.'

'Then I'll ask.'

In Mundhi, space was a precious thing. The family slept in the same room. One day their mother had announced that in future she would make her bed next door. No one asked why. The children wrangled over how the beds should be divided. Afra wouldn't have minded being alone sometimes except Fatimah considered it an honour to be close to her older sister. And if Shafi worshiped Fatimah, Fatimah adored Afra, seeing in her everything she wanted to be. Afra indulged her. At night, the girls lay under their rough blanket and talked, sharing all kinds of secrets.

Shafi called across the room. 'Fatimah! Fatimah!'

The girl got out of bed and crept to his cot to soothe his monsters away. Calling for his sister in the night was common; they'd shared the same bed most of the boy's life. Any change left him feeling alone and afraid. Fatimah crept back under the blankets and snuggled against Afra. 'He's all right, the dark scares him sometimes. He'll sleep soon.'

Afra was touched by the little mother lying next to her. The bond was strong between her and her brother. She loved Shafi too, and he loved her, but his devotion he kept for Fatimah.

'Your head is older than your body, sister.'

They laughed. The old bed shook. When their giggling subsided they lay quiet.

Fatimah said, 'Will you marry Jameel?'

'I hope so.'

'If you marry him I'll see you every day.' She rushed on, lost in her vision of tomorrow. 'You'll live in Mundhi. Don't go away from me. Don't go away from us. We need you, we'll always need you.'

Though she couldn't see her face, Afra knew Fatimah's eyes were wide, asking her to reassure her the way she had with Shafi. She kept her voice low and took her sister's hands in hers.

'Wherever you are I am. And wherever I am, you are too.'

'Again, so I'll never forget.'

'Wherever you are I am. And wherever I am you are too.'

***

Jameel rose later than usual – he wouldn't be going to the fields today. He fed the animals, thought about breakfast then changed his mind. He wasn't hungry. He was too nervous to eat. It could be put off no longer. He had to speak to Afra's mother and today was the day.

The sun had already begun its daily safari. Early morning, with the cool of night still in the air, when the world looked clean and clear, was Jameel's favourite time. On a morning like this it was easy to be optimistic. Instead, his insides rolled, his legs trembled and he felt sick in his stomach. A dozen times he banished the feeling, while he washed and dressed in a white kurta and loose-fitting pyjamas. When he was ready he sat on his bed. It was too early to be visiting, those not working in the fields would still be at their chores and anyway, he needed to think. He looked around at his mother's house, his house now; was it right to expect Afra to share a home smaller and less comfortable than her own?

His father died when Jameel was a baby leaving his mother with the task of ensuring they both survived. She honoured the responsibility at a cost. Year after year of grinding labour wore her out. But her son lived.

The end came quickly. Old before her time, her body had no resistance to the pneumonia. Too ill to work, she reluctantly took to her bed. From then, Jameel watched her slip out of the world as quietly as she walked through it. Could he be asking his beautiful Afra to repeat his mother's life?

He sat with his chin resting on his knees and gazed at his universe. This and the stretch of land outside the village – a legacy from his grandfather – was all he could boast. So little in the eyes of the world.

He thought of the woman guiding him through the first years of his life, refusing to recall her ashen face, fevered and frail. One evening she called him. 'Jameel, there's something I want you to do.'

The boy had learned it was better if he didn't question her.

'On the floor in the space where I keep my clothes you'll find a cloth and a letter. Bring them to me.'

He found them, they weren't hidden; an envelope with faded writing on the front, and a dull red and grey square of material tied in a parcel. Young Jameel had picked them up and carried them to the bed. The cloth clunked. She thanked him in a rasping whisper.

'This letter is important. It's from my mother's brother in Lahore. He was a village boy like you. Now he's a successful businessman with a restaurant in the city. If you ever need a place to go, go to him.'

She repositioned herself and pulled on one corner, loosening the knot. She smiled. 'See this.'

Blue-veined hands unwrapped the treasure. Jameel moved closer, spellbound by the performance. His mother drew the rag aside to reveal the secret. Thirteen-year-old Jameel felt her excitement, and with the last fold removed, the mystery was laid bare.

'There. Aren't they the most beautiful things?'

Her son tried not to show his disappointment. On the white sheet lay pieces of wood, round and carved. His mother's eyes welled with tears, not of sadness, tears of joy.

'Do you know what this is?' She shifted her gaze from the prize to his face. 'I wasn't always as you see me now. I was beautiful.'

Jameel thought his mother was going to cry but no, she was savouring the moment from a time he'd never known: a past she'd never left. Her outstretched fingers found the wipe at the side of the bed and dabbed the perspiration on her brow with a bony hand.

She patted the bed. 'Jameel, come closer. Sit here. Sit by me. I've a story to tell, and though it means nothing to you now, it will. You'll be a man then and you'll understand.'

Jameel edged forward. His mother called on the last of her strength and spoke, clear and unhurried; for a time almost well again.

'I remember the first time I saw your father so clearly it might have been yesterday. I'd seen him before of course because our families lived in the village, but the first time I really saw him he was walking alone from the fields. Everyone else had returned to the village. Tahir had kept on working. His head was bowed; he was weary. Back then, he was young and strong and handsome. Oh, so handsome! I puzzled why I'd never noticed this before. It couldn't have happened overnight. Something must have changed to make him so manly. Now I know the change was in me not him. He crossed the high land with the sun falling behind him, looking to where I stood, and went on to Mundhi. Later, I often asked him if he saw me. He always answered no. Tiredness had dulled his mind, he said. All he saw was a warm bed and sleep. It would have suited the girl I was if he had answered yes, of course, but a man like Tahir had no need to lie about his love, he showed it in a hundred ways, even on our last morning.

'I watched him. He was watching too. For months we went on with this delightful nonsense until we met on the path south of the village. People use a million words when they speak of love, yet real love just is. Someday you'll know.'

Behind the hollow eyes and parchment pallor Jameel glimpsed a girl. Time was cruel indeed.

'One night Tahir and his mother – your grandmother – came to my father's house. I was sent out with my brother and ordered to stay away. I didn't hear what they said. Eventually, I returned, cold and tired, to find everyone acting as if I'd said something clever and they were pleased with me. We married. Later, we were blessed with you.'

She paused, drained. 'And so to this.' She nodded at the pieces of wood. 'Your father's family had nothing: no money or cattle and little land.' She spoke without bitterness or pity. 'But he had a love for me the strength of ten. More than enough for one life. On our wedding night he presented me with these.'

She lifted the bundle of ebony rounds and counted. 'One, two, three, four, five…ten, eleven, twelve. Twelve, six for each wrist.'

The boy wanted to be impressed.

'These are hand-carved bangles. A set, two sets in fact. They belonged to your grandmother, given to her by your grandfather, and to him by his mother. They're very old and very precious. Not in the way the world measures value, the way the heart weighs such things.'

The effort was becoming too much; a new attack of fever gathered on her brow.

Jameel tried to inspire her to health. 'Put them on, mother.'

Her eyes closed. Her chest rose and fell. 'Your father's love and your grandfather's, and even before them is in this wood. Now they're yours.'

Jameel said, 'Let me see you wear them.'

The woman smiled. 'I did wear them. For many happy years I wore them. The bangles have new work to do. Your grandmother believed they have the power to bring lovers together. Then the charms move on to unite others who need their help. As time passed, I knew it was true.'

She clasped her son's hand in a feeble grip. 'This is my gift to you. Choose well and when you give them to your girl she'll love you forever. It can be no other way. Tell her the story. Girls like stories about love. And believe. We are what we believe we are, Jameel.'

He refolded the cloth and tiptoed from the room. His mother drifted to sleep, wasted to nothing; tiny under the sheet. What a story. Not exactly the treasure he'd hoped for. Thoughts of girls and love would come to Jameel Akhtar, but not yet.

***

He slid off the bed, alarmed to see he had creased his new white kurta.

Remembering the story made him want to check. The bundle was on the floor just as he'd left it and he had no doubt who would wear them.

He could put it off no longer. Jameel straightened his clothes in a final unnecessary gesture and set off. Afra's mother saw him across the village. His crisp outfit told her all she needed; he was coming to see her. She would have preferred to avoid the conversation they were about to have but wouldn't shrink from it. This boy had risked his life to save her children from a terrible attack, and maybe a worse death. He was a brave one all right. Since his mother died, he'd become a man, nevertheless she would set that aside. It had to be.

She greeted him, feigning surprise. 'Jameel. Why aren't you out in the fields? Are you all right?'

Jameel answered with his own brand of fakery. 'I'm well, Mother, and the fields will wait for me.'

They went inside, out of the late morning sun. The room was bigger than his with better furniture. Hot tea appeared, made with half water, half milk, sweetened with four teaspoonfuls of sugar. She laid a cup on the table in front of him. 'I'm curious. Why does a handsome man pay a visit to an old woman today? Tell me.'

'You're not old, Mother. And you have the power to make me happy.'

She accepted his compliment; this was difficult for him. 'How can I do that?'

Jameel sipped; the tea was too hot. He was already tired of this shilly-shally. 'I've come to you about something so important to me, that when I think of it, I can scarcely breathe.'

He rushed on, unable to hold back, forgetting the speech he'd rehearsed over and over in his head. 'If my own mother was here, she'd speak for me and find the words I cannot find. But she isn't. All I can do is follow the only voice I'm sure of: my heart.'

The woman's expression remained impassive. She had a heart voice too but its message was buried. She didn't speak in case she heard herself say things she mustn't say.

'You are wise. You know why I visit in the middle of the day. Or maybe you wonder if I'm ill. Could that be why Jameel isn't in the fields? And the answer would be yes, I am – and I've never enjoyed it more. I'm on fire from dawn 'til dusk and into the night. You have the cure.'

'Your heart must read many books, Jameel.'

'Afra is the reason I feel this way. I expect the whole village is aware of it. Even when we were children, playing together, I knew I had to watch over her. You've known me since I was a baby, you know my worth. Now I'm a man, to care for her is why I'm on this earth. There can be no other reason and I need no other. I've waited until I can wait no longer. I'm here to ask permission to marry her. Hear me, and let my life begin.'

The heartfelt plea left her unmoved. 'Jameel, I knew the moment I saw you. Of course I did. I'm old, not a fool. I see the way you look at my daughter. And I remember the service you did my family, here in this room with the dog. I've little enough to live for. Without your bravery that day...' She let the thought go unfinished. 'Now you're asking me to return your gift. Right deserves to be rewarded, though in life it's not always so.'

She lifted her eyes and met his. She had to end it, now and forever. 'My answer to you is no. You cannot have my permission.'

For all his anxiety, he hadn't expected rejection. 'But why? You know me, I'm Jameel.'

'And why I answer as I do.'

His confusion deepened.

'You're a good boy. But you're nothing in the world.'

"Nothing in the world." His worst fear spoken to him.

'And you'll stay nothing. Afra's young and beautiful. She can have any man. I must protect her from the impetuousness of her youth and make her look beyond a village boy. She thinks she understands life, she doesn't. Neither of you do. There are other girls for you, Jameel, more suitable girls, who'll give you children and make you proud. But not Afra.'

The assessment of his worth stunned him. His white pyjamas felt ridiculous. The woman picked up her cup and drank the sweet liquid, cool now.

'And this is your final word?'

'My final word.'

He had entered the room – the scene of his bravery – full of purpose. Now his head hurt. He needed to get out. He felt faint. The mother kept her eyes on him. She'd wounded this boy and she wasn't sorry. Better to learn your place in life early. Better to have foolish notions driven out while there was time to recover and go on.

'It's not about you or me; it's the world we live in. From time to time, we'll see each other in the village. Let's not pass without a word. Let's not become bad friends. I like you. I've always liked you. I refuse because I see your future. In time…'

'I'll never forget Afra.' He was near to tears.

'She's destined for more. She deserves more. I deserve more.'

They were out in the compound. 'What you can offer is not what she needs. You'll have a small life and be content with it. My daughter will go on to a big life with a rich husband. That will never be you. I've said I know you, Jameel. Now you know me.'

She went inside and closed the door, leaving him with the chickens and the donkey and the dust.

Chapter 3

The moon crept from behind a cloud and cast its silver light on Mundhi village.

Tonight it was no friend of Afra. In bed she'd had the usual whispered talk with Fatimah, but her mind was somewhere else. She hadn't seen or heard from Jameel. She asked about him. Nobody knew where he might be. His house was in darkness.

She closed her eyes, listening to her sister breathe, willing sleep to come. For hours, she lay wondering, until she could stand it no longer. The shared bed creaked. Afra slipped from it to her clothes lying on the chair and grimaced every time the door moved against its hinges. During the day these sounds didn't exist, as if the sun soothed the complaining old wood. Outside the air was cool. The smells that lingered were the aromas of life in Mundhi; chili and cumin; ginger and mint, rosewater and kaora. Afra shivered and closed the door, aware of the consequences if she was discovered. A female skulking in the middle of the night would be severely punished. Women were the embodiment of family honour. Even an accusation was enough to guarantee ruin. To be caught would bring retribution she dared not think about. In Pakistan what she was doing was very dangerous.

She crept through the village, keeping to the shadows. A dog barked and her heart stalled. She quickened her step. The moon played hide and seek; for the moment it was hiding.

Afra gathered her garments round her and sprinted to Jameel's house. She reached for the handle and pulled. The door was locked. Fear gripped her. Had he gone off without telling her? She listened then knocked. No one answered. She knocked again, louder than before, and put her mouth to the keyhole. 'Jameel, Jameel. It's Afra.'

Nothing.

Maybe he was ill. She crouched in the doorway and knocked again, harder. 'Jameel. Jameel.'

A sound, quiet, growing louder. Then footsteps.

In the sky the moon broke through, a key turned in the lock, the door opened and there he stood. 'Jameel. Are you all right?'

His eyes darted over the houses looking for signs of discovery and helped her to her feet. 'Quickly. Inside.'

She felt herself pulled from the entrance. The door closed behind them. He disappeared and returned with a candle, sheltering its flame with his hand.

Afra said, 'I was worried.'

The candlelight was weak but strong enough to show his face. It seemed different. 'You're not well.'

His reply was harsh. 'Why have you come here? Don't you understand the danger you're in? If we were found like this, whatever they did to me, it would be worse for you. You must go before you're missed.'

Afra didn't hear. The face she loved was thinner, lined, and his eyes were swollen.

'What's happened to you?'

'Nothing. At last I'm awake. And I see.'

'See what? What do you see?'

'A clown who would deceive himself and you. Yesterday I met him for the first time though he's never been far, and knew him for the dreamer he is.'

'Jameel?'

'I want you to go. So far you've been lucky. You could still be caught. I want you to run.'

'You talk in riddles.'

He placed his hands on her slender shoulders. 'Afra, my eyes have been opened to who I really am. I have no business inviting you to share my life. I thought it was a good thing. I was mistaken, it's wrong. In time we would be forced to recognise it, and by then it would be too late.'

'But I love you. I was sure you loved me.'

'Love is not enough. If it were we'd be as rich as the Moguls. A happy life needs more, and I have no more.'

She pushed his arms away. 'You talk nonsense. Love is the only thing that matters, everything else is an illusion. Why do you hurt me with this? You've forgotten all we've said. I'm angry with you, Jameel. I may not walk home with you today, I'm so angry.'

She was close to tears. He stepped back and stretched out his arms. 'I asked your mother for you, she refused. She told me things I didn't want to hear. That I was nothing in the world. I couldn't tell her she was wrong.'

'I'll speak to her. She'll change her mind.'

He smiled, slow and sad. 'But I won't. I can't. You deserve better than I could give.'

The girl was in shock. Everything had changed, and so fast. They were at the door. 'I'll speak to her. She'll hear me.'

'Afra Afra, it's not a time to speak, it's a time to listen, so listen to me. Our love cannot be now. That doesn't mean it can never be. What do you say to Fatimah, "wherever you are, I am, and wherever I am, you are too?" Well, that will be you and me.'

She sobbed. Jameel disappeared into the other room and returned with something in his hands. He guided her nearer the candle and peeled back the corners of a faded red and grey cloth. 'What is it?'

'Magic.'

He held up the bangles; light skimmed off their polished surfaces. 'They belonged to my mother, and before that to my father's mother, and to hers. Twelve, six for each arm.'

'They're beautiful.'

Jameel took her hand and slid six of them onto her wrist. She caressed them. 'What kind of magic?'

He drew her hands to his lips. 'They have the power to bring two people together. You take half. The rest will stay with me. On the day we're together again, I'll give mine to you. You must wear them always. If you don't it'll mean you've lost hope. Believe in the power, guard my gift, and remember.'

'Let me say it.'

He kissed her forehead. 'Say it then.'

'Wherever you are I am, and wherever I am you are too.'

They hugged each other. How she wished to hear him ask "Tomorrow then?"

'I'll speak to my mother.'

He shook his head. 'Keep the bangles safe. They'll guide us back to each other. I must leave Mundhi. It's for the best.'

'Oh! No! I can't go!'

Afra tried to break back into the room; he caught her. It was light now. People would be out in the village. For her sake he had to make her leave. 'As long as we believe, the bangles will not fail us.'

He pushed her away, closed the door and leaned against it. With Afra gone the room was a shell. The scrap of land would be sold; a week, two at the most. That would give him something. Jameel wished he could go at once. Leave Mundhi forever. He blew out the candle. This was the saddest day of his life, but his mother had been right.

Girls liked stories about love.

Chapter 4

Hamid Ghazili said nothing, he only looked.

Jameel looked too. His eyes saw the same narrow piece of earth he'd seen every day of his life. Unworked for almost a week, the corn leaves drooped, determined to put on an unimpressive show. The older man stroked the stubble on his chin. Beneath the turban, his weathered face told the story of a life lived under the sun.

Jameel matched his unhurried air, gazing east to where the Great Indian Desert reduced life to a daily battle. That was not the Punjab. Here, agriculture flourished in the subtropical climate; hot summers and cool winters. Hamid spat on the ground and drove the heel of his sandal into the dry earth, confirming some suspicion. Jameel watched dust drift in a tiny haze and wondered if he should spit. Would it mark him as a man who knew a thing or two?

The farmer paced the land. Jameel didn't follow; he knew every stone and felt no sentimental pangs at being rid of it. Once, it had played a role in his plans. Those plans had changed. Destroyed by Afra's mother. Jameel had locked himself away, crying in the night. When Afra came to him he'd found the strength to rise above the desolation in his heart and pretend to be strong for her. But there would be no return to how it had been.

What was said couldn't be unsaid.

A message to Hamid Ghazili had brought them here. Jameel sat on the ground and held up a hand to shield his face, fixing on the figure of Hamid, pacing and counting in the distance. The price was fair though the farmer's opinion deserved respect. If their business was successful, Jameel would have some money at least.

The house would remain unsold; no one in the village needed a house.

Hamid completed his inspection. The prospective buyer stood as he had at the beginning, tracing the land with his eyes, surveying the scene. The seller did the same, unsure what he was supposed to see. The farmer clapped Jameel on the shoulder and the deal was done.

A car sped along the dirt road, reflecting sunlight in brilliant flashes; it would reach the village before them. Mundhi was a long walk from the main road – motorcars were a novelty. Hamid and Jameel watched the wheels throwing up dust and stones. The dark blue BMW swept under the arch, travelling too fast to see inside. When they reached the compound it was there, wisps of smoke trailing from under the bonnet.

'Three days, maybe four,' Hamid said, 'then I'll have the money for you.'

Longer than Jameel wanted but it would have to do. Hamid shuffled towards his house while across the baked earth, Afra was about to feed the chickens. The vehicle had attracted her attention along with a dozen others, mostly women. In the middle of the morning, the men were out on the land. The birds squawked. She threw a handful of seeds to the ground and watched as two men got out. The driver went to the front and lifted the top. Steam rose in a column. He put his hand in his pocket and produced a handkerchief. At his second attempt the radiator cap released, hissing. His companion lit a cigarette from a gold lighter and blew smoke into the air. Both had the same high forehead and hooked nose, the same moustache and jaw line. They wore western-style suits and white shirts without ties. There the similarity ended. The one smoking was dominant.

The driver talked to a woman across the compound. Whatever was said sent her back to her house. His brother strolled in the sun, prowling the dusty earth like a jungle cat, scanning the ochre rooftops, assessing the modest dwellings. Jameel saw the challenge in his eyes and knew in his bones he didn't like this man. The stranger sensed it, tossed the cigarette away and ground it in the dirt.

The woman returned with three plastic bottles filled with water and gave them to the driver. From the squares of land in front of each house, people marvelled at the car: a sleeping beast in the middle of their village. Afra – her face uncovered, her hair hanging long and black – was just as curious as the rest. She tossed more feed over the wire fence while the insatiable birds complained. The older brother saw her though she didn't notice him at first because her attention was with the car. The driver said something and both men grinned. Afra realised they were talking about her and drew back. No man in Mundhi had ever looked at her that way.

Jameel saw the strangers enjoy the effect they'd had on the girl. More words passed between them then the elder brother got into the vehicle while the other laid bottles of water on the back seat – extras for the journey – and closed the door. He spoke to Mirvat Khan, wife of Yusuf, pointing to where Afra had been. She answered his question and, a minute later, tread-marks on the baked earth were the only sign they'd ever been there.

Jameel observed it all: the arrogance of the man, the coldness in the eyes. And the face. A face he'd prefer to forget.

Chapter 5

The land was sold. Without thinking it through he'd given away his only source of income. There was nothing for him now; he would leave Mundhi.

Hour after hour he lay on his bed, staring at the overhead fan, listening to the whir of the blades cutting through the air, taking stock of his situation. Afra would never be his no matter what his mother had said. The tale of the bangles had been a necessary distraction from reality.

As the only male in his family, he'd worked while others learned to read and write. Where could a young man like that, without money or property, find a place in the world?

Jameel was afraid.

Morning brought little change. He mooched around his house; the house no one wanted to buy. And all the while, her words drove shafts of terror through him.

nothing in the world

He considered ways to end the whole hopeless mess. Each solution brought pain for Afra. He disregarded them, save one. Jameel remembered the rabid dog and how far it had fallen. If he threw himself down the well who would know? He brushed the nonsense away. What would his mother make of her brave boy, then? Or Afra? No. He wouldn't give in so easily.

'Afra's mother is wrong. Her opinion doesn't matter.'

For the first time in days he felt hungry. When he'd eaten he went for a walk through the village; the sounds of children playing and the smell of coriander, garlic and onions frying in cooking pots, floated on the air. Evening was falling.

At the common ground in the centre of Mundhi, his brain refused to accept what he saw. The car was back, outside Afra's house. Big and black in the gathering dusk. A light shone behind the gossamer window hangings. Jameel crept to the courtyard wall; chickens stirred behind the wire fence. He felt ridiculous crouched where he had no business to be. Voices drifted from inside, too low to make out. He heard the murmur of females and the deeper bass tones of a male.

An hour passed. It was dark now; the back of his legs ached. Chairs scrapped the floor telling him that whoever was inside was leaving. Time to retreat. And not a moment too soon. The door opened and three people came out – two women and a man. Jameel couldn't see clearly yet he saw enough. One of the women was Afra's mother. The man was the stranger who'd stared at him with unspoken disrespect.

The tail-lights disappeared. Jameel stepped from his cover. He knew the reason these people were in Mundhi – they were arranging a wedding. Tears streamed down his face; he made no attempt to brush them away. This was the final nightmare in a week of bad dreams. His shoulders slumped in defeat. With the strangers gone, Mundhi was quiet. The silence folded round him.

'What has changed?' he said, and answered his own question. 'Nothing.'

***

It was too early for sleep. Afra sat on her bed in the room she shared with her sister and brother. When she heard the knock on the door that evening she'd answered it. A fat woman with steel grey hair and a severe expression stood in the fading light. She looked Afra up and down, taking her time. 'I wish to speak with your mother.'

'Come in.'

The woman squeezed herself past. Afra noticed the car and recognised it. Someone was inside. Her mother wiped her hands on a cloth and stepped forward to meet the visitor. She bowed her head. 'Jee ayan nu.'

The visitor returned the traditional reply in a flat voice and maneuvered her bulk to the wooden seat that doubled as a bed. The children watched, subdued. She sat down, unsure of its ability to take her weight and spoke. 'What I have to say is only for you.'

'Of course. Afra, Fatimah, Shafi. Go. I'll call when you can come back.'

The children went to their room. Shafi scrambled on to his cot and Fatimah sat on the edge of the bed. Their sister lay on the other side with her hands over her eyes.

'Who's she?' Shafi asked.

'Strangers.'

'Who is she, Afra? Why is she here?'

Afra didn't want the children to see her face. 'We'll know soon enough, Shafi. Soon enough.'

The younger ones began some game their bigger sister couldn't follow. Afra had lied. She realised why the woman was in their house, and what she wanted. Before the night was out, she'd know her name. They heard the front door open and close. Whoever had been in the car was next door being presented to her mother.

Afra shuddered. Her fingers caressed the bangles on her arm, trying to find comfort in them. They felt heavy and cold; pieces of carved wood; only decoration. Later, a door slamming wakened her. She opened her eyes; it was dark. Fatimah was beside her and Shafi snored in his cot. How could she sleep while her whole life was being decided a few feet away? Her mother called. 'Afra, come here!'

She tiptoed from the sleeping children. Her mother stood in the middle of the room, smiling, happy, the burden carried for years had been lifted.

'Sit down. A lot has happened tonight.'

Her daughter did as she was told.

'Since your father died I've lived with a terrible dread. Without a man to look after us, we've never been far from disaster. One hard winter, one failed crop or a broken leg, enough to cast us down. If your father had had a younger brother, I would have married him. Not for love. For security. Night after night, I've prayed good fortune would find us, and it has.'

Her daughter listened, saying nothing.

'The woman who was here is Noor Dilawar Hussein, mother of Quasim. He's her eldest son – she has three – and a daughter, Chandra. They drove many miles to be here. They're very rich and live in a big house. You'll meet them all soon.'

Afra played her denial of the inevitable to the end, asking her question in fading hope. 'Are they coming to Mundhi?'

'No, they won't come here. You will go there, to Lahore. Quasim wishes you to be his wife and I have said yes.'

***

Even if she was allowed a voice, telling her mother no would've been too hard. Her dreams had been answered – a rich husband for her daughter. True, it meant her oldest girl would move far away but that was a common thing.

The family would receive the 'bride price' in exchange for her fertility and the loss of her labour, ensuring Fatimah, Shafi and their mother would be released from threat of ill fortune, real or imagined. It was a happy day.

For Afra it was the end of her world.

Jameel: it had taken so long to appreciate his worth. She saw him, tall and handsome. Lost to her forever. This Quasim was just the latest lash of the whip. She threw herself on her bed wishing she was dead. Shafi snored in the corner unaware of his older sister's despair. Fatimah felt Afra collapse next to her and spoke, her voice an urgent whisper in the dark. 'Afra, what did they want?'

The big sister told the little sister her news. 'And what about Jameel? You can't marry him too, can you?'

'I'll never marry Jameel. That was a dream. That dream is over. In a few days I'll leave Mundhi.'

'So where will you go?'

'They say to Lahore.'

'Can I come too? Can me and Shafi come to Lahore with you?'

'No, Fatimah. I'm going to my new home, to my new family, and I must go alone. Besides, who would look after our mother?'

'But Afra, when will I see you?'

'I'll visit you.'

'When?'

'Often.'

'Every week?'

'No, not every week. When I'm settled in my new life, I'll visit you here.'

The little one insisted. 'When?'

'As soon as I'm able, trust me.'

The girl fell silent. She fumbled to find her big sister's hand in the dark. Her fingers brushed against the rings. 'What's this?'

'A present from Jameel. A beautiful gift. Let me tell you about it.'

And the legend of the bangles worked its wonder on Fatimah as it had on others before. When Afra finished the sisters lay still.

'You mustn't lose them or you'll never find Jameel.'

'I won't.'

The quiet between them was something they'd remember the rest of their lives. Afra broke it, pressing home the advantage the tale had given, setting a child's worry to rest, even for a time, unaware Jameel had used the story to calm her own breaking heart.

'And anyway, when they've worked for me and I have all twelve, I'll give them to you so you'll find the man of your dreams.'

'You'll give them to me? They'll be mine someday?'

'One day, yes, they'll be yours.'

'When will you leave?'

'Soon.'

'Where is Lahore?'

'North. It's in the north.'

'Will I ever go there?'

'Yes.'

'Will I visit you in your new house? Is it a big house?'

'I'm told it's a very big house, a fine house, and of course you may visit me there, you and Shafi.'

Fatima was satisfied. Afra was glad.

'I'll miss you.'

'Why? There's no need. Have you forgotten already?'

Fatimah whispered. 'Wherever you are I am...'

Her big sister replied. '...and wherever I am, you are too.'

Chapter 6

His battered brown suitcase bounced against his thigh. It weighed little; there was almost nothing in it. In truth, it wasn't really his. It had belonged to his mother. Jameel had never used it, there was no reason to; he'd never been away from the village. The night air was cool. Low cloud covered the sky, keeping the stars from shining their light on the reluctant adventurer. Jameel heard his footsteps on the dirt road. A lonely sound. Soon, Mundhi was out of sight.

He might as well have been on the moon; he couldn't feel more alone. Eventually he reached the asphalt road – his first goal – and set the suitcase at his feet. A lorry whooshed past, pulling at his clothes, dragging him against his will. The speed and power of these machines startled him. He needed to be careful.

It was surprising how fast two pinpoints of light could appear from nowhere and become a thundering monster, flashing by to be swallowed by the blackness. Drivers and their passengers. Strangers on a journey. Where were they going? What would become of them? The very questions he asked about himself.

He edged nearer the lip of the road and stuck out his hand. Nobody stopped. They saw him too late and were travelling too fast.

After an hour he was tired, thoughts of giving up and returning to the village filled his head. He remembered his house as a warm place and his bed a wonderful luxury. But no, he wouldn't be defeated so early. Another set of headlights shone larger by the second. The lorry approached at the same awesome speed as the others and zoomed past the young man. Jameel forgot it, his attention already on the next opportunity, no more than specks of light in the distance.

A hissing sound made him turn; the truck had stopped. He ran towards the glow of brake lights and the vehicle humming with power. A tarpaulin covered its load. Jameel mounted the first high step and grasped the handle. The door swung open. The man behind the wheel waved him to hurry and he clambered on to the worn seat.

The driver said, 'Lahore?'

'Lahore.'

The cabin smelled of cigarettes and oil. Jameel was impressed by the multi-coloured ribbons and chaotic colours, the trademark of truckers in Pakistan.

In Mundhi, Afra and Fatimah lay with their arms round each other. Across the room Shafi snored in his cot. Next door, their mother drifted in dreamless calm for the first time in years.

And in Lahore, another family slept, satisfied with the bargain they'd made.

***

The driver didn't speak during the first hour. His face was lean and sallow with thick stubble covering his jaw; the glow from the instrument-panel lit his tobacco-stained teeth.

Jameel's eyes adjusted as the road was revealed in golden light. He could make out shapes, gradually realising they were cars and lorries that had crashed. Driving in Pakistan was a dangerous business. The absence of conversation reassured him. The man offered him a cigarette. He refused, happy to watch the ground pass under the giant wheels, glancing at his new friend, and hugging himself in the warmth of the cabin. It was an adventure. He was on his way to Lahore and a new chapter in his life. Mundhi village was far behind him. His fingers played with the bangles on his wrist – not really something a man would wear, but for the moment the safest place – and tried not to think of what he had lost.

The lorry turned into a large flat area where other trucks were parked. It crunched over the unlit ground and pulled in beside them. The driver pulled on the handbrake and turned off the engine, opened the door and jumped out. His passenger did the same, trailing behind through the maze of stationary workhorses and the smell of diesel oil and cooling rubber.

Lights shone from a low building. They headed for it. Clearly, this man was no stranger here. Jameel followed him through a door into a bright room where men sat at tables, eating, smoking, and drinking mugs of tea. The driver said hello to people. Jameel felt grown-up. And to think, this had been going on while he was asleep in Mundhi.

Other lives in other places.

A big world and he was in it.

The driver spoke to a man behind the counter. They knew each other. A tray of food and two mugs appeared. He picked up the tray and weaved between the tables towards a space at the back. Jameel tried to look as if he belonged. They sat down and shared the meal between them: a spicy chickpea and potato curry, lentils in coconut milk and aloo paratha. Cooking smells and men talking met in the air, and Jameel sensed the brotherhood of the road. He tore off pieces of roti with his right hand to scoop up the food. After minutes of frantic eating, the driver waved to someone at another table then spoke.

'My name is Mazur.'

'Jameel.'

'And Lahore is where you're headed? We can travel there together.'

This was welcome news. Jameel celebrated with a drink of the tea. Mazur said, 'You know Lahore? You have business there?'

Jameel interrupted his eating. 'I have a plan.'

Mazur watched him devour the bread. One glance told all he needed about his new companion. 'It's always good to have a plan.'

He lit a cigarette while the young man emptied every plate in front of them. They sat like that, one smoking the other eating, with no more talk until the driver asked another question. 'What is your plan, my young friend?'

'Jameel.'

'What's this plan of yours, Jameel? Maybe I can help you with it.'

He waited until everything in his mouth had been chewed and swallowed before he replied. Mazur recognised the naive boy. In thirty years on the road, he'd met Jameel many times.

'I'm going to my mother's uncle. He has a restaurant and maybe a job for me. I hope so.'

'Well yes, that's certainly a plan. But tell me Jameel, is he expecting you? Does he know you're on your way to meet him?'

'No, we've never met. I only know his name is Gulzar Hafeez.'

Doubt shadowed his face. Mazur had no wish to feed it. 'It's a start. And where does he live in Lahore?'

'He wrote a letter to my mother saying life went well with him. I believe he's an important man in the city.'

Mazur drew on his cigarette, hearing hope in place of fact. Jameel tipped the mug to his lips and emptied it.

'Do you have this letter? Can I see it?'

Jameel fished inside his shirt and brought out a single page, old and dry. Mazur saw the date: the letter had been written before this boy was born. 'This is good. Your relation prospers. M M Alam Road has many fine shops and restaurants.'

He stubbed out his cigarette, leaned forward and put a hand on the young man's shoulder. 'Listen to me, Jameel. When we get to the city we'll go our ways and never meet again. What I say will help you. You've never been anywhere like Lahore. It can be a cruel and dangerous place full of thieves and fools who survive by preying on those even more foolish than themselves. Do you have money?'

The question made Jameel uneasy.

'Split it up. Some in one pocket. Some in another. Even keep some in your shoes. Only bring out a few coins. People will be watching, make them believe you have nothing of value or soon that will be the truth. I'll drop you near the train station. Go to the left-luggage counter and leave your case. They'll give you a ticket.

It won't cost much. If you go around carrying a suitcase, you may as well shout out 'Come and rob me, please!' Don't go with anyone or wander down alleyways or side streets. Okay?'

None of this had occurred to Jameel. Could Lahore really be so different from Mundhi village where everyone knew everyone and crime was unknown?

Mazur wasn't finished. 'And always walk straight and tall, as if you know your way. Anything else will tell these sharp-eyed jackals you're a stranger. They live off the unwary. Ask someone who looks respectable to point you to M M Alam Road, near Gulberg. As I say, there are fine restaurants there. If your great-uncle is indeed an important man they may know him.'

The driver saw fear in the boy's eyes.

'Do you understand? The city has enough lost souls. Make sure you aren't one of them.'

Jameel's hand closed over the money in his pocket.

Mazur hoped the boy would heed him. His mother's tale sounded like the kind of glamour that girls often saw in an older male relative – a loving but inaccurate assessment of character and achievement. Lahore was a big city. What happened there happened in any big place. People arrived believing a better future was waiting for them. For a few that dream came true. For many, the good life would elude them as day by day they accepted less than their expectations, until their existence was worse than the one they'd fled. With nothing to stay for and nothing to return to, they filled their days waiting for death.

Mazur glanced at the wreckage of their meal. 'Finished? Then let's go.'

The transport cafe was busier than it had been; drivers came and went all the time. As they were leaving, the man behind the counter produced a brown paper bag containing four warm and greasy roti and handed the parcel to Jameel. 'Here. You'll need this later.'

They made their way to the lorry, avoiding the coming and going in the unlit parking ground. Fifty yards away, traffic sped to unknown destinations. Jameel hoisted himself up easier than the first time. The cabin door wasn't locked. He pulled it open and scrambled in. Mazur turned the key, the engine rumbled into life and the monster edged through the dark towards the road. It seemed hours since they'd left it. They built up speed and rejoined the race through the night.

'So, Lahore,' Mazur said. 'He doesn't know it yet, but your great-uncle's waiting for you.'

He forced certainty into his voice, grinning at his subdued young passenger. Jameel didn't answer. He crushed the bundle of money tight against his thigh and tried to remember why he'd ever wanted to leave the village.

A car zoomed past and disappeared into the future. Jameel watched it go and caressed the reminders on his wrist. Resentment at Afra's mother and sorrow for his lost love were powerful emotions, but no match for the fear stirring in him.

He stared stone-faced, wishing he was in Mundhi.

***

In the early morning light, a thick grey cloud hung like a gathering storm over the city. Further off, the sky was clear. Lahore was defined by the darkness above it. Mazur pointed to the ominous blackness. 'Smog. Lahore Dust they call it. Smoke, dirt, and production waste. It covers Lahore like a tent, so bad sometimes you can only see a few yards ahead.'

'And what do people do about it, Mazur?'

The driver lit a cigarette with one hand; it glowed and filled the cabin with blue smoke. 'They do what I do. Admit it's killing them without believing it.'

'How many people live here?'

'Too many. The truth is no one knows. Ten million they say, though there's no way of telling how many Afghan refugees or immigrants from Iran have settled in Lahore.

'Ten million?'

'Ten million plus. Lahore is an overcrowded, polluted hellhole. I love it.'

'How long have you lived here?'

'I don't live here. I often stop here. Today my business is small. I'll be in the city only a short time, then on to Islamabad. But I know Lahore well. I've walked in its gardens, eaten from its tandoors and whored in Heera Mandi many times.'

Mazur grew quiet, revisiting his past. He pulled the truck off the main road and crawled to a halt behind cars, lorries, bikes and carts. 'Traffic's a problem, that's why they have so many underpasses. They help, but only a little.'

Mazur's words were a commentary on the scene outside. Jameel had never seen so many people or vehicles, so much activity, crammed into one place. Everyone was hurrying somewhere. The streets were like canyons, carrying one human tributary after another.

'Do you know what Lahore is famous for?'

'No.'

'Carpets.' Mazur paused for dramatic effect and failed to get it – his passenger was only half-listening. 'Carpets.' He tried to generate interest. 'Hand-made. Carpets are big business in Lahore.'

Mazur let the history of carpets go untold. Jameel's jaw hung open, his eyes fixed on the pageant so different from Mundhi village. His new friend studied him while they waited. A nice young man. He hoped he'd find his relation and escape whatever he was running from.

They made progress through the crowded streets. 'I'll let you out here. The Central Railway Station isn't far. Do as I've told you. Get rid of the case, and be careful in this place. Then you can begin your search. What's the name?'

'Gulzar Hafeez.' Saying it made it seem more real.

'Okay. Here, don't forget this.' Mazur handed him the parcel of roti.

Jameel opened the door and climbed down. No one paid any attention to his arrival in the twenty-third largest city in the world. His friend for a day passed the suitcase to him. Jameel looked up into the cabin. Mazur smiled. 'Good luck, and remember, walk straight and tall.'

'I'll try.' He was afraid to let this good man go; the bump in his shoes didn't reassure him. 'Thank you, Mazur.'

He closed the door, stepped back and was swallowed by the crowd. At first the truck didn't move then it joined the flow and disappeared.

For a night, the cabin had been Jameel's world; he'd felt safe. Now where he stood was noisy, bustling and intimidating. Wild-eyed people hunched behind steering wheels, only interested in overtaking whatever was in front. Every expression was taut and intense.

The young man from Mundhi might as well have been invisible. He put the case under his arm, gripped the bag of roti and let himself be swept in the direction Mazur had pointed, in step with strangers for the first time in his life.

Chapter 7

Fatimah and Shafi lay curled on Shafi's cot, one at each end, watching their sister fold her few clothes into a battered canvas bag. The atmosphere was solemn. Now she was gathering her things together they realised in a way they hadn't before.

Afra was leaving.

Shafi was the least affected, tugging strands of stray thread from the bedcover. He was too young to feel the pain his sisters felt but he managed a sad face. It was hardest for Fatimah. She was about to have her role model, big sister and best friend drift out of her life and she was miserable beyond tears, unable to imagine a day without her guiding hand and calming words. Afra pretended to be cheerful for the others.

Jameel was gone from Mundhi; she didn't know where. Walking home from the fields talking to him might never have been. Life had shaken them apart.

'When?' Fatimah asked.

'Soon.'

'How soon?'

'An hour, maybe less.'

Fatimah put her face in the pillow. The less definite 'soon' sounded further away. In the room next door, their mother struggled to stay resolved. She knew the sorrow she'd brought to her family. They would never understand none of this was of her choosing and that force of circumstance had dictated the road. How much better, how much easier it would have been for them to live together in Mundhi. She imagined her children grown, married with children of their own. Climbing onto her lap, their trusting faces shining up at their grandmother. She pushed the images from her mind. Mrs Dilawar Hussein was returning today and though she wished it could be different, it couldn't be.

Better to let the girls have their moment together, there was no telling when they'd meet again. She made tea and stared into the unlit fire. Her daughters thought her heartless. If they only knew. In the Punjab it was common for a girl to marry into a family far from her own. Sometimes, the new bride would leave and never see her parents or brothers and sisters again. Although that was the way of it, custom didn't lessen the pain.

Afra collected the little she had and drew the strings of the bag together. 'I'm going out. I want to take a last look at the village. There will be nights when I'll want to be able to make Mundhi appear in my head. I need to remember it. I won't be long, I promise.'

Outside in the yard, the chickens squawked and ran around, fussing over nothing. Uncu the donkey lolled in the shade, his slow movements so different from the behaviour of the birds. His eyes were untroubled, to Afra, almost wise. Donkeys weren't clever creatures yet Uncu accepted his life without struggling against every turn in the road. He didn't complain, he made the best of it and, in the heat of the day, slept when he could.

Perhaps this docile beast – too dull or too enlightened to worry – had something to teach. She opened the gate and went into her village for the last time, walking to the end of Mundhi and back again winding between the houses to where she and Jameel had been together.

How she'd hated to see him sad and cast down, not the Jameel she'd always known. But even in his anguish he'd found the strength to give her the bangles and tell her their story. Afra caressed the six carved hoops at her wrist.

"As long as we believe, the bangles will not fail us."

She gazed at the deserted dwelling; this was where they would have lived and been happy. Without him, just bricks and mud.

***

Everyone heard the car pull up; its tyres crackling over the earth, louder than the powerful engine under the bonnet. Fatimah tensed at the sound while her older sister pretended to be unaware of the vehicle's arrival. The opening and closing of a door made denial impossible.

They'd come for her.

Afra picked up the bag, tucked it under her arm, opened the door and went into the yard. Her mother came through the other door. A stillborn smile passed between them. A man with the same hooked nose as his brother lounged by the driver's door. In the back seat, a veiled figure sat upright, detached from the scene. Her son walked round the front of the car and nodded to Afra's mother. He took the bag from her daughter, his eyes lingered on the face under the hijab he'd heard so much about.

She caught his interest and the hairs on her neck rose. The family stood, gripped by the finality of it. No one spoke. Even Shafi had gone shy, hiding behind his sister, his childish way of dealing with unpleasantness.

'So?' Afra tried to sound positive.

Her mother hugged her. 'I'll miss you, we all will.'

'I know.' She turned to her brother and sister. 'Look after our mother and each other. Next time we meet I'll know if you've been good, so be good.'

Shafi peeked out. 'We're always good.'

His big sister fell to a crouch, level with his face. 'I know you are, Shafi, because like me, you're afraid of Fatimah.'

It would take a lot more than that to cheer Fatimah today. Afra put her arms round both children as their mother looked on in stoic wretchedness. The driver pressed something into her hand. She took the wad of dirty notes without looking at it, knowing the bargain was complete.

Fatimah cried, 'Tell me, Afra! Say it!'

Afra took the child's hand in her hands. 'Wherever you are I am.'

Fatimah's eyes filled with tears. 'And wherever I am you are, too.'

'Firdos!' The woman called from inside the car, bringing the magic of the moment to an end. The youngest of her three sons held the door. Afra got in. The engine thrummed into existence, the car turned and passed the group standing in the dust outside the house. Afra waved. They waved back and were left behind. Mrs Dilawar Hussein didn't acknowledge her in any way; her face remained hidden behind her hijab and Afra felt her heart beat faster. She tried to relax, wondering how long it would be before she saw her family again.

And Jameel, where was he?

All she could do was take hope from his words, borrow wisdom from Uncu, and make these her travelling companions. She touched the wood, wishing its power would work for her. His name slipped from her lips. 'Jameel.' Stern eyes fell on her. She pretended to sleep.

By the time they reached Lahore, day had become night and the mother of her future husband hadn't spoken. The city glowed in the dark, an orange aura radiating from it. Despite her sadness and fear, Afra had slept part of the way. Now they were in the city Firdos slowed the car, mindful of his passenger. There wasn't much to see; the well-lit streets were quiet. Perhaps it would look better in the day. Would this woman be better? She doubted it.

They drove on through the city, for what seemed almost as long as the journey from Mundhi until the car stopped outside a house where lights were on, the only one in the street. Firdos opened the door on his mother's side. Mrs Dilawar Hussein levered herself off the seat using a cane. Afra had forgotten how fat she was.

The son and his mother behaved as if the girl didn't exist. Firdos carried the canvas bag, hurrying after the older woman. She took his arm for support and said something. He replied – the only words either had exchanged since the irate call when she'd grown tired of the touching goodbyes.

Afra let them go on at their slow pace and studied the house that was very different from a village house: bigger, with a flower garden in front. A man appeared at the door, the light from within sketching the outline of his frame. He came forward to welcome Mrs Dilawar Hussein, offering unneeded assistance. She heard the woman tell him to stop, that she was all right and still he hovered and fussed round her. Now, Afra was ignored by all of them.

The others went inside, one holding his mother's arm, the other smoothing imagined obstacles out of Mrs Dilawar Hussein's path. If Afra had had somewhere else to go she would've fled there and then, but she didn't, so she followed them. The room was smaller than she expected, with threadbare carpets and ugly furniture. It smelled like someone ought to open a window. The two sycophants busied themselves settling the matriarch into an ancient armchair while a woman stood ready with a cup of something, her shoulders hunched, tired and unhappy. Could this be Chandra? She held the cup with both hands, afraid to spill even a drop, and glanced at the new girl, then away.

Afra's mother had said this family were rich and lived in a big house. This couldn't be it. Nothing about it said money had been spent here. In truth, she had no idea what rich might look like but, like everyone everywhere, assumed she'd recognise it. Mrs Dilawar Hussein accepted the drink without thanks, her eyes boring into Afra above the rim of the cup. The men watched the older woman, waiting her instruction. Her voice and her power filled the room. 'You'll stay here until the wedding. Bilal will be responsible for you.'

A sly smile from the man who'd opened the door identified him as Bilal. His gaze lingered on Afra a moment too long. There was something feral in the black eyes, the pockmarked cheeks and the oiled hair, plastered against his head. Someone who slept in his clothes and was a stranger to soap and water.

'When will my wedding be? Will it be soon?'

'Soon enough. Until then you'll help Nadira, Bilal's wife.'

The driver got up, keys dangled from his finger. 'You're tired, mother, I'll take you home.'

'Not just yet, Firdos. Bilal, call your wife.'

Mrs Dilawar Hussein gave out orders like a general. The men accepted it. Bilal clapped his hands. 'Nadira!' His wife reappeared in the doorway. 'Take her to her room. And her bag. Tomorrow she can work with you.'

Nadira motioned Afra to follow. No one said goodbye, good night, sleep well or any of the usual words of welcome or friendship. Bilal's wife was already halfway up a staircase, the canvas bag bumping against each step. At the top, three doors led off the small landing. Nadira opened one, turned on a light and went in. There was nothing except a small bed with a single sheet and a sink. If a carpet had ever covered the floor it was gone, leaving bare boards, marked in places where heavy furniture had rested on them. Nadira laid the bag down and pointed, her wrist was thin as a reed. She didn't speak to the guest. She was afraid; her whole being shouted it. A voice seeped through the floor – Mrs Dilawar Hussein, grumbling again. Nadira trembled and ran from the room.

Afra sat on the hard bed; rust peeled from its iron frame. The sink was blocked and something brown pooled on the bottom. Then there was the smell.

She put her head in her hands and cried.

Chapter 8

Lahore Central Railway Station in the heart of the city was built during the British colonial era. Jameel hadn't seen anything like it. Inside people were everywhere; hurrying, carrying luggage, clutching tickets and checking the timetable suspended from the roof. Signs meant nothing to him. A soldier in uniform showed him where to go.

Jameel lifted the suitcase on to the counter. 'I want to leave this here.'

The attendant gave him a ticket and carried the luggage into the back. During the whole transaction Jameel was the only one to speak.

He kept the bag of roti. On the street, a red and yellow bus passed. Blank faces stared at him. The visitor studied them, fascinated. Now and then, he asked someone if he was headed right for M M Alam Road. Every set of directions he was given added another layer of confusion. Jameel felt his belly rumble and decided to stop not knowing he was in the City of Gardens, that Lahore was famous for its gardens and parks.

It was warm; shafts of sunlight pierced the black malaise above. He sat on the grass and pulled a roti from the bag – cold and no longer soft. He broke a wedge off and ate it, grateful to Mazur. The contrast amazed him; the bustling madness yards from the peace and tranquility of here. And he wasn't the only one who was hungry. People sat in groups, eating and talking, shaded by jacaranda. A man with a caged parrot walked by, stopped to examine Jameel and moved on. Further away, another character gathered a crowd by making a coin balance on top of a box. With a flourish he brought out a handkerchief and placed it on the ground. From his pocket he produced teeth, lifting them carefully between the tips of his fingers and laying them on the cloth.

He closed his eyes in prayer. 'My friends' he said to the group of curious strangers, 'there is little in this world better than good teeth. If you've been given healthy teeth, then you are blessed indeed.'

He gestured to the collection. 'These belonged to important people.' He picked one up so the crowd could see it better. 'This came from a Maharaja, and very glad he was to part with it because it caused him a great deal of pain.'

Then he paused and eyed the onlookers as though he suspected they harboured secrets they refused to share and nodded at some inner realisation. 'If you have a tooth that troubles you – that aches from time to time – your worries are at an end.'

A pair of pliers appeared in his hand. 'I can rid you of this sorrow. You'll feel nothing, I promise. For the merest donation – a rupee or two, not more – your pain will be gone.'

He waved the pliers in the air. 'What do you say? Come on. Step forward.'

The audience drifted away. They'd gone as far as they could go with him and his performance and weren't interested in becoming part of the act.

Jameel was already becoming used to the city, the frightened visitor replaced by an interested observer. He lay down and curled up with a hand closed round the notes in his pocket and slipped into a dreamless sleep. On the green carpet, with the sun on his face, he thought of nothing, not even Afra. When he wakened it was dark, and the park – so welcoming in the day – was an eerie place.

He grasped for the crumpled paper: it was there. Jameel didn't check his shoes; he could feel the bulge in each one. He breathed, relieved to have survived his nap unscathed, got up and lifted the bag of bread. Only one roti remained – he must have eaten the rest. His legs were stiff. After the heat of the day the evening air chilled him.

The street was no quieter than before, except now everything was lit up: the shops, the signs, even some of the vehicles. Jameel approached an elderly turbaned man standing in a group of people who stood in a line, some shuffling, one reading a book, others looking bored, resigned to waiting for the bus to arrive.

'Excuse me, which is the way to M M Alam Road, please?'

The man lifted an arm and pointed.

Why did people not speak? Did they know he was a stranger? In Mundhi, everyone talked to everyone, stopped to share a moment with a neighbour, and smiled. In this Lahore, words were like gold. He hoped he would never be in too much of a hurry to say hello because that would be a lonely life.

'Near, very near,' a shopkeeper told him mysteriously in answer to his question.

Fear returned. The enormity of his task became clear. What if this? What if that? Negative thoughts, the currency of the defeated, pounded his brain. He was searching for one man, a man he'd never met, in the midst of ten million.

ten million plus

Even if he found him, what kind of welcome could he expect?

Jameel tried not to dwell on these things, preferring to remember Mazur's advice about walking straight and tall. A sign on the wall above his head said M M Alam Road. It told Jameel nothing. He asked a man on a bicycle balancing a tray of eggs in one hand. 'You're already there,' the stranger said.

The avenue overflowed with places where people sat eating at tables behind big glass windows. They talked to each other, ignoring the world outside, and didn't seem to mind they could be seen. Jameel walked up one side and down the other, taking his time, finding a different wonder with every look. His heart knocked in his chest. The search was about to begin.

He stopped in front of a window and peered through the glass. A man, a woman and two children sat at a table covered by a white cloth, eating and laughing. The woman was beautiful. Not as beautiful as Afra, but beautiful nevertheless. Her companion was fat, his clothes were new: a successful man.

nothing in the world, a good boy, but nothing in the world

Would her words follow him forever? He shook them away and concentrated on his progress. A red sign attracted him. He pulled his courage round him like a coat, opened the door and went in. A waiter in neatly-pressed shirt and trousers came forward.

'A table, sir?'

The question took Jameel by surprise. '…No thank you. I'm looking for someone, perhaps you know him?'

'What's his name?'

'Gulzar Hafeez.'

'Just a moment, please.'

Jameel took in his surroundings: a lot of white. Food appeared from behind a swinging door, carried on trays by other smartly-dressed people. It was cool in this place and he could hear music. His clothes were crushed and creased compared with everyone else, a long way from how they'd been the day he'd spoken to Afra's mother. His throat was dry. He realised he must look shabby and fear crashed like breaking glass against his heart. To add to his insecurity, the older man coming towards him wore a suit and a tie: someone who walked straight and tall. He was bald and smiled with his eyes when he saw Jameel.

'Good evening. I am Mohamed Abdul Qadir. This is my restaurant.' He waved at the white space. 'I'm told you're looking for Gulzar Hafeez. Can I ask why?'

'I have business with Mr Hafeez. I'm Jameel Akhtar.'

'I see. Then I cannot help you.'

He raised a hand, encouraging Jameel to go, and though he still smiled there was no welcome in his eyes. The conversation had lasted seconds; the outstretched arm was an invitation to leave. Jameel's hand touched the door handle. He turned, all pretence at worldliness abandoned. 'He's my only family.'

Mohamed Abdul Quadir's expression changed. 'Stay here,' he said.

Jameel was still holding the paper bag with the last piece of roti inside and wanted to throw it away. Instead, he found a spot on the floor to study. Mr Quadir came back with a young man. 'This is Ali. He'll take you where you want to go.'

Ali seemed keen to help. He was about the same age as Jameel, wiry and alert and dressed like his boss.

'You mean you know him? You know where he is?'

'Of course.' Mr Quadir beamed. 'Everyone knows Gulzar in M M Alam Road. Besides, he's one of my oldest friends.'

***

Ali knew where he was going, at home with the mass of people swaying like corn in fields as far as the eye could see. He waved Jameel to follow, weaving against the current of humanity flowing along the pavement. The boy from Mundhi village knew he'd always remember the journey; the excitement of pushing against the crowd, the traffic only feet away; the smells and the colour and the joy of being on an adventure in a city of ten million people. He'd even forgotten to feel afraid, learning that the best times were when he lived in the moment.

Ali stopped to let him catch up. Ducking and diving past people who didn't deviate from the course they were on was a talent. It took agility and confidence. And youth. Jameel followed the grinning boy, struggling to keep him in sight, aware he might be leading him to a new life. His guide stood in the doorway of another restaurant – the street was full of them – and waited for Jameel to arrive.

Like a magician presenting a trick, he put his palms together, bowed and was gone, carried away on the flood of bodies.

The door was made of heavy dark wood with a gold plaque in the centre. Three steps led up to it. Jameel climbed to the second. From here he could see the way he'd come, a friendless stranger. Now, he was about to meet the uncle his mother had spoken of with such pride. If nothing else, he'd have someone whose blood was his. There was a second door, he pushed it and entered another world.

Inside was filled with the sound of voices and the clink of glass and china. A man in a dark suit spoke to him. 'Salam. We've been expecting you. Follow me.'

Jameel returned the greeting and trailed behind. They passed through a room full of diners. Other men carrying food hurried by. No one paid any mind to the young man from Mundhi village. A carpeted corridor led to another door. The leader knocked, opened it and went inside. 'He's here,' he said and left.

Lately life was full of people who appeared and disappeared – Mazur, Mr Quadir, Ali, and now this person. Maybe in a big city you eventually meet everyone.

ten million plus

He edged into the room. A figure faced away looking out of a window, arms folded behind his back. He wore a business suit and his fingers fiddled nervously with his shirt cuffs. Jameel was too young to realise that this was a big moment, not just for him. The man who turned to greet him was tall and wrinkled with a bushy grey moustache suspended over his mouth. 'Jameel?'

'Great Uncle?'

His uncle rushed to him and placed his hands on his shoulders. 'Jameel!' He hugged him and led him to a chair, holding his wrist, afraid he might escape. 'Let me look at you.' His fingers touched the bangles. 'What are these?'

'From my mother.'

'Your mother's? You must tell me all about her. Everything. But first let's eat, young people are always hungry. And call me Uncle.'

He lifted a telephone and spoke. 'Set my table for two tonight, Wasim. An important guest has arrived.'

They stared at each other until the table was ready. When they were seated Jameel said, 'Do you always choose this table? Wouldn't it be more fun to sit at a different one each night?'

Gulzar Hafeez stroked his moustache. 'Look. Tell me what you see?'

Jameel hooked an arm over the back of the chair and scanned the room from one side to the other. People were eating, waiters rushed around, and when the doors swung back, he could see into the kitchen. But what was he looking for?

'I can see everything.'

'So can I, and that's why I sit here. Sometimes, I eat nothing at all and I still sit here'

'So you can see everything, I understand.'

'And so everyone can see me seeing everything. Do you understand that?'

'No, not really.'

'You will, Jameel.'

A waiter brought a glass jug of water and a card with writing on it. Gulzar Hafeez took charge, calling out a series of dishes the waiter noted on a pad. He read what he'd written and hurried to the kitchen. Gulzar poured for them. 'I want to ask you about Inas, your mother… is that all right? If you're here, does it mean she's dead?' His voice was different from the one that ordered a meal from a piece of card – that was a confident voice – this one was tempered by sadness and respect.

There was no need to reply.

'I've so many questions. For now just tell me this: did she have a good life? Was she happy?'

Jameel replied with care. 'Until my father died my mother had a very good life. They were happy. She was happy. After, it was more difficult, but she didn't lose her spirit and taught me never to lose mine.'

Gulzar Hafeez pursed his lips. 'I knew your father, of course. He was only a boy. I'm sure he grew into a man I could like. Looking at you I see my sister. Perhaps because that's what I want to see.'

He clapped his hands. 'Anyway, here comes our food.'

Gulzar unfurled the white linen square next to him and placed it across his knees. Jameel did the same. From then on, plates arrived in an endless procession, each dish more aromatic and spicy than the one before. Jameel hadn't known food could taste like this. He ate, copying his uncle. Gulzar noted the performance;

the young man was a stranger to eating in public. But he learned quickly. He was sensitive and proud, clever and respectful too. He liked him already.

When the table had been cleared they sat in silence, comfortable with each other. The restaurant was almost empty. Gulzar had more to ask. 'So, now you're in Lahore what're your plans?'

'My main plan was to find you. The city's so big, much bigger than I imagined. I'm amazed at my good fortune.'

The honesty gave Gulzar hope. He had no other relatives in the world except Inas' son. He didn't want this boy to go out of his life. No one could know the guilt he'd suffered. One letter in all that time. Building his business always produced reasons to keep him away and he'd been derelict in his duty to his sister.

In Lahore, he was Mr Hafeez, a successful businessman, but inside was a village boy hiding behind a façade, afraid his polished charade would be discovered.

'That's because it was meant to be. You're travelling on *your* path. Lahore, even the world, isn't a confusing place to a man following his destiny. Things come easily. Why would they not?'

'I was hoping you might have a job for me, as a dishwasher perhaps. I could learn to do that.'

Gulzar gulped back his emotions. 'You're in luck. I do have a job for you. Though I'm afraid it's not as a dishwasher.'

They talked after everyone had gone, chatting like old friends. 'Tonight, you'll stay with me, and every night. My home is your home, if you want.'

'I do, and I thank God for finding you.'

The day had begun in a transport café with Mazur, a kind man, and was ending in a restaurant in Lahore with another kind man. Jameel felt the bumps dig into his feet.

'Can I ask a question, Uncle?'

'Of course.'

'Do you keep your money in your shoes?'

His uncle pondered his answer. 'I used to. There was a time when I kept all my money in my shoes.'

Gulzar looked round his favourite restaurant, one of six he owned in the city. 'But I stopped doing that a long time ago, praise be to Allah.'

***

The noise came with a blast of brilliant light that hurt his eyes. He buried his face in the softest bedclothes he'd ever known. *Swoosh!* The room was awash with day. The brightness bored through the covers trying to reach him. He lay, unable to find the will to move. The bed was large and warm and safe, he didn't want to leave it.

'Wake up, Jameel.'

Gulzar clapped his hands. Jameel stirred; a gentle hand shook him. 'Time to come awake.'

He wasn't usually a sleepyhead. In Mundhi, he'd often be up and out before the sun, especially in summer when work started early and finished around noon. After that, it was too hot. Today was different. The night spent travelling in the truck, and the smells and sights and sounds round every corner in the city, had drained him. Also, he'd sat talking with his uncle into the small hours.

The room had gone quiet. He guessed Gulzar must have left. He'd be back soon. Jameel crept from under the covers and sat up. He was alone. The heavy curtains hanging from the ceiling to the floor had been shrugged aside, allowing sunlight to blaze through the windows. His head began to clear and he marvelled at the good luck he'd enjoyed since the truck stopped and he'd climbed aboard to see Mazur's welcoming face and impatient gestures.

It had been dark when they got to Gulzar's house. Jameel was close to exhaustion. Gulzar had called for tea and bombarded his nephew with questions about his mother and the village.

Gulzar Hafeez was rich – the bed gave some idea of how rich – his answer about keeping money in his shoes had been a joke. Jameel shook his head in disbelief. Could it really only be two days since he'd walked in the dark towards the road?

Footsteps echoing off wood and walls told him someone was coming.

'Uncle?' But it wasn't his uncle. It was a boy carrying a pile of clothes. He set his load down and disappeared.

Jameel had left his clothes on the chair. They were gone. He sank into the crisp white pool. The ceiling seemed miles away, a fan purred in its centre. Up where the walls ended, intricate patterns and designs stretched all the way round. A fireplace with a fire ready set dominated the far wall. It was a magnificent room.

The house was silent. Perhaps his uncle had gone out. No doubt an important man had business to take care of which wouldn't wait for a sleepy guest.

More footsteps, far away at first but growing louder, then his uncle burst in, arms open, a grin on his face. 'At last, the boy's awake!' He'd lost none of the previous night's enthusiasm. 'How did you sleep? Well?'

'Very well.'

'Good. Very good.'

'But someone has taken my clothes. I folded them over there. Now I can't find them.'

'But you have clothes. Many clothes.' He pointed to the bundle the boy had brought. 'Try them. If they don't fit or you don't like them, we'll get more.'

Jameel was stunned.

'New clothes are only the beginning. Later today we'll start to make our plans.'

'Plans for my new job?'

'Plans for your new life, my boy.'

Part Two

In the heart of the city

Chapter 9

The knock at the door brought Afra out of a shallow sleep. The light went on. It was Nadira. The night hadn't soothed her anxiety. She spoke in a whisper. 'Get up. You must get up, now.'

Afra propped herself on an elbow. 'What time is it?'

'Almost five.'

'And you want me to get up? Why?'

Nadira's face was uncovered. Afra saw it for the first time. She'd thought she was a woman; the stoop of her body led her to that conclusion. Now her error was clear. Nadira was young, a girl.

'Up. Quickly. We've work to do.'

Afra swung her legs out of the bed. On the soles of her feet the bare boards felt coarse and cold. Nadira crossed the room to the mound of clothes on the floor, a jumbled heap Afra had been too tired to fold. She lifted the garments and handed them to her.

'Put these on. Please. My husband's brother, his cousin and a friend come to the house every morning for breakfast. We must be ready for them. Come on.'

Afra dragged the clothes on. It felt like minutes since she'd taken them off.

Nadira said, 'I'll see you in the kitchen. Hurry.'

Why was she acting like this – telling her to be quick and talking in frantic whispers, like an old woman chivvying a child? She wasn't more than fifteen or sixteen. Strange behaviour. Afra finished dressing, threw water on her face and tiptoed downstairs, through the room with the faded armchair that had held the complaining Mrs Dilawar Hussein.

Nadira handed her a knife. 'Let's get started.'

***

Three hours later the men arrived, greeting each other with enquiries about how life progressed since the day before. The kitchen Afra had entered was not the place these men saw. It had been transformed into a warm welcoming space, swept and clean. A table sat with four chairs round it. The men dropped into their seats without a hello or good morning to the girls working at the stove, busy putting the finishing touches to the breakfast.

Bilal laughed with one of the men as his wife laid plates and fresh roti on the table. His face reminded Afra of a rodent. He looked as if he didn't wash and his teeth were dark with decay. The smell of new baked bread filled the kitchen; the men joked about how hungry it made them. One draped an arm over the back of the chair and stared. Afra saw him, but pretended she didn't.

'Bilal. How lucky are you? Two females to keep you happy and here am I, alone every night, dreaming of women I've never seen.'

He shook his head in mock disbelief.

'The new one belongs to our cousin, Quasim. She'll be his wife, the arrangements are made. He's asked me to look after her until then.'

'He must be more trusting than I remember, or maybe he doesn't know you.'

They sniggered and made crude gestures, enjoying the new girl's embarrassment under the veil Nadira insisted she wore. In Mundhi, Afra often wore the hijab but not indoors. The men talked through breakfast and drank cup after cup of tea. As they were leaving, Bilal called to his wife. 'Keep her busy. This place needs cleaning.'

The women washed plates and cups and cleared away what was left of the food.

When they were alone, Nadira relaxed. 'Time for us to eat,' she said.

Good news. Afra was hungry. She hadn't had anything since Mundhi. Nadira brought the remains of the breakfast: it wasn't a lot; fresh chapatis filled out what the men had left. But the tea was hot and very sweet, the way Afra's mother made it and just the way she liked it. They ate and drank in silence. Her new family had offered nothing, not even water, after the long journey. She made funnels with pieces of bread and filled them with food, tore off other bits and soaked up the juices. Between them, they ate everything. Nadira didn't take much though her bony arms said it would be better if she did. When the food was finished they sat, curious strangers.

'How long have you been here?'

Nadira counted on her fingers and gave up. 'I don't know. A long time. Or perhaps it isn't, perhaps it only seems long.'

Afra revised her opinion. Nadira was fourteen at most: stick thin, frail even, her eyes dull and old. Village life could be hard, women wore themselves out early. Afra had seen it. Too much work and loneliness made them give up. This girl was going down the same path. People stayed alive because they wanted to and died for the same reason. 'Where are you from, Nadira? Are your family near?'

The girl-woman gave a sad smile. 'From a village in the north. There was only my mother and myself, and she was old. I don't expect to see her again. She may even be dead, her health was never good.'

'So how did you find your way to Lahore?'

'Is that where we are?'

'Of course, the city's all around us,'

'Is it? I haven't been there.'

'You are there!'

'I've never been out of this house. Bilal forbids it.'

Surely that couldn't be true? But she knew it was. The food in her stomach felt heavy and bitter. Fear made her want to be sick. This child wasn't a wife or a companion, she was a prisoner. Nadira was a shadow shortening on the ground: a slave in the heart of Lahore.

***

For a week, at Nadira's bidding, Afra rose before the sun and began the chores that would send her to bed more tired than she'd ever been. By the end of the day, the house didn't look any better than it had at the start; the place was beyond cleaning. Despite their shared adversity, no real friendship developed between her and Bilal's young wife. Nadira lived in constant terror, the way a dog beaten too often cowers even under a friendly hand. Afra didn't realise what she was seeing would soon be her life.

One night she heard a scream. Half asleep, Afra imagined Shafi was having a nightmare. Why didn't Fatimah comfort him? Hadn't she heard his cries? An angry voice brought her awake. She gathered the sheet to her and listened to the deep timbre roll like thunder round the house. Then, the unmistakable sound of flesh on flesh cracked like a whip through the bedroom wall. A woman pleaded in vain against a relentless tirade.

And the blows fell.

Afra's instinct was to make it stop. Instead, she lay on the bed with her fingers in her ears and prayed the tyrant would grow tired of the beating. Eventually, it ended. In the morning, Nadira shook her and whispered the call to work. 'It's time, come on.'

Afra hauled herself up and dressed, so emotionally drained, she might have been the one who'd been attacked. What she'd heard numbed her. Nothing like it happened in her village. Did it?

Downstairs, Nadira already had pots of water on to boil and was grinding a spice mixture with a stone. She didn't greet the new girl. Afra started making the dough that would become the morning's bread. When Bilal's wife crossed the kitchen to get oil to fry the powdered spices, Afra glanced at her and gasped. Nadira's left eye was closed and she was trembling.

'I heard.'

Nadira didn't respond. Afra wanted to put her arms round this girl and take her pain away. 'I heard. And now I see.'

The victim kept her chin buried in her chest and sobbed.

'When did this begin?'

No reply.

'You can't stay, you can't. One day he'll kill you.'

'He did that the day he brought me here,'

Nadira turned. Her face was swollen, marked purple and yellow and her lip had split. 'What you see is the smallest part of my pain. I long for the warmth of the funeral flames against my skin. Until then, don't offer hope to me, there is none.'

Afra was stunned.

accept, find the shade, live on

Stupid words.

Nadira had been brutalised into accepting there would be no shade for her. One part living, three parts dead. They worked in silence after that, as far apart that morning as they'd ever been, divided by a common plight.

Around eight, the breakfasters arrived. Bilal joined in the ribald humour of his friends, unaffected by the harm he'd caused. To see him sit there laughing through mouthfuls of food anyone would believe his soul was clean and pure. So, evil enjoyed a joke. Nadira's eye went unnoticed under the hijab. The rest of the day was spent like other days, scrubbing and cleaning without improving anything. Afra saw the house as a manifestation of its owner. Washing wouldn't cleanse it.

When Bilal returned in the evening, Nadira took his meal to him. She and Afra ate together after he broke wind to announce he'd finished. They didn't speak; neither wanted to hear what the other had to say. Soon after, Afra went to bed, worn out from work and worry.

The noise of the door opening brought her awake. Footsteps bent a series of groans from the old boards. She was facing away from the intruder but smelled him. The threat made her conscious of her nakedness and she tensed. The steps came nearer, each one louder than the last, almost to the bed. In seconds, he'd have her. Yet, she wasn't afraid. This monster's intentions were clear and she was alone in the house. Nadira couldn't be counted on – she'd told the truth – she was already dead.

Afra threw back the sheet and launched herself at the outline of her attacker, determined that whatever came later, she'd have the first of it. She barged into him, bowling him over in the dark. His body met wood. He cursed. Afra dived past, heading for the door and who knew where after that. Her one thought was to get away. Bilal tripped her and she fell. Younger and more nimble, Afra recovered first. But he was stronger. He hit her in the side and she slumped against the wall.

Then he was crushing her. They grappled; a mess of fists and blows. Bilal grabbed her hair and dashed her head against the door. Afra almost blacked out; his foul breath brought her back. Disgust gave her the will to fight though it could only end one way: it was a contest she couldn't win.

Bilal's knee jammed her legs apart and they locked like tangled marionettes, panting and gasping. His grip tore hair from her scalp. Suddenly she stopped struggling.

'Go ahead. Go on. Finish what you've started.' Afra taunted him. 'Go on. Go on.'

Thick fingers pulled at her. She ignored the pain. 'But I'll tell. I'll tell Quasim. I'll tell Mrs Dilawar Hussein. You're afraid of her, aren't you?'

Bilal tightened his grip.

'I'll tell, I'll tell, I'll tell, I'LL TELL!'

'No one will believe you. You need witnesses. I see no witnesses, do you?' His hand closed round her throat. 'You'll be dishonoured, not me. Who would believe you?'

Time was running out, and what this coward said was true. Her heart crashed against her breast; her throat was on fire. She whispered, confident and knowing, 'Oh, Bilal, they'll cast me out for certain, but make no mistake, they'll believe me. They'll believe me because they know you. They see how you live.'

Bilal faltered. Afra pressed her advantage. 'Do you think I care what happens to me? I'm like your sad little wife, already dead. I'd kill myself and think I'd had the best of the bargain. You wish to live with Mrs Dilawar Hussein on your side. All that will be over.' She laughed in his face.

He didn't loosen his grip. His knee still crushed her naked thighs but something had changed. Bilal ran his tongue over cracked lips as his fevered mind weighed her words against the animal urge that had driven him to her room. Lust was slinking away like a fox chased from the chickens.

'Now or never. Violate me and I'll be dead before the sun comes up, I promise.'

In the dark, he was certain she was smiling. Bilal threw her aside and spat. 'Whore!' The door slammed behind him. Afra sat against the wall and closed her eyes. For the moment the nightmare was over.

Nadira must have heard though she didn't mention it. The four men ate their usual breakfast and Afra imagined Bilal was quieter than on other mornings.

Two days later, Mrs Dilawar Hussein arrived with a woman. She seemed in better spirits. The woman curled her lip at the faded furniture and peeling paint. This was Chandra, soon to be her sister-in-law. Chandra was tall like her brothers. Both women wore hijabs so their faces were hidden. The matriarch spoke. 'Nadira, why have you got Afra working? She's a guest.' Said lightly, the most gentle of chastisements.

'Go please and fetch some tea – you know how I like it – and cups for the three of us.'

Bilal's wife ran to the kitchen. The matriarch patted the seat. 'Come here child, I have news. Sit beside us. This is Chandra, my daughter. She has agreed to help you prepare for the wedding.'

Over her veil, Chandra's eyes gave nothing.

'When will that be, Mother?'

'That's what I'm here to tell you. In two weeks you'll marry Quasim and join our family.'

The mother and daughter removed their veils. Chandra had the hooked nose and piercing eyes that must have come from her father. Afra guessed she was about twenty, older than herself. The mother was different today, not the fierce autocrat of their previous meeting.

'Two weeks, not long. We've a lot to do. Chandra will guide you. She's here to let you two get to know each other'

Chandra allowed the smallest of smiles when her name was mentioned. Afra bowed her head. 'I'm happy to meet you, sister, and glad you're here. Your assistance will be most valuable.'

'We must go,' Mrs Dilawar Hussein said, 'another appointment I'm afraid and Firdos is waiting.'

'Thank you for coming. And you, Chandra. I look forward to seeing you soon.'

Afra was sincere. Now it was arranged, she desperately wanted the marriage to be a happy one. Her heart cried out for a friend. Perhaps Chandra would be that friend?

The visitors hurried for the door. 'Stay as you are, child. And don't let Bilal frighten you, he's harmless really.'

Afra knew a different truth.

When they'd gone, she thought about the visit – short, friendly, and strange. She returned to the cleaning. There was no question of leaving Nadira with it, whatever her mother-in-law said.

***

Firdos steered the car through the traffic. As the youngest brother one of his jobs was to chauffer his mother and sister around. Although it was becoming more common, women were discouraged from driving in Pakistan. He kept his resentment hidden. Chandra sat at the window and looked out at the city. Her mother took up more than her share of the seat. When Bilal's hovel was left behind, Chandra spoke. 'Why do I have to pretend to a stupid village girl?'

'Because Quasim and I wish you to.'

'What will my friends think of me? They'll laugh behind my back, and who would blame them?'

Mrs Dilawar Hussein sighed. Young people were so tiresome. 'Chandra, listen to me. How many times must I explain? This wedding is very important to your brother. He's thirty-six, time for him to marry. Like you, I wish his eyes had been dazzled by someone else, someone more like us, but they weren't. This girl is what he wants, so she's what he'll have. That's one thing. The wedding is another. Our friends and people he does business with will be there. Quasim can't just announce he's married, there needs to be ceremony, and the bride must seem happy.'

She turned to her daughter. 'You enjoy what comes from your brother. I don't hear you complain about your comfortable life. Well, now you're needed to play a part, make a contribution. You'll befriend this one and help her. Before the day and on the day. The world must see a shining bride. After…' She shrugged a meaty shoulder. 'That's another story. We'll have no need to pretend. In time, she'll produce a son for Quasim and her purpose will be served.'

Chandra didn't argue. If her mother told her brother about her attitude….. No, she'd obey because she must, and because she'd seen Quasim's anger. Not something easily forgotten.

Chapter 10

The weeks had passed quietly after Bilal's attack. He must've known about Mrs Dilawar Hussein and her daughter's visit, he'd become less abusive, even to Nadira; still an arrogant tyrant, that wouldn't change, but preferring to ignore both girls most of the time.

One evening Bilal delivered a message. Afra was lying on the bed when she heard his heavy step climb the stairs. She froze. The footsteps stopped outside her door, two knocks and the rusty old door handle began to turn, moving in slow motion. She sat up, terrified. Bilal didn't come in, he stayed hidden behind the frame.

'Woman!' He asserted an authority lost in the dark. 'Be ready tomorrow, you're going out. Chandra will come for you in the morning.'

The door closed, the threat was gone.

Chandra arrived full of enthusiasm for the day ahead. Afra felt like her old self. She laughed. 'This is exciting.'

'Yes it is,' Chandra said, 'for me too. It isn't every day I get to choose wedding outfits. You won't mind if I pretend they're for my wedding, will you?'

'Of course not. Is that why we're going out, to choose clothes for me?'

'Why else? In ten days the whole world will be staring at you. You'll be the centre of attention. You must look like a queen. Her wedding is the one time everyone expects the woman to outshine the man. We mustn't disappoint them, must we?'

'No, we mustn't.'

'And see, Quasim has bought you a wedding gift.'

A gold cage sat on the seat, inside a bird with deep blue feathers and reddish-brown breast stared out.

'This is for me?

Chandra was amused. 'When you know my brother better you'll realise how fortunate you are to be his wife. I'll take this to the house and put it with the other presents. Now let's have fun.'

And it had been fun, a time to savour. Afra saw the expensive garment she was wearing, one of several they'd bought and remembered the compliments from the older girl.

'Quasim will think he's dreaming when he sees you.'

In one shop after another Chandra searched the racks, mindless of the cost. 'This is the one I'll have.' She modelled a red embroidered shalwar kameez. 'When it's my turn to be married, I want this one.'

A moment later she whooped with delight. 'This is it, Afra.' She held up a long skirt covered in beads. A tunic with more decoration matched the skirt. The ghagra blinded her with its brilliance. 'A queen I think I said, this one was made for an empress.'

Afra let herself to be guided by Chandra, after all her family was paying. Chandra forgot she was playing a part, following her mother's command. She loved spending money on clothes, even if they were for a stupid village girl.

***

Quasim hadn't attended the first event: the mendhi. No males did, only women. There had been no sign of him since he'd visited Mundhi with his mother; he didn't see the yellow dress Afra wore without make-up. Many of the guests, all friends of the Dilawar Hussein family, wore green outfits in keeping with tradition. Two hours before it began, a woman came to the hotel to paint Afra's hands with a paste of henna powder and oil, creating art on her fingers and palms. At the mendhi, Afra sat between Chandra and her mother. Mrs Dilawar Hussein nodded and smiled at the sweets and desserts presented to the bride-to-be: symbols of celebration and happiness.

The females ate and danced in the hotel's smaller reception room. Afra hadn't been in a hotel and only ever danced with her sister and brother. She thought the whole thing marvellous. Even Mrs Dilawar Hussein appeared to be enjoying it. Hours later, alone in the room at Bilal's house, she felt low. The dress was gone, left in a bedroom at the hotel where she'd changed at the beginning of the evening.

No one mentioned Afra's family and though she would've loved her sister and brother to attend, it was a hopeless wish. How could they? They were many, many miles from Lahore. The journey and the expense involved made it impossible. Afra would be the only one from her family there. And a sadder thought: her mother must have realised that the day she agreed to the bride price.

Two days later was Shaddi, the wedding day. Nadira woke her to prepare breakfast then the bride-to-be went to her room and packed her canvas bag. She wouldn't come back to this place, no matter what. Poor Nadira was doomed to spend the rest of her life here, as shackled as any beast of burden, as condemned as the vilest criminal, without hope of reprieve.

She saw the delight on Quasim's face when she appeared, a vision in gold. Chandra had placed the last of the heavy jewellery round her neck and stepped back to admire her work. 'Like Cleopatra's triumphant return to Egypt,' she'd said, and guided her to a mirror in the corner. Afra had gasped, where was the peasant girl from Mundhi?

'Chandra, I'm beautiful. Thank you.'

Quasim's friends stood waiting to accompany the couple to the feast. To Afra they were strangers. Quasim's eyes shone, he looked her up and down and spoke to his sister. 'You've done a wonderful job, Chandra.' He took in the finery but missed the eyes pleading for recognition, appraising her without warmth.

The couple made their entrance. Afra's smile faltered, she forced it in place. The rest of the day was a blur. A band played, dish after dish was brought to the tables; tandoori chicken, saffron rice with nuts and fruit, naan; on and on. The bride and groom sat on either side of the matriarch, who scrutinised the waiters and the guests as if there was reason to mistrust both. No dancing or singing this time, just eating and talking and laughing. Quasim was relaxed, at home surrounded by his family and friends. Afra could see his brothers: Firdos, the driver on the journey from Mundhi and the shopping trip, and the one who'd asked Mirvat Khan for water. Zamir. Their eyes met and she recognised something she neither understood nor welcomed.

Someone placed a table in the middle of the room. Quasim and Afra walked to it. A priest recited prayers. He asked Quasim if he accepted Afra. Quasim nodded. A witness laid some papers on the table. He signed, his young wife made a mark and a cheer went up around the hall. Mrs Dilawar Hussein joined the newlyweds, supported by Firdos and Zamir.

Chandra answered her sister-in-law's unspoken question. 'Photographs.'

Photographs were a novelty. In her whole life Afra hadn't ever had her picture taken. She smiled, Quasim smiled back. Perhaps it would be all right after all. A man with a camera danced in front of them, calling out instructions, moving the group around. Quasim and Afra stayed at the centre no matter how the others were placed and replaced. She searched the crowd hoping to see a familiar face.

Then she did and was sorry.

Bilal sat at a table at the back. Alone, of course. His eyes undressed her the way they'd done every day in that hellish house. Afra pushed the image of his poor wife away. Nadira was beyond help.

Bombarded by one new experience after another she could be forgiven for not thinking about Jameel and Mundhi, already so far away. Even the bangles were forgotten, under the gold tunic out of sight, eclipsed by shining clothes and cloying sweets.

And then they were on their way home. Quasim leaned forward to direct the driver. The car swept off the leafy boulevard through a set of high gates, over a gravel drive to a grey imposing building set well back from the road and stopped.

"They're rich and live in a big house." Her mother's boast. This was it.

The driver rushed to open the door. Quasim strode up the steps and through the heavy door. Afra followed; as a wife she could expect to do a lot of following. Inside were gorgeous wall-hangings and more cushions and divans than she could count, a staggering contrast to Bilal's vile hovel.

Quasim took her hand and led her up a long staircase, faster than she could walk. His hand held hers in an unbreakable grip. At the top they hurried along a corridor. She stumbled and fell. Quasim picked her up as if she weighed nothing and headed to a door at the end, threw it back with his free hand and swept in. Afra didn't see the room, didn't notice its expensive curtains and carpet, or the chandelier made of a thousand glass tear-drops hanging from the centre of the high ceiling, there was no time. Quasim carried her to the bed and let her fall. She was shocked by her husband's urgency, he'd said nothing all day, most of the time he had ignored her.

Hands ripped her tunic. Beads scattered across the floor; she felt the chill of gold against her skin. His body knocked the breath from her lungs and blocked the fading daylight. She didn't fight him. She didn't respond. An image of that night in Bilal's house flashed behind her eyes; this was not Bilal.

This was Quasim, her husband.

More clothes were stripped away, his body covered hers, his lips found her neck.

And then it was over.

He collapsed, panting. She was pinned, unable to move. He pushed himself off and lay on the bed, eyes closed, his face hard and unlined. Afra struggled from under him and covered herself with the remnants of the outfit made for an empress lying shredded on the floor, its beauty spent, like Quasim.

'Wash and come back to me,' he said.

Behind a door she found a grey and white marble bathroom with a mirror covering one wall. Hot water gushed, condensation frosted the mirror, she rubbed the glass and there she was: Afra, wife of Quasim, naked and empty in an ornate room.

'Afra.'

It would get better, of course it would.

He called again, louder. 'Afra!'

She dried herself and went back to the room and the bed. He lay on his side, savouring her body and signalled her to join him. She slipped the bangles off her arm and pushed them out of sight with her foot. They wouldn't be part of this. He lunged, kissing and biting her, making sounds in his throat. Rough, uncaring fingers scratched her skin bringing a hundred tiny discomforts. Afra released herself. Tomorrow she'd search for the shade, if there was any, she'd find it. Find it and live on. And if there wasn't: accept.

Across the city, Jameel dreamed, unaware of what was happening just miles away. He'd never know how much she needed him.

Chapter 11

'Jameel!' Gulzar Hafeez opened an arm to include the stranger standing behind him. 'Meet Pir, Pir Ahmed.'

A brisk round-faced man gave a formal, not unfriendly nod. Gulzar didn't allow awkwardness to take root. 'Pir comes to us highly recommended. He'll be with us as long as we need him. In fact, I've hired him on a full-time basis. The faster we get you to where you need to be the better.'

He beamed at the tutor, confident his decision would be welcomed. Jameel's eyes darted from one to the other. He was missing something. 'And where is it you want me to be, Uncle?'

'Not where, Jameel. Not a destination.'

His nephew didn't know what he was talking about, except he was talking about him. 'I want you to travel on a journey with Pir. When the last step has been taken you'll be a different man, standing in a different place.'

Gulzar was accustomed to speaking uninterrupted. He threw an avuncular arm round Jameel's shoulders. 'When we met it was a great day for me. At last I had someone. You'll never know how many times I've wondered what my life has been about. All the years, all the work, for what?'

'But you're successful.'

'Am I, Jameel? In some ways, yes. On the outside I've made a great show of it. How sad to disagree. What you see here is good. It's fine, I like it, I chose it. I'm fortunate to have it and, even if I could, I wouldn't change it. But it's not enough.'

He poked a finger at his chest. 'In here, it's not enough.

'Building my business was all I cared about most of my life. I swore I'd never be poor. That thought drove me on, disregarding everything else, even cutting myself off from what little family I had. There was only my sister and me. I decided to rise above my background and become a rich man without realising the village was the power that moved me forward. Fear of going back drove me on. 'So I never went back though I almost did, several times.'

The confession, revealing and profound, was above Jameel's head.

'I let my family down. I prospered while they struggled and the more time passed the harder it became to do the thing I knew was right. Go back and help in any way they needed.'

His eyes brimmed. 'A call from my friend Mohamed gave me a second chance.'

Gulzar sighed and placed a hand on his nephew's arm. 'You asked if I had a job for you, remember? Well, I have. As soon as you're ready two things will happen.'

The light was back in his eyes.

'I'll retire and you'll take over from me. I'm sorry but it's the only job I'm prepared to offer you.'

Jameel reeled at the prospect. He was being given a position it had taken his uncle his whole life to achieve. Anxiety boiled to the surface. 'How can I possibly do this? I know less than nothing.'

'At the moment that's true, and why Pir is here.' He beckoned the tutor into their circle of two. 'Together we will transform Jameel into Mr Akhtar, the businessman. Any questions?'

nothing in the world; nothing in the world. A good boy, but nothing in the world

Jameel rubbed his hands together. 'When do we start?'

His uncle grinned. Even Pir smiled a little.

***

Gulzar stifled a yawn and patted his belly. The inescapable proof of his over-indulgence sat beneath his kurta; he had eaten too much at dinner again. His nephew sat across from him, studying symbols in a book, copying them onto sheets of paper.

'How did it go today?'

'Pir's a wonderful teacher but he expects too much of me.'

'He expects you to give what you have.'

'Can I ask you a question? Have you ever been in love?'

'I've been in love many times, Jameel, though never for long. The demands of my businesses always won me back. Many good women have slipped away. I realised too late. Why do you ask? Are you in love?'

'I was. I lost her.'

'That happens. Then again, real love refuses to be put aside. The answer to your question is that I've been in love many times, but really, never. If I had, I'd be a richer man, whether it lasted forever or ended in a day. Who is she?'

'A girl from the village.'

'Well, soon you'll be able to offer her a life. If it's love, real love, it'll wait.'

Jameel considered what his uncle said. 'She may be already married. Her mother rejected me because I was nothing in the world, that's why I left Mundhi.'

'Jameel, let me tell you something. Pir is instructing you in things he understands. Writing, reading, numbers. Important things, for sure. Then I'll show you how my businesses work. More important things to know. By the end, your head will be rolling around on your shoulders under the weight of it all. You'll have knowledge, a mountain of it, yet your education will be incomplete.'

'There will be more?'

'Much more, so be sure to leave room because it's gold.'

Working with Pir was hard enough. After that it would be his uncle's turn, and then? He wasn't sure he could handle it.

'Surely everyone can't need to know all this to get on in the world?'

'No, indeed. Most people know very little and still struggle by. The reading and writing, perhaps, and haven't you noticed how even the dullest dullard can count his money? Beyond that, few understand.'

'What don't they understand?'

Gulzar shrugged. 'Themselves. Who they are. Why they feel the way they do.'

Jameel's face fell; he'd hoped for more. Something he could find in a book.

'Everyone knows who they are, don't they?'

Gulzar stretched. 'Unfortunately, no. Most people have no answer to a question like that. Most have never asked, so how could they?'

His uncle liked to talk and sometimes.... Jameel returned to his study.

'Pir and I will show you all you need to master business. We'll be your teachers and you'll learn from us. By the end, you'll be further than most ever get. You'll have knowledge, quite a bit of it. The world is full of knowledge, it's all around us. But happy people aren't all around. Have you looked? Did you see many? No Jameel, your education will be complete when you know who you are.'

Gulzar wished he hadn't gone down this road, it was too early and Jameel was too young. 'Wisdom, not knowledge. When you have wisdom you'll be the complete man.'

'And what's the difference?'

'All the difference in the world. Knowledge comes from the outside, wisdom is within.'

'I don't follow.'

'Of course you don't. How could you? You're at the start of your adventure. You don't know what you don't know. Let me give you an example. This woman, tell me again what she said.'

'She told me I was nothing in the world.' Jameel's face flushed.

'Mmmm.' Gulzar stroked his moustache. 'And you believed her?'

'It was Afra's mother.'

'And you believed her.' A statement not a question.

'She's known me all my life.'

'Wrong. She doesn't know you, how could she, she doesn't know herself. She doesn't know anything worth knowing about you. Her values are material values. Her judgement is flawed. Did she know that soon you'd be a rich man? Did she know that? And if she had what would her opinion of Jameel have been then, eh?'

He knelt beside the young man and his books. 'You let the views of this woman drive you from your home and your love, yet they're the worthless words of an unenlightened soul. Do you see?'

'A little, I think.'

'If we allow the opinion of others to matter we're in their power. What they think of us becomes what we think of ourselves. The only opinion of you that matters is your own.'

Jameel yawned and dragged himself to the door.

'But why do I have to learn so much? Reading, writing, numbers. About business, about myself. Why? I'm an honest man, prepared to work hard, isn't that enough?'

Gulzar rubbed a tired hand through his hair. It was easy to understand why Jameel, or anyone for that matter, would balk at what was in front of him. Maybe he was wrong to push the boy so hard, so fast. 'You must find your own answers, of course. All I can do is tell you what life has taught me.'

Tiredness hung on his nephew like the clothes of a larger man. 'So, I must be smarter than everyone else?'

'No, Jameel, no one is saying that.'

'What then?'

'Two things.'

'What are they?'

'Trust in God, and at night, tie up your camel.'

Gulzar was a good man. Jameel loved him already. A good man but crazy as a desert storm. 'Goodnight, Uncle,' he said and closed the door.

Chapter 12

She lay on the bed listening to the fan whirring above. She wasn't tired, well, maybe just a little. It was only two in the afternoon. That morning she'd felt unwell. The feeling passed as quickly as it had come. Bilal and the doomed Nadira seemed far away. Mundhi and her mother were even harder to recall. Jameel and Fatimah and Shafi she stored deep in her memory; thinking about them brought too much pain.

Afra placed a hand on her wrist. None of the family had commented on the wooden symbols, too busy with their own lives to pay attention to the new wife. She had no idea what those lives were. The men went off to their business. Chandra was always out somewhere – the relationship she'd hoped for with her sister-in-law hadn't survived the wedding day. Chandra ignored her, or at best, flashed a diluted smile. Just when she believed she'd found a friend, what a pity.

Mrs Dilawar Hussein never spoke to her. Afra wasn't unhappy about that; the woman disapproved of everything and spent the day fussing and fuming or complaining about the cook, roaming the house in a state of permanent dissatisfaction.

When she joined the family for dinner, conversation was between the brothers, the women said nothing, at least not to her. The meal was served on a polished table in a room kept for that. Everyone used special cutlery. Afra watched and learned.

Food was prepared by the cook and brought to the table by Zana, the servant. Zana was a teenager. So far, nothing had been asked of Afra. She had no work to do and no one to talk to. The days were long, the nights longer. Quasim's initial animal enthusiasm had become a more measured toying – no more enjoyable for that.

He took his time satisfying himself; it could have been any woman crushed under him. No tender words escaped his lips, nothing to temper his brutish actions.

For all that, he treated her like a jealously-guarded possession, even with the rest of his family. Chandra and his mother wore saris wrapped round and draped over their shoulders, occasionally Chandra wore jeans. Quasim insisted his wife cover herself from head to toe.

Afra had no say in her clothes, they appeared in the wardrobe the day after the wedding, heavy black and brown shrouds that itched and scratched.

Things were very different from the house in Mundhi; for one, it was many times larger. Afra still hadn't seen most of the rooms. In time, Zamir and Firdos would bring their wives to live here and the corridors would echo with the laughter of their children. It was hard to know if anyone else was in the building it was so quiet; traffic on the road outside was no more than a distant hum, most times, not even that, and at night the gates were closed against Lahore.

Afra had been out of the house just twice, each time Quasim met with a business associate. On the first occasion, she was kept in a room while the men talked; no one offered her anything to drink. The second meeting was shorter. They went to the outskirts of the city. Quasim said, 'Stay in the car' and locked the doors. Afra wondered why he bothered to bring her. It should have been good except it was another lonely experience. She missed the argumentative chickens disputing every crumb and Uncu lying in the shade, too stupid to be unhappy. Her one companion was the cage bird. Afra fed it scraps saved from breakfast. If Mrs Dilawar Hussein was having her afternoon nap, she lifted its golden prison from the window to the garden. It liked the sunshine and sang a clear melodious song that stopped when she took it back inside.

Ten weeks since the wedding and already she was bored. This new life demanded little and gave less. Quasim returned in the evening and told her what he wanted her to do or not do. Conversation, as she'd known it, didn't exist. Walking from the fields, waiting for Jameel to ask the same question every night seemed wonderful now. A picture of him kicking stones rose behind her eyes.

tomorrow then?

She saw his face the time she'd been cross with him and hated herself for her impatience. That look was the saddest thing. Afra cried. He'd been her best friend in the world. Nobody could say where he'd gone. Maybe Karachi. Afra had heard it was a dangerous place and prayed he was safe.

She rolled on to her back, an arm over her eyes, shutting out the light. The bangles brushed her face. This would never be home. Home was wherever Jameel was. The fan calmed her, lulled her, she felt tired. In the middle of the afternoon, how could that be?

***

Afra felt herself falling into space, her head cracked the wooden floor and she landed on her back with her clothes bunched around her waist. She opened her eyes, shocked. The kick buried itself in her side like a hammer. 'Get up!'

Another blow crashed into her bare thigh. 'Get up!'

Quasim towered over her. 'Get up, woman.'

She struggled to her knees. What had happened? The last memory she had was of feeling tired, then this. Her head spun. Something bitter rose in her throat. Quasim grew tired of waiting; a hand hauled her to her feet before she was ready. Her legs collapsed. She staggered and tried to focus. 'Quasim?'

Her skin bruised under his grip, fear made Afra vomit. Her husband watched. Quasim, the ranting madman was replaced by a more terrible twin; an unsmiling torturer; a man who could cripple her without anger. She wanted to scream. Who would hear or help even if they did?

'Quasim.' The words sounded thick and slurred. 'What's wrong?'

The blow came from nowhere and caught her on the temple. He lifted her and threw her to the bed. 'Do you know what time it is? Not even five o'clock. And you sleep.'

'I was tired, just tired. I closed my eyes, that's all.'

She begged him to listen. Quasim hauled her to her feet, drew back his arm and struck. Afra doubled in agony. Pain like she'd never known exploded in her belly. He spun her round and let go. She crashed into the far wall and blacked out.

When she came to, Quasim knelt beside her holding a glass of water. And he wasn't angry anymore. 'Drink this.' He placed the glass to her lips, his hand steady. The liquid ran down her chin. Moments ago, he'd been beating her, now he nursed the damage he'd done. 'I want you to stay here. I'll say you're not feeling well.'

She lay against the wall and heard him shut the door behind him. Afra crawled under the sheets and her body closed down. Sleep was the medicine it found.

***

In the dark, she heard the steady rhythm of his breathing. Her back ached and her arm throbbed where he'd gripped it while he struck. Images of the attack came unbidden. The top of her head felt torn open yet these injuries hadn't brought her awake. Something more serious was wrong; her stomach was on fire. Somewhere inside lay real hurt.

Afra eased herself off the bed and limped to the bathroom. Her husband slept, untroubled, snoring the night away. The pain was intense, her head swam, she was going to faint. She lowered herself to the floor, to the cool tiles, while the furnace in her belly raged. She lost consciousness again.

When her eyes opened it was light. The floor was cold against her skin. Her body hummed with pain but the hurt in her stomach was gone. A metallic smell filled the room and the inside of her thighs were wet. Afra pulled her clothes away and saw the blood.

Tears fell. She raised herself on to the toilet seat and scooped water from the bowl. More tears came. Her sobbing echoed in the bathroom as the last of the foetus was washed away.

If Quasim knew he'd blame her for losing his child.

Not hers, not theirs. His.

It would never be born. And she was glad.

Chapter 13

After six months in the house, things changed.
No subtlety was employed. Mrs Dilawar Hussein had
no use for it. Since the miscarriage, Afra was obedient and
said nothing unless spoken to. It worked. Quasim hadn't wanted
a partner or a friend – he would never want those things. His
motives were less complex. All he needed was a sexual vessel and a
son. The first she could supply, even tolerate, so long as she took
her mind to another place during the act. It made her smile to
imagine what the brute would think if he knew that during sex
his wife was busy feeding chickens in Mundhi.

She'd been bought for another purpose, and in that, Quasim
was destined to be disappointed. Afra believed any hope of a baby
had been washed away in the night. That was one secret. The
other circled her wrist. Many times every day, she ran her fingers
over the delicate engravings, drawing hope and strength from
them, praying they'd lead Jameel to her.

Mrs Dilawar Hussein broke the breakfast silence, spitting a
question at her eldest son and answering it herself. 'What use is
she? No use!'

The anger was naked. Afra didn't raise her head although the
woman was talking about her. 'Six months and nothing.'

The son kept on eating. Afra suspected he'd already heard this
rant. 'There's time,' he said.

'You think so? I believe we've made a bad bargain.'

Quasim didn't defend his wife while they discussed her as if
she wasn't there. The hijab gave her something to hide behind.
Chandra listened to the exchange between her mother and
brother. There would be no support from her. In six months, she'd

spoken just twice. Zamir and Firdos seemed to want no part in the debate either, they concentrated on their food. Quasim sighed, uncomfortable with the conversation.

'What would you have me do?'

His mother sneered. 'I expect you're doing all you can. This girl has cost us.' She glared at her daughter-in-law. 'From tomorrow, she can start to pay it back. We'll have our money's worth, one way or another.'

Quasim didn't argue. He reached for another chapati, broke off a piece and dipped it in gravy. Soon after, the men left to go to their work, where they sold agricultural machinery – tools, fertiliser and the rest – to farmers in the country beyond Lahore. Quasim, the eldest, was the boss. The third and last time he'd taken her out with him, he had a meeting with an important customer. Afra stayed in the car yet again, while her husband went inside a metal-framed building with 'Dilawar Hussein' painted in large letters on the side, and she'd known she was looking at the source of the family's money.

With breakfast over, the women had drifted to their own parts of the house. Zana hurried to clear the crockery and debris. The rest of the day passed like every day, in silence. Afra understood the older woman's unhappiness; she'd been brought to their house to give birth, and be an unresisting body in the night. She was failing and would continue to fail, thanks – though Mrs Dilawar Hussein would never know – to her son. The family's reaction would be horribly predictable. Afra remembered the treatment meted out to her for nothing. What her punishment would be for losing the child wasn't a thought worth keeping.

Next morning, when she followed her husband to breakfast, there was no place set for her. Five chairs stood with the table. The others ignored her until their mother arrived. She beckoned Afra to follow her. They walked through the house, downstairs into a steamy dungeon. Zana and another woman Afra had never seen worked at a stove. The sour smell of burned fat and stale spices wafted in the air. The matriarch spoke to the cook, glanced at Afra and nodded. Mrs Dilawar Hussein marched away.

The cook looked her up and down. 'Find a brush and get started. I hear you've a debt to pay. I can find plenty of ways for you to work it off.'

***

'Clean! I want it clean!'

The pail of rubbish, swept from the kitchen floor, was kicked across the cold stone slabs; scraps of food bobbed in puddles of dirty water. Afra didn't argue. The kitchen was clean, certainly cleaner than when she'd first been pressed into service with Zana and the cook. They were gone.

Early one morning she'd found the kitchen in darkness. She put water on to heat and mixed the dough for bread. After an hour, no one had shown up and the truth of her station became clear. She was the servant. And the cook. The other women had been kept on long enough to teach her what was required. They probably hadn't known, though even if they had, what difference would it have made?

Quasim's mother appeared in the doorway, casting round for something to be dissatisfied about, always able to find it. Afra, on her knees, hadn't noticed her standing over her. Mrs Dilawar Hussein brought her foot down on the edge of the bucket. The pail of water got the same treatment, swamping the trash, creating a bigger mess.

The contrast between the women was stark. One screamed, the other cowered like a frightened dog.

In the dining-room, the brothers talked while the new Zana laid the food in front of them. Quasim ignored his wife. It took several trips before everything was out. When the last of it was on the table, she knelt in the kitchen and gathered the remnants of vegetables and fruit. Making her mind blank was the only way to survive. Questions weakened her will to carry on. Two especially: What had she done to deserve this?

And would she ever see Jameel and Mundhi again?

To the first the answer was clear: nothing, she'd done nothing.

The second was equally clear: not in this life.

Zana's departure meant someone had to do her work. Mrs Dilawar Hussein had informed her daughter-in-law that someone was her. Afra followed the overweight woman round the house, hearing the never-ending list of tasks. 'Do you understand what your duties are?'

'I think so.'

'Thinking will not be good enough. Do it and do it right.'

The work was too much for one. She was being ordered to do the jobs of three people; all she could do was try. There was no way to finish everything this crazy woman demanded. She'd be dead from exhaustion in a month.

'And I almost forgot, there's one more room I want you to see. Follow me.'

Afra did, up two flights of stairs the older woman struggled to climb. The second staircase was neither polished nor carpeted with walls that hadn't been painted in years. The mother's chest rose and fell; she coughed and spluttered. At the top, they reached an unvarnished door. 'Open it.'

Afra gripped the handle. The mechanism was slow. Behind it was a box worse than the one at Bilal's house. A child-sized bed took most of the space, a sink and a toilet, chipped and marked and foul-smelling, took up the rest.

'This is your new room. Before you do anything else bring your things up here.'

Afra sat on the bed. Damp from the cover seeped through to her skin. In a cracked mirror above the sink, she saw a face: Nadira's.

***

The door had no lock and was always open for Quasim. He seldom came near her and when he did, it was only for a few minutes; he no longer found her desirable.

She'd lost track of time and couldn't say how long she'd been in the house. In fact, it had been more than three years.

During winter, when the barren room was freezing, Afra paced to keep warm. Once she went to the kitchen and huddled in front of the oven where it was warmer. But it wasn't worth the risk, so she suffered in the cell at the top of the house.

In the summer months, the opposite was true. At night, there was barely a breath of air. And all the time she worked like a dog. Days seemed to last forever, attending to chore after chore before she fell on the bed and slept, often too tired to eat whatever the others had left.

The unremitting toil stripped the flesh from her bones: the light within her dimmed. Her hair, once thick and lustrous, came out in handfuls. Her teeth suffered under the burden of labour and the poverty of her diet. Sometimes they hurt more than she could stand, stealing the precious hours of rest from her before the body-breaking, mind-numbing cycle began again.

And, at times, the past crept up on her in distant memories: Fatimah and Shafi wrestling Jameel to the ground amid wild shouting and screaming. Did they ever wonder what had become of their sister? As for Jameel, would she look up and find him ready to take her with him?

She smiled a small unhappy smile. Whatever else happened, that wouldn't be it. Even if he found where she was, her jailers guarded her too well. She wouldn't have the strength to flee and would rather die than have Jameel see what she'd become. No, when daydreams came, she swept them away like the leavings on the kitchen floor: the useless things of yesterday.

***

Afra didn't wear the bangles now; the work was too rough to expose her only possession to it and they slipped off her stick of an arm. She kept them under a loose floorboard, putting them on when she most needed to feel their strength against her skin. Quasim didn't come to her room – not even sometimes – and for that at least, she was grateful. If experience had taught her anything since coming to Lahore, it was that there was always something worse. Not long ago, she'd felt sorry for Nadira.

The change in Zamir and Firdos went unnoticed. Quasim's younger brothers watched. They wanted her. Neither discussed his lust because to desire a brother's wife was an abomination. Each waited and planned for the moment when the servant was least expecting their attention.

Zamir was first to take the treatment of the woman to a new low. The middle son was similar in looks to his older brother, but very different. Where Quasim was arrogant and smart, Zamir was just arrogant. His life had been one of silent resentment towards the head of the family since their father's death. No matter how much Chandra and the two boys disagreed with him, only their mother dared speak with anything other than respect.

Zamir knew Firdos had a secret. Late at night, he crept out of the house to visit the prostitutes in Heera Mandi. Zamir had seen him more than once. He wouldn't go there – it wasn't safe in any number of ways – yet he was readying himself to play an even more dangerous game. And Zamir Dilawar Hussein had a secret of his own; he was thirty-one-years-old and had never been with a woman. The prospect scared him. Women were alien creatures to the second son. He didn't see them as people, only as objects of desire.

Here in the house, day after day, year after year, he studied his brother's wife, imagining her under the unflattering clothes. Their very shapelessness aroused him. Zamir had wanted to possess her from the first but if he acted on what was in his heart, he'd dishonour his brother. As time passed, he felt thwarted in this as in everything, making him reckless and, considering what he itched to do, recklessness made him stupid. Feelings of injustice swamped his brain, while thoughts of caution or danger or consequence were forgotten. Zamir believed he felt lust. He didn't. What consumed him was hatred: of his brother, his father, his mother, the whole family. The whole world.

The second son of the Dilawar Hussein family looked normal. No one suspected Zamir was insane: Afra was the vehicle for his revenge.

One morning at breakfast, he put a hand to his head and slumped forward. 'Zamir,' his mother said with her usual impatience, 'are you all right?'

Zamir pushed his fingers through his hair. 'I don't know. I feel ill.'

'Girl! Bring some water for Zamir.'

Afra ran to the kitchen, filled a glass jug and returned. At the table everything was as it had been. Zamir bent forward looking unwell, his family stared at him.

Quasim said, 'Are you sick, brother?'

'I feel it. I'll lie down for a while.'

Whatever his brother's shortcomings, Zamir never missed a day's work. The others finished their breakfast and left. In the kitchen, Afra started to clean, ignorant of the danger she was in. Upstairs, Zamir lay relishing the opportunity he'd created.

By the middle of the morning Afra was almost finished downstairs and had forgotten all about her husband's brother. As far as she knew, everyone had gone, leaving her to her crushing routine. Three pots of prepared vegetables were ready to cook. She assessed her work, folded a cloth and laid it near the sink.

Suddenly she realised she wasn't alone.

Zamir stood in the doorway. He grinned. The girl was unafraid, past the point where her safety concerned her. It was all too clear. Zamir hadn't been unwell, that had been a ruse. 'Can I help you, Zamir?' Her voice was clear and strong.

The brother couldn't know death held no threat for her. All he saw was a way to redress the injustice of his life. When he dominated her he'd be asserting his place in the family.

And at last, a battle he could win.

The thought inspired his sickness. His brother's wife would pay for the pain of being the second son. He took a step forward, his mouth dry. For Afra, here was something to lash out at after the abuse borne without protest. When the brother crossed the line he'd find her waiting.

'Can I help you?'

He moved further into the room and lunged at her. Rather than escape, she met his force with her own. The weariness fell away in a rush of anger. They struggled in the middle of the floor. Afra's fingers tore skin from Zamir's arms. He howled and hauled her off her feet. Opposition was unexpected, his assault needed to leave no sign otherwise he'd be unmasked. They fell, Afra on top. He lost his grip. She struck him on the side of the head. Hard blows.

Zamir had the most awful thought of his life. Could this kitchen waif defeat him? He mustn't let that happen; the last scraps of his self-worth screamed against it. His tortured mind drove strength back in a crazy rush. He threw the emaciated body across the kitchen's stone floor, scampering after it like an animal. Afra's head hit the ground. Zamir tried to strangle her but she broke free. Her eyes fixed on her attacker, filled with rage equal to his own.

Desperate souls struggling to square the inequality of their lives.

He straddled her exhausted, semi-conscious body, panting and sweating and ripped her underclothing away. Zamir had won. Afra lost her strength as victory brought him a fresh supply. He dragged his clothes off. She searched for the place she ran to when Quasim towered above her and fled in her mind to a dusty village in the Punjab.

tomorrow, then?

She whispered to a nervous boy kicking stones. 'Tomorrow.'

Zamir didn't hear, he was where he was feared and respected, where his word was law. The rise and fall of the girl's breasts told of the battle she'd fought and lost. Zamir's success coursed through his veins, filling the emptiness in him. He was the winner, a hero with the strength of ten. A god.

He forced his victim's legs apart. Afra waited for the final degradation.

Nothing happened.

She opened her eyes. His arms tied her to the ground but his face showed pain greater than her own; contorted and lined, fractured by a dawning humiliation worse than any he could inflict on her. Zamir cried, helpless, childlike. He buried his face in her shoulder and wept against her neck. The winner had become the loser. His life-force shrank away unspent.

Afra realised she could be in greater danger. When the monster put aside his self-pity he'd cast around to find an outlet for his rage. She squeezed from under his body shuddering with the shame of impotency. Zamir continued his lament, more alone than the friendless slave running from the room to hide in the heights of the house.

Next morning, when Afra brought the breakfast to the table she was afraid to look at Zamir. She needn't have worried. Her husband's brother was just as reluctant to acknowledge her, using a newspaper to shield himself. The failed abuser melted into the family group, content for the moment to bide his time and nurse his hatred, husbanding it the way others kept odd buttons, for the day it was sure to be needed.

Chapter 14

Gulzar heard his son on the telephone to the bank and realised it was time to step aside. Jameel spoke with the confidence of someone who knew his business. And he did; from the bottom to the top.

He'd arrived in Lahore, a dreamer of small dreams: a broken-hearted refugee with an ambition to be a dishwasher in his great uncle's restaurant. After six months, he'd achieved his modest goal. During the day, he studied with Pir, while at night he washed dishes, mopped kitchen floors, and fell into bed dog-tired. Hours later the process began again. From there he progressed to peeling potatoes and preparing vegetables, boning chicken breasts and carefully shelling prawns.

He asked no special treatment and got none. Nobody toiled harder than the young man from Mundhi.

It took Pir three and a half years to complete his work. One day he announced himself satisfied and left. Then the real learning began with a less-forgiving master. Gulzar lived and breathed his empire and insisted his protégée do the same. His philosophy – Jameel was to discover he had one for every occasion – was simple, and he voiced it again and again. It was his mantra: "Attention to detail. A thousand small tasks done well. Anyone can be mediocre. Let's be proud of what we do, eh?"

In the fifth year he became Gulzar's deputy. They went on walks together round the city, sampling food, discussing problems with the managers and experiencing the customers' experience. Gradually the older man faded into the background as Jameel's stronger younger hands took the reins.

The call ended, Jameel replaced the receiver.

'Congratulations. You're ready. At the end of the month you'll become the MD. I won't be hard to find if you need me. I'm certain you won't. It's all yours, now.'

Jameel wasn't as surprised as he appeared, he'd seen this coming but was shrewd enough to play his part. 'Are you sure I'm ready?'

'More than ready. I've gone as far as I can. The business needs fresh blood. I've watched you thinking, scribbling away. Time to let whatever's going on in your head out into the world.'

His son nodded. 'I've been waiting for the right moment to say it. We should move into the hotel sector. We'd need a partner of course. Vertical expansion it's called.'

Gulzar smiled: this from the boy who only a few years ago hadn't eaten in a restaurant. 'Is it? No rush. Put your proposal on paper and we'll discuss it. Anything you need, just ask.'

'As a matter of fact there is something. Someone.'

***

Mohamed Abdul Quadir's smile was warm. He came towards his visitor and shook his hand. 'Jameel. Gulzar talks about you all the time. How is the old rascal?'

'He's fine. I want to speak about Ali.'

'Really? Let's sit down and you can tell me.'

'Ali's been with you a long time. He'd never leave if he felt he was letting you down. I'd like to ask him to work with me – he'll say no of course. Unless he has your blessing.'

'And what can you offer him that I cannot?'

'You have a large family. Ali won't rise above his present position. I intend to make him my right hand. Not just an employee, an important part in an expanding business.'

'Does Gulzar know?'

'Yes. He supports my decision as long as I haven't risked your friendship.'

'You and Ali are close. You'll make a great team. He's the best manager I've ever had. I'll be sorry to lose him.'

'You won't be losing him, you'll be helping him. And me.'

Ali appeared and embraced Jameel. 'Come for some decent food for a change?'

Jameel laughed. 'I want more than that. Walk with me.'

His friend didn't ask where they were going, as always he just grinned. When they came to the heavy dark wood door with the gold plaque in the centre Jameel bowed and opened it. 'Where it began, remember?'

'I remember all right.'

They sat at a table and ordered vegetable pakora. Ali became serious. 'Why have you brought me here?'

'Can't you guess?'

'I'd rather you tell me.'

'Okay. How often have we talked about how great it would be to work together?'

'Very often. But that's all it is, talk. It isn't going to happen and we both know it.'

'Wrong. I'm offering you the chance to make it happen. There's a job with your name on it. Come and work for Ravi Restaurants.'

Ali shook his head. 'I already have a job, Jameel.'

'Not like this.'

'I'm flattered of course but Mr Quadir depends on me.'

'I've spoken to Mohamed. We have his approval if you're willing.'

'I'd love to manage one of your places, who wouldn't?'

'I'm afraid that's not what I have in mind.' He heard himself and was reminded of Gulzar shaking him awake on his first morning in Lahore.

plans for your new life, my boy

'Then what?'

'I have an idea, a big idea and you will be part of it. We already have enough restaurants. I intend to go into the hotel business. How does assistant general manager for the group sound?'

***

The air was cool, cold even; winter was on its way. Afra shivered, fully-clothed under the single sheet. Her teeth chattered; her feet were stone. If she didn't fall asleep soon, she'd creep downstairs and spend what remained of the night by the kitchen stove.

In the darkness, the creak of the floorboard was like a gunshot. Someone was climbing the staircase, testing each step. Not Quasim, he had no reason to conceal his approach or his intentions.

Her mind searched for an alternative and shuddered. Zamir. She'd been lucky the first time. She pulled the cover away, dog-tired and hopeless. There was no window in the room, otherwise Afra would've opened it and jumped.

The floorboard groaned again. An unlocked door was all that stood between her and the madman, come to complete what he'd started. This time, he'd make no mistake.

No fury raged through her now, that torrent had passed, but when Afra fled the kitchen she'd taken something with her, and kept it near. The footsteps stopped. Zamir stood on the other side. The rusted handle turned. She crouched to meet the intruder, her hand closed round the kitchen knife.

Afra sensed rather than saw him and drove the short sharp point into the dark as hard as she could. He screamed. Steel sliced flesh a second time. He screamed again. Zamir fought to find the door, panicked by the pain his attacker had inflicted, fearing more and worse. He crashed out of the room and down the stairs with no thought of stealth. Afra ran her finger along the blade and smiled. It was wet.

In the morning, she washed the knife and put it with the others. Twice she'd repelled Zamir, perhaps there was a force watching over her after all. Maybe the power Jameel had spoken of. She carried the breakfast plates into the dining room. Everyone was there. Zamir ignored her.

Thirty minutes later Mrs Dilawar Hussein left, then Quasim. Neither knew anything of the second son's ambitions. If they had, Afra would be deemed as guilty as her attacker. Both would suffer for dishonouring Quasim.

Zamir and Firdos were last to go. The youngest son was reluctant to put weight on his left leg. Afra had been mistaken, it hadn't occurred to her the attacker might be Firdos. Her situation was worse than she had imagined. Better to have it ended. These men wouldn't forget. And where there had been one smarting animal, now there were two.

***

Seven years after Afra's mother sold her into slavery, Chandra told a lie. Not a new experience for the Dilawar Hussein daughter, but what it brought couldn't be undone.

One evening Afra strolled in the garden between the tall palms and frangipane. The staccato racket of a broken exhaust made her look towards the traffic. At first, she didn't see Chandra or the man talking by the gates. When the couple registered with her weary brain she dismissed them. Whatever the daughter did was nothing to do with her. She lifted the cage – the bird had been silent today; the taste of freedom hadn't been enough to make it sing. Afra took a last look at the sky and reluctantly went inside to begin the final preparations for dinner. Chandra's companion was tall like her, dressed in western-style clothes. They spoke in animated whispers, his eyes never leaving her face. She was as taken with him. They gave their attention to each other, relishing their status of fascinating and fascinated creatures.

They stood inside the open iron gates, so involved they failed to notice Quasim's car edging through the traffic. When Chandra saw it she ran to the house and the man walked away before the head of the Dilawar Hussein family turned into the drive. The vehicle braked at the front door, screeching tyres spraying gravel. Quasim jumped out, looking to where the stranger had been. 'Chandra! Chandra! Here! At once!'

Quasim stormed into the main room, impatient for his sister to obey. Waiting stoked his anger. Chandra appeared, surprised and perplexed. She faked concern. 'Quasim, what's wrong?'

Her brother wasn't a man for games unless he made the rules. 'Who was that man? Don't lie, I saw him. Who is he?'

Chandra was at the crossroads. The fork chose itself. 'What man? There's no one here but me.'

'I saw him.' Quasim spoke with quiet certainty. 'At the gate, I saw him.'

Chandra knew his volcanic temper, and understood the need to take care. She answered with respect. 'Brother, you saw someone but please believe me. I know nothing about a man. Where was this person?'

'In the garden.'

The head of the family was unused to being questioned. Chandra was smarter than her brothers but they wouldn't discover that from her. 'I haven't been in the garden today. It's too hot.'

'There was a man.'

'What did he look like?' She used the question to distance herself.

'He was tall. Well-dressed. I didn't see his face. He made off as soon as I arrived.'

His sister realised she was safe; he'd witnessed nothing.

'How strange,' Chandra said, playing the role of Quasim's partner in solving the mystery, covering her tracks by hiding in plain sight. 'What business could anyone have in the garden? Unless – '

'What? Unless what?'

His sister shook her head knowing her next words would set her free. 'You saw a man in our garden. You assumed he was there to meet me.'

Quasim listened. His sister smiled. How easy he was to manipulate. 'Yes.'

'What if this stranger was meeting someone else?'

'Who? There's no one here.'

Chandra let him get there by himself, that way he'd stay convinced. Quasim struggled to the obvious conclusion. She helped him, and watched his lip curl in distaste.

'No one? Not no one, brother.'

***

The water churned in a rolling boil; the vegetables were almost ready to drain.

'Afra.'

She jumped, startled, and turned to see an unusual sight: Quasim. He never came to the kitchen. Apart from their mother, none of the family did.

'Quasim. I didn't hear you.'

He pointed to the pots crowding each other on the stove. 'Busy, I see. Always so busy, eh?'

Afra knew better than reply, she detected anger in him and saw it in the tightness of his jaw. Quasim surveyed the scene. 'It's a beautiful day outside. Sunset is such a relaxing time, so comforting.' He paused. 'And so romantic.'

He ran a fingertip over the kitchen table inspecting it for dust; from a man as cruel as Quasim Dilawar Hussein it was a terrifying gesture. This was not the Quasim who used to creep into her bed for five minutes.

'Don't you think it's romantic, Afra?' His tone made her sick with dread. Her husband rarely called her by name. She stood fixed to the spot, not certain what the right answer might be. He moved closer and glanced at the spluttering water.

'Were you in the garden earlier?'

'Yes, of course. I often walk there; it washes the tiredness out of me.'

Quasim wanted to kill her.

He closed the few feet between them, grabbed a handful of her hair and dragged her to the stove. Afra's cries echoed in the kitchen as a hundred shafts of pain cut into her head. He forced her face into the largest pot. Water boiled inches from her face. Tiny droplets stung her cheek. She felt her skin blister. 'Quasim, please! What have I done?'

'I don't know.' He tightened his grip. 'What have you done?'

'Nothing, Quasim! Nothing!'

The head of the Dilawar Hussein family calmly tortured his wife. Her cries, her pain, left him unmoved. He pushed her head lower. 'Who was the man you met in the garden?'

She screamed. 'No one! No one! I met no one!'

As fast as the attack began it stopped. Afra collapsed on the stone floor, her body rocking in anguish. Quasim towered over her, emotionless; indifferent to the damage he'd inflicted. His polished shoes were covered in a film of dust. 'I believe you,' he said, and left.

At the end of dinner he spoke to his brothers. 'I need to talk to you.'

Zamir and Firdos didn't ask why, they'd know soon enough. Fear crawled through both of them and for the same reason. They'd heard the screams, the crying and the pleading, and worried their assaults had been revealed. Only Chandra was detached. She felt nothing for the woman's trouble and had already forgotten she was the cause.

The men moved into a room of couches and divans. Quasim said, 'Brothers, I have a dilemma and I need your help. Tonight a man was inside the gates. I saw him and he ran. At first, I was certain he was meeting Chandra. She claimed no knowledge of this stranger and I believed her, I still do. But there was a man. He was meeting someone from this house.'

'Who, Quasim?'

'He may have been meeting my wife. You heard me question her.'

'What did she tell you?'

'What I expected – that she saw no one, met no one.'

He shrugged at the obviousness of the defence. Zamir saw an end to his anxiety. 'You don't trust her?'

'She's a woman, Zamir.'

The brothers nodded.

'How can we help, Quasim?'

'Is it possible this wife has betrayed me?'

Firdos said, 'Absolutely. Where she's from everything is possible.'

Zamir reinforced the lie for his own selfish purpose. 'A few weeks ago I thought I saw her talking with someone near the road. I would've spoken earlier but I couldn't be sure. The evidence wasn't enough to justify such a serious accusation, so I stayed silent.

Though it wounds me to say it, I believe she plays you false.'

Quasim placed a hand on his shoulder, Zamir bowed his head. 'You're a friend as well as a brother. I appreciate your reluctance to cause me pain.'

Quasim was resigned to a truth that suited all of them. Zamir seized his chance and pressed for the action that would redeem him. 'She needs to be gone. Tonight would not be too soon.'

Firdos was eager. 'What are you saying?'

'Quasim is head of our family, this isn't work for him. We'll take care of her. The world will hear she ran away after her husband told her three times he was divorced from her. I'll be a witness.' He turned to Quasim and took his hand. 'I'll swear she was no longer your wife. You'll be free of her. The family will be free of her. Dishonour needs an answer. Say the word, and it's done.'

Quasim was touched by their loyalty. How often he'd been quick to judge them. How often it passed him by. They were good. In that moment of twisted solidarity Quasim was certain. 'Do it,' he said. 'Do it.'

Chapter 15

Zamir came to the kitchen where Afra was drying pots. 'Come with me.'

She knew better than ask why, this man wouldn't explain. His brother was waiting in the car. Zamir opened a door. Afra got in. Firdos engaged the gears, let out the clutch and drove through the gates. Soon, traffic thinned and the streets were quiet.

Afra said, 'Where are we going?'

The brothers didn't reply, their silence told all she needed. By luck she was wearing the gift from Jameel, held on her stick-thin wrist with string. An unnatural calm settled over her. Her breath came soft and even. Afra was ready, more composed than the beasts with her. She saw release.

Firdos eased the car into a yard.

'Out.' Zamir spat the instruction, in control at last. The girl did as she was told. Behind her she heard Zamir, impatient for his brother to open the door. Firdos found the key and let them in.

The corrugated building was crammed to its high roof with metal islands of shelving, packed with sacks of fertiliser, pipe, shiny spades, forks and other equipment she didn't recognise. Drums and containers, too many to count, hugged one of the walls; different shapes and sizes of black tanks capable of holding thousands of litres of water huddled together deeper into the store. Near the door, wooden posts, metal fencing, rolls of chicken wire and iron supports – new arrivals that would be sold before long to make way for other loads of the same. When the men left after breakfast every day this was where they came. Afra was seeing what the world saw: the respectable face of the Dilawar Hussein family. Zamir pushed her into the warehouse.

It was cold. Afra didn't mind. The trials of seven years would end tonight in this place.

They watched her like jackals, confident the kill belonged to them. Each had a score to settle because, in different ways, she'd humiliated them. These men meant to murder her. They didn't know she'd died the night Jameel closed the door on her.

One sorrowful note rang in her heart.

as long as we believe the bangles will not fail us

It had all been untrue. Just a story about love for a silly girl.

***

Zamir stepped away from the woman on the ground. 'Bring her here, Firdos.'

His brother dragged her across the floor to a coil of rope. They laid her backwards over the wheel. 'Get something, wire, anything to tie the bitch.'

Zamir panted instructions, eyes blazing with his triumph. He'd overcome his difficulty, violence had brought his desire to an irresistible height, and in victory, he was more cruel than he'd ever been in defeat.

He punched the helpless form, casual in the way he wounded her. Firdos added blows of his own. Then Afra's final ordeal began in earnest.

'Do you want her again?'

Firdos shook his head. Unlike his brother, he liked his women to know what he was doing to them. This one was a piece of bloodied meat. It had been fun an hour ago but he'd had his revenge, now he was tired.

Zamir rested his hands on his thighs. Banging on the roller door interrupted the silence. 'Bilal. Let him in.'

Zamir had called his cousin before they left the house, told him what he wanted and offered him money. Bilal, always anxious to ingratiate himself with his more successful relations, had been happy to oblige, and money was never unwelcome. Firdos unlocked the door. A smiling Bilal stepped into the light.

One look told him everything. Zamir ignored him. The Dilawar Hussein family didn't rate this man – he was a low-life peasant, lazy and crude. But useful for what had to be done.

Bilal imagined himself part of the plan. 'Where do you want me to take her?'

'Away. One-fifty, two hundred miles south, into the Punjab. The further from Lahore the better.'

'Is she dead?'

'Not yet,' Firdos said. 'She will be. Soon.'

'And if she isn't?'

'You'll see she is, Bilal.'

'Quasim?'

Zamir remembered why he disliked his cousin. 'Quasim knows nothing except that yesterday he spoke three times to divorce her. I heard him myself. In the morning, he'll discover she's run off in the night.'

Bilal had known Zamir all his life; he was as cold as a cobra. Concern wasn't in his nature. 'Get her into my car. I've a long drive ahead of me before morning.'

'Bring it as close as you can. Anyone might be watching.'

Bilal left. Firdos said, 'Can we trust him?'

Zamir laughed. 'Of course not. The Bilals of this world can't be trusted. His involvement is our guarantee otherwise we'd be in his power. I can think of little worse than allowing that scavenger, who unfortunately has our blood, to have something on us. He'll kill the woman, take his money and remember that we hold his secret just as he holds ours.'

Firdos didn't share the loathing and mistrust of Bilal but his brother's logic convinced him. While they slept in their comfortable beds, Bilal would be miles away.

Zamir went into the shadows and returned with a beaker. Firdos saw his brother and blanched. Zamir strolled to the unconscious woman tied to the rope drum, looked at her bowed head, sighed and spoke, gently shaking her shoulder as if he was rousing her from a deep sleep. He whispered. 'Afra. Afra.'

She didn't stir.

'Afra.' He slapped her cheek. 'Afra, wake up.'

A moan came from her bloodied mouth. Zamir slapped her again.

'It's time to say goodbye.'

Zamir waited for her to raise her head. Bilal stood at the door, fascinated. Firdos didn't try to interfere; he looked away.

'Goodbye, Afra.' Zamir threw the contents of the beaker in her face.

Her scream echoed off the metal walls. More followed. She tried to tear herself free, writhing and pulling at her bindings. Zamir stayed where he'd been, he didn't retreat an inch, even with the stench of burning flesh in his nostrils. His view of her suffering was unsurpassed. Eventually, the screaming stopped and Zamir turned to the others, satisfied with his work.

***

One hundred miles south of Lahore, Bilal realised the risk he was taking. If he was stopped, how would he explain his passenger? Zamir and Firdos could deny any part in it and he would be left to suffer the consequences alone. Like the shallow villain he was, Bilal processed events only as they affected him. He travelled unfamiliar roads, cursing himself for not asking for more money, especially from that family.

Sprawled in a heap over the back seat lay what was left of the woman. She hadn't made a sound. Bilal wondered if she was dead. The car filled with the smell of acid and scorched flesh; he rolled down a window to let it escape.

One hundred and forty miles.

Bilal looked over his shoulder at the bunch of rags in the back and felt no pity. He remembered her in his house, years ago. She'd been something then; young, beautiful, spirited, too. But this was now. The only thought in his creature mind was whether she had anything worth stealing. Bilal decided to cut the journey short. Thirty miles later and more than one hundred and seventy-five from Lahore, he pulled over on a deserted country road and hauled her onto the grass verge. The moon broke through and he saw her face. What a waste. How he'd wanted her when Nadira cleaned for him. Now a new one made breakfast and warmed his bed when he wished. But this woman had been special.

Bilal rummaged through her clothing. On a wrist he felt jewellery. Bangles. Wooden and worthless. He took the slender neck in his hands and squeezed as hard as he could. It changed little as far as he could tell. She was dead.

The car accelerated into the night. The despised cousin had only one regret about the black deed he'd joined in.

He should have asked for more money.

***

An hour after Bilal headed back to Lahore, a farmer keen to make an early start drove by and noticed the bundle at the side of the road. Whatever had happened, he didn't want involved. The nearest hospital was twelve miles away. He took the woman to it, dumped her outside, and went about his business.

His conscience was clear.

***

Nurse Idris Phadkar had almost completed her walk round the grounds. There were times she just had to escape. Nursing was satisfying except on long nightshifts like tonight when everything was routine. She was ready for a change, a move to the big city, Islamabad or Karachi, maybe. Somewhere like Lahore, less than two hundred miles but a world away. Lahore. She could be happy there. Then she heard it.

Part Three
Honour Killing

Chapter 16

Pearl Continental Hotel, Lahore

I turned in my seat and looked out into the foyer, empty except for straight-backed uniformed staff on their way to attend some well-heeled guest. I'd go soon. With these prices, I'd go very soon.

A woman was rearranging the huge fresh flower centrepiece of the marble and glass atrium, selecting long-stemmed exotics from a shallow wicker basket, building them into a floral masterpiece. In the morning, guests would admire the ostentatious show without wondering how or when it got there.

Pointless.

I was done with pointless endeavour. During the last three years in Pakistan – the politically-volatile arse-end of nowhere – I'd been pretty much done with any kind of endeavour. At a shave off six feet tall, dark hair and dark eyes, there was just enough to hint at the man I'd been before life started stealing from me. My tan lightweight suit, crumpled at the front and crushed in a thousand lines at the back, complemented the stubbled jaw and bloodshot eyes.

But so what?

My finger moved, a gesture no more strenuous than a bidder at Sotheby's, and George, the bow-tied barman, responded as fast as any auctioneer. Another Johnnie Walker Red Label, amber through the heavy cut glass, arrived on the cork coaster in front of me. George wasn't his real name. I had no idea what it was. In my head, I called him George. And George understood the needs of a drinker like me. More than once poor service had forced me to take my troubles elsewhere.

At thirty-eight I'd ceased worrying how I looked or what impression I made. Fuck it! It was all I could do to file my twice-weekly report to London and rarely checked to see if any of the stuff was used. I didn't care. I'd become a brooding introvert, very different from before.

Before. I didn't go there anymore.

At the end of the bar, 'George' was polishing glasses. Almost time to go. No problem. Time to stop drinking here – not time to stop drinking, that was another couple of hours away. The voice cut through the silence of the deserted lounge. 'Ralph! Ralph Buchanan! Well I'll be…'

A man, casual in jeans and polo shirt, was standing three yards away, wearing a pleased-to-see-you smile. 'Ralph Buchanan,' he said again in soft disbelief. 'What're you doing out here?'

I didn't reply. I had no idea who I was talking to. Wait it out my brain told me: all will be revealed. 'You don't know me, do you? 'Course you don't, why would you? Eden, John Eden. *The Guardian.* On my way back from Hong Kong.'

Was this supposed to mean something to me? I played along with the two journeymen meeting on the road charade. 'Hi John, what you doing here?'

'Stop off. Friends I haven't seen in an age. Didn't think it was through choice, did you, Ralph?' He laughed. 'Even the locals aren't here through choice. So what brings you to Pakistan, of all places?'

I'd had my story ready before I even arrived. Time to try it out. 'Al Qaeda,' I said, and went into my act. 'Got recruitment stations and training camps in the north. The military will get the camps, satellite will tell them where they are. Recruitment's done where those birds don't go – on the streets, in the communities. I want to find out how they do it and how much the government knows about it. They've got a pretty pro-western public face. The thinking is, there's another agenda. Not everyone's a friend, that's a given, and how friendly the friends are is unknown. It's a large canvas, lots of potentials, loads of interest. No breaks yet. When it does, it'll be a biggie. I'm in for the long haul.'

Fantasy. Eden lapped it up.

'Wow! But why am I surprised? We used to call the front page Ralph Buchanan's page. No change there.'

The smile missed my eyes. I wanted this meeting to be over. The barman was turning lights out one at a time. Eden wanted to talk. 'D'you know the last time I saw you? Four years ago at the Dorchester. You must remember. You were the star of the show.'

The night at The Dorchester: hard to connect it with who I was now – a guy in a crumpled suit, hugging the bar.

'Well, great to see you. Maybe we'll bump into each other at another gong-giving.'

I forced out a positive. 'Could be.'

He headed for the lifts. Eden was someone who'd probably never done anything more than report what was already known and cruise on the company's expenses. Funny how a chance meeting could spoil your evening. 'George' had gone, slipped away during the conversation, back to his real life as George the husband or lover, the son or the friend. Good old George, getting out of this place at the double. Quite right, too.

There was a time I would've enjoyed the interlude with John Eden and the opportunity to bask in another's admiration. Things were different these days. I toyed with the last of my drink.

you must remember, you were the star of the show

And I did remember; of course I remembered.

***

Four years. Only four. My drinking was a problem even then.

The main function room of The Dorchester was laid in tables of twelve. Men in dinner suits and bow ties with ladies wearing months of agonising and planning. The room filled with the steady hum of conversation. When you boiled it all away, most industries were tight little communities, islands in the stream, where everyone knew everyone else, with relationships, good or bad, going back years. The newspaper business was one of those islands.

Award ceremonies became parodies of themselves, it was unavoidable. The original intention – to recognise achievement – is lost in soul-searching acceptance. Everyone from God down gets a mention. Winning affects people, changes them. The sincere seem unstable, the unstable are seen as tortured talents, and the vain morph into models of humorous self-deprecation, and usually make the best speeches.

The occasion was heavy with the pomposity everyone in the room claimed to abhor. A couple of martinis in my room [four was a couple but who was counting?] relaxed me enough to enjoy the car ride to Park Lane. I watched the city pass by through rain spattered windows. It was a long way from Glasgow, and before that, the local newspaper that had given me my start. Ambition had driven me south to the capital. And I'd made it.

The speech would be short and sweet. No fake humble. No self-important rambling. I'd won and I'd deserved to win, that was all there was to it.

The liveried concierge opened the car door with one hand, an umbrella in the other. I got out and walked the dozen or so steps to the busy lobby. The Dorchester hosted functions 365 nights of the year; they ought to be pretty good at it by now.

'Good evening, sir.' The uniformed sentinel accepted my embossed invitation and crossed off my name against the room-setting pinned on a board.

'Have a good evening, Mr Buchanan.'

The standard line. Welcoming and personal. Unless you'd heard it a thousand times. The table was near the stage, just far enough to allow some palaver on the way up; overacting was allowed, after all, it was an awards ceremony. My colleagues were already there. They beamed, pleased to see their golden boy.

Even in the best hotels, the task of feeding hundreds depends on logistics and process, rather than the silky nuances of a teaspoonful of sauce. I wouldn't remember a thing I tasted that night, but I'd remember sitting next to Christine Douglas, the paper's political commentator. Christine: vivacious and sharp; petite and dark-skinned, with a toned-down afro. I'd had a thing about her for years. She was too savvy to go for my kind of charm. No matter, there were plenty who did.

Her hazel eyes were warm above high cheekbones. 'Looking forward to your moment in the sun, Ralph?'

'I suppose I am.'

'You suppose?'

'Yes, I suppose I am.'

'Mmmm. Nervous.' It wasn't a question.

'Don't be ridiculous. Why would I be nervous?'

'Maybe because it's the greatest moment of your professional life. I'd be a little uptight. Most people would.'

'Well, I'm not.'

I heard myself sounding like an ass, stiff and pompous. And nervous?

'Ralph. You're too self-sufficient, d'you know that?'

'Sounds like a virtue to me. Have they changed it? Is virtue the new vice? Christ, I need to keep up.'

She shook her head. 'This is your night. It's okay to be a bit razzed.'

'I'm not fucking nervous, I'm fine.'

She reconsidered. 'No, not nervous. You're too egocentric for that.'

I borrowed from the doorman. 'Enjoy your evening, Christine.'

At the bar of the Pearl Continental I wondered what had become of Christine Douglas. I hadn't kept in touch with any of my former colleagues since my banishment to this fucked-up, god-forsaken place. No one had contacted me.

The parade of grateful scribes went on and on, accepting their awards, thanking their mothers for having them and their colleagues for putting up with them. I wasn't entirely jaundiced. Some of these people worked year after year, doing a good job, never seeking a spotlight. They deserved their trophy.

The award was a handsome thing: a sculpted hand holding a quill, finished in silver, mounted on a heavy polished mahogany round. It would look good on anybody's cabinet.

Donald Munroe, the balding, thick-set president of the awards committee came to one of the high-points of the night. 'This evening we've been paying tribute to men and women in our business whose continuous commitment, talent and resolve ensures we remain loyal to our responsibility as custodians of the truth. The history of newspapers is punctuated with the names of those whose diligence and courage set them apart. People who unearth the real story, the story that doesn't want to be told. Tonight a new name will be added to that list.

'In the summer of 2008, a newspaperman began to suspect something was amiss with MEDICAL, Europe's largest pharmaceutical company at that time, and 'MM', their best-selling dehydrated baby milk product. MM – it stands for Mother's Milk – or rather, it did – was the market leader. Worldwide sales totalled hundreds of millions of euros, dollars and pounds.

'A sharp increase in the percentage of baby fatalities alerted him. Eighteen months of hard work, inspired deduction and a refusal to take no for an answer finally paid off. What he learned led to the lawsuit we've been reading about almost every day since.

'The water used in the process was run off a contaminated source. Using insider testimony as a lever, he prised the lid off the biggest scandal in the history of medicine and proved MEDICAL knew the water was bad but did nothing about it. That company gambled with the lives of our children. Now, it faces billions in damages. For the sake of the many families involved we hope litigation reaches a swift conclusion. The behaviour of that company and the justice it will meet serves as a warning to others, themselves charged with a sacred duty, not to betray the faith of the consumer. In healthcare trust is the first prerequisite.'

I could still hear the hush.

'If it were not for one man, that betrayal would still be going on. The awards committee considered long and hard on the recipients of tonight's awards, as they always do. In every category, people were able to lay impressive claim to being the outstanding journalist in their field. In this case, the contribution almost defies categorisation. It gives me pleasure to present the British Newspaper Industry Award for Outstanding Investigative Journalism to Ralph Buchanan.'

The President led the applause.

I shook unfamiliar hands. Christine may have given me a kiss, I can't be sure; the next few seconds were lost to me. The view from the stage made the hairs on my neck stand up. At every table, people stood, clapping and whistling. The ovation went on for minutes. I was stunned. Christine Douglas had it right on two counts: it was the greatest moment of my professional life, and I *was* nervous.

That was when I decided to change the speech. When the tumult died, I faced my peers. 'Mr President, members of the committee, my fellow journalists, ladies and gentlemen. Hearing Don Munroe speak just now was like listening to someone else's story. I'd forgotten some of it. The many dead ends, the almost constant uncertainty, the feeling of being wrong about the whole thing and the price paid by loved ones living with another's obsession. Some days it seemed that when one door closed behind us, another slammed shut in our faces. I say 'our' because investigative journalism is a team game. On day one there were four of us. By the end there was just me. But the work the guys did along the way kept the pump primed. This award is theirs as well as mine. Larry Franks, Alva Estiban, Tony Fascionni, wherever you are, take a bow.'

The audience responded on cue. Everybody loves a good sport. I didn't know if I thanked my mother, or God, or anyone else. It seemed so long ago, and until that point it had been wine and roses all the way. They'd loved that team game nonsense, hadn't they? Changing the speech, getting the humble in there. Good decision.

I flicked my fingertip off the empty glass. It made a 'ping' sound. How you could tell it was the real McCoy; it sounded right. I slid off the leather stool and made for the door.

Of course there were some things that test didn't work for.

Chapter 17

The taxi dropped me back at the flat. In Lahore there were people about even at this hour. I switched on the light and made straight for the bottles – Dewar's, Chivas Regal, Bells – sitting together in a corner of the kitchen. Had I bought them yesterday or the day before? Who cared? Scotland produced rivers of it. And if that ran dry, there was always the Japanese stuff.

I took an unwashed tumbler from the sink, let the tap water fill it and spill out. Clean enough. The measure was more generous than the ones from George. I stared into the glass – a burnt-amber eye stared back – and swirled the drink around the edges. The meeting with John.... whatever his name was... Eden, that was it... started me down a path I hadn't travelled since leaving London. I closed my eyes and followed it the rest of the way.

Back at the table in The Dorchester, my colleagues had given me a winner's welcome. "Congratulations", "well done" and "outstanding" followed me. Christine Douglas touched my arm. 'Good speech.'

'Oh, unaccustomed as I am, blah, blah, blah.'

'Very generous.'

'Christine,' I put a hand on my heart in mock hurt, 'I'm a generous guy. Thought you knew that.'

She turned away. The champagne came in a never-ending conveyor, our table's allocation supplemented by gifts to the man of the hour. The line of back-slapping well-wishers went on and on. I needed to go to the lavatory. I grabbed hold of the silver gong inscribed with my name, struggled out of my chair and squeezed past tables and chairs, shaking hands without seeing whose.

The journey took a long time, too long my complaining bladder told me. At last, I made it to the back of the room. The male graphic on the door guided me. I was drunk. Not legless, but drunk, nevertheless.

The toilets were empty apart from a man at the latrine. I stood a few feet from him and sat the silver hand and quill on top. It almost fell into the trough. I caught it. Emptying my bladder seemed to go on forever. When I finished, I picked the award off the porcelain and looked at the other guy. I recognised him: Tony Fascionni, beefier round the middle than when we'd last met. He was watching me but his eyes showed no sign of welcome. He looked at the silver gong.

'Wonder Boy! Well, well.' His voice was a mocking thing.

'Tony, I didn't know you were here tonight.' Lame in the face of his contempt.

'Oh, I'm here, Wonder Boy. Didn't win anything. Didn't light up the night like you, but I'm here. Caught the speech. Nice. Good of you to give the rest of us a mention. Appreciated.'

'You should've come up, Tony.'

Fascionni grinned and nodded. 'Thought about it, Ralph. Decided against it. Didn't want to steal your thunder. Know how you like your thunder.'

In the flat in Lahore the memory chilled me.

'Besides, nobody likes a party pooper. If I'd got up there, might have had to say something. Might have opened Tony's big mouth and told our friends and neighbours how it really was. That would've been – what's the word? – inappropriate, that's it. A room full of newspaper people in there. The truth would've been unwelcome. To make this circus work takes a whole lot of people telling the same lies. Anything I had to say on the subject of MEDICAL would be inconvenient. Like pissing in the bride's mother's new hat: no big thing but enough to spoil the occasion, know what I mean?'

'Tony, you were a part of it in the beginning, you and the guys. You should've stood up.'

'Fuck off, Buchanan. They like the story just the way it is. Like it the way you tell it. The truth isn't the popular option.'

Fascionni jabbed a finger at me. 'Anyway, what would I say? How we worked for each other, protected each other, protected our sources?'

He was breathing heavily, on fire with his anger.

'Or would I tell them it was Alan – not you – who made the connection in the stats? That it was Frank and me who interviewed every fuckin' soul while you got your shoes shined?'

'Unfair, Tony. Alan spotted the change in the stats, I made the deduction. And of course, you and Frank worked, worked hard, but it was me who pulled it together. Me who wrote the progress reports. Make that, no progress reports. I took the flak for nothing to show, persuaded them to let us stay with it, so unfair, Tony.'

'Unfair. You want to talk unfair, Ralph.' He laughed without humour. 'Tell Jo-Jo's mother about unfair. Call her up and tell her this is his night, too.'

The conversation played in my head.

'Didn't hear his name mentioned, wonder why? Jo-Jo Reynolds. Nice kid, remember? Came to us one afternoon and told it all on tape in front of witnesses. And what did Jo-Jo ask in return for delivering the whole mess?'

Fascionni's neck bulged, his voice a shrill accuser. 'He asked not to be named. But you let it out. Told those MEDICAL murderers what we knew. Told them the source. You remember all this, don't you Ralph?'

I said nothing.

'You named him, and they dropped it to the unemployed workforce. The boy was hounded. Only stopped three months later when they cut him down from the kitchen pulley.'

Fascionni was almost in tears. 'And they gave you an award for breaking a confidence. As soon as Jo-Jo opened his mouth we had them, and we should've protected him. That was it for Frank and me. Alan had already gone. Couldn't stand you, even before Jo-Jo cracked up.'

He was in my face. I could smell his breath now, and feel the tiny dots of spray hitting my chin.

Back in the past Fascionni rubbed his eyes, tired of carrying this around. 'You killed him. He helped us and you killed him. Why did you give them his name? Why?'

'They wouldn't believe me. Wouldn't believe we could prove it. I lost it, got angry, it just came out. It was an accident.'

'No, Ralph, you were drunk and it slipped out. Had one of your liquid-lunches before the meeting.' He shook his head. 'There're always accidents with people like you. Always some other poor fuck who gets it.'

I edged round the journalist, nearer to the door. What happened next took me by surprise. A slap. The most humiliating thing. Four years later and thousands of miles away the colour rose in my face. Fascionni had grabbed my lapels, the silver paperweight fell from my hand into the trough; water and urine flowed over it. 'The trouble with you is you're a cowboy. Worse. A fuckin' dangerous cowboy.'

He looked past me. 'Don't forget your gong, Ralph. Enjoy the rest of your night.'

That sentiment again. The door banged. I lifted the award and wiped it on the roller towel. The exchange had shaken me. Remembering it had shaken me.

In the flat in Lahore I lifted the bottle of Dewar's and put it to my lips.

***

I woke up in stages, stiff and cold with the postcards from hell arriving. Half-focused snapshots of the night before. Unconnected fragments of memory floating on a sea of anxiety. I fought against the incoherent movie playing in my head and opened my eyes. Light flooded in.

Not the men's room at The Dorchester. Thank God for that.

I uncurled from the armchair in slow motion, kicked something with my foot and looked down. A bottle lay on its side, another had rolled across the room, both empty. The symptoms of the night's excess hit me; thick mouth, headache, nausea, weakness.

Starting the day in this condition had become the norm even before I arrived in Pakistan. In the fridge I found a beer, took a drink and carried it to the chair. It helped, it always did. 'Here we go again, Ralph.'

Before the drinking started in earnest, a hangover was the price of a night on the town, and with it anxiety and depression that only more alcohol assuaged. And the morning drinking began. A beer before breakfast, then a couple. Cornflakes and the Famous Grouse.

I sat up, in no hurry to go anywhere, and looked round the room. It was a mess. I didn't know when I'd last cleaned the place. Clothes, papers and magazines lay where they'd been left and a stale smell filled the small space; an open window would make a big difference. The kitchen was tidy, unaffected, I never used it. No cooking meant no mountain of plates or congealed food welded to their greasy surfaces. None of that. Except for a couple of glasses, it was fine. That couldn't be said for the bedroom; sheets lay on the floor and the air was musty.

'So what?'

I gulped down the beer.

A hangover was par for the course. A couple of drinks would send it on its way. That was the pattern. Never completely sober, topping-up until the evening session. The emotional consequences were something else – the cycle of anxiety to depression and back again – plagued the daylight hours. I'd gone from newspaper 'superstar' to maintenance drinker. I didn't discuss it with myself, but I'd lost my way, wasted my gifts and evaded my responsibilities. Nobody knew it better than me.

A guy with a great future behind him.

The decision to do nothing today was easy. I got another two cold ones from the fridge, pulled the top off one and sat back down. Last night I'd talked to a guy who knew me.... Seaton, Eaton, a name like that. The whisky mist held firm. What had he said? Something about The Dorchester hotel. It wouldn't come. Christine Douglas was in there, how strange, and Tony Fascionni. Crazy stuff. A blur. John, was that it? John

Eaton? No, not right. Memory mocked me with glimpses and fragments, like the moon playing with the clouds. Eton, John Eden. Got it. He'd been at the awards, that's how he knew me. And that sparked off… what?

Oh, fuck! Fuck! A flash flood washed through my blacked-out mind, sweeping yesterday into plain sight. Not all of it but enough, more than enough. The star of the show the guy had said. Tony Fascionni had a different take. I felt the flat of his hand and my response screamed in my brain. I'd stood there and taken it.

because it was true, because it was deserved

When Jo-Jo Reynolds kicked the stool away we'd both started to fall. The rope broke his neck, I had continued down. And I was still falling.

Jo-Jo was only the beginning. Chic Logan had given me insight into the business at the beginning. Chic was an old-timer, ready to spend more time with his family. After thirty-five years his coat was on and he was headed for the door. One day he saw me writing my copy, glancing at my notebook for the few facts so I could tease them into a piece of work. He walked over and pulled up a chair. 'Mind if I sit down?'

'Hi Chic, how's it going?'

'Fine, Ralph. Going fine. What do you have?'

'Man kidnapped his own child. Caught driving a stolen car trying to leave the city. I interviewed the arresting officer. It's all here.'

'Mmmm, sure about that?'

"Course I'm sure. What d'you mean?'

'Nothing, except you're in an awful hurry.'

'I'm doing something wrong?'

'Don't know, Ralph. Can't say you're doing it wrong 'til I know what you're doing.'

'But what, Chic?'

'Tell me again what the speed writing's about.'

I repeated what I knew, suspecting the backside was about to fall out of it. 'A kidnap, the guy's own daughter. Stole a car, got caught. All straight from the horse.'

'And that's your story. That's it?'

'What's wrong with it?'

'Nothing, far as it goes'

'Very helpful, Chic. But what's wrong with it?'

Logan unbuttoned his jacket. 'Seems to me it isn't the story. I mean, where's the mother?'

'Covered that, she's dead.'

'Even better.'

'Chic, you want to help? So just tell me. I'm here to learn.'

'Okay. I'm sitting here, minding my own business when you burst in, rush to your desk and start writing. Everybody else's moving just enough to keep the circulation going. I come over and ask what you've got. You tell me, and now I know.'

'Now you know what?'

'I know you've got the same everybody else has, the story that sits on top, the obvious stuff. The real tale's underneath. A good newspaperman appreciates that nothing starts where you think it starts. What happened to get it to where it is now is the interesting part. Why is the key.'

He paused to let me catch up. 'Why is the father doing this? Where was he taking them? Where is his car? If he doesn't have one, why is that?'

He took a breath. 'It's called digging for the truth because it's underneath. When you can answer those questions you might have a handle on it.'

I'd learned something. 'Thanks, Chic, I've got it.'

Logan smiled. 'My pleasure.'

In Lahore, I realised how much of that applied to me. How had I got here? How had it come to this? I knew some of it, the rest was a nightmare. Changing the speech, probably the last good decision I'd made.

No, not probably, definitely. From then on it had been one shit move after another.

***

The phone call came out of the blue. Would I meet her? Reluctantly, I agreed.

She was early by ten minutes and it was easy to understand why. A woman who looked the way she did didn't need to set up her entrance. Any time was the right time. Doctor Simone Jasnin walked without hurry across the hotel atrium to the bar. I saw her take in the unshaven face, the unwashed hair and clothes that cried for an iron.

She was sleek, manicured and stylish, in a maroon and grey silk sari; elegant and fragrant in an unforced way. I guessed she was single through choice. My head ached. I managed a wisp of a smile and stood to greet her. 'Doctor Jasnin?'

'Mr Buchanan.'

'Can I get you a drink?'

'Yes, thank you. Sparkling water, no ice or lemon.'

I caught a waiter's attention and ordered; water for her, Chivas Regal for me. I'd no use for small talk, even on a good day, and her perfection made me edgy. Or maybe it was the alcohol from the night before. 'So, what can I do for you?'

'I'd like your help.'

I studied her; the hair, the eyes, the mouth. This was a beautiful woman. In the past, I would've chased her until she let herself be caught. 'You'd like my help with what exactly? How can I help a doctor?'

She bristled. 'As I told you when I called, my name is Simone Jasnin. I work in rural areas. I lived here when I was young. My father was Pakistani. After he died my mother moved back to France. I decided to return and make a contribution to my father's country. It's my country, too.'

She stopped. The waiter placed our drinks in front of us, arranging the white paper coasters in a tiny performance of gentility. She'd paid no attention when I ordered, now her eyes lingered on the double whisky as the doctor in her observed me.

'You're half French?'

'And half Pakistani. But Pakistan is my home. I think it always will be. I love her. That's why I'm here, Mr Buchanan.'

'Because you love your country? And you believe there's some way I can help? Why me?'

'I asked around. I was told you were good. You may know little about medicine, though MEDICAL might disagree if they still had a business worth having, but you do know about injustice, and that's why I need your help…to bring a gross injustice out into the world.'

I listened, more interested in her than her words. 'And this injustice is?'

'The treatment of women in Pakistan,'

I finished my drink and searched for the waiter. She hadn't touched hers. I didn't offer another. 'The treatment of women almost anywhere is an injustice.'

The waiter interrupted my platitudes and went into the same ritual, this time adding a bowl of nuts to the table-top choreography. 'Would you like me to explain the conditions many women endure in Pakistan?'

'Of course, if you want to, though I doubt there's any way I can help.'

She stood. The coloured silks of her sari fell in an elegant cascade. I saw the depth of her brown eyes and realised I'd said the wrong thing. She looked at me and at the glass I was holding. 'I'm boring you, I'm sorry.'

There was a time when I would have handled this meeting effortlessly, committed myself to nothing, and still be taking her to dinner this evening. The woman in front of me was a medical professional, her tone clipped. 'I'm disappointed not to have been able to interest you in the plight of millions of people. Perhaps it wouldn't have made a big enough story for you.'

'Doctor Jasnin…'

I'd reaped as I'd sown and it didn't feel nice. She cut me off. 'No matter, I'll look for someone else to help with the problems that concern me. You have your own I see.'

The remark caught me off guard. 'What problem?'

'The one in your hand, Mr Buchanan.'

I watched her go, angry with myself and her. After a few steps, she turned and spoke. 'Actually, I lied a moment ago. I wasn't told you were good. I was told you used to be good.'

Chapter 18

There were easier ways to go about it but this was the way he preferred. Three nights a week he made the journey, always on foot. He didn't visit the same places at the same times, for what would be the point of that? The element of surprise was important if anything was to be gained. Gulzar Hafeez was his father and he'd taught his son all he could, including his cardinal rule: stay in touch with what's going on in the business.

'Tell me what you see.'

'Everything, I can see everything.'

'So can I, and that's why I sit here.'

'So you can see everything, I understand.'

'And so that everyone can see me seeing everything. Do you understand that?'

But insight couldn't be got at a distance; it needed to be gathered first hand. There were many things to know and learn: about the food, the suppliers; about the customers who visited the restaurants and the people who worked in them. Trading, profit and loss sheets gave up their truths to anyone able to interpret the columns of figures and percentages. That kind of knowledge was invaluable, of course, and could be mined without leaving the office. Yet it didn't hold the essence. It had no smell, no feel. It was the mechanics of business – no substitute for instinct. Real success was achieved by watching and listening. Management by walking about the business gurus called it in their books. Jameel's guru had known what they preached before they'd even been written.

Gulzar was wistful. 'How I wish I could teach you everything, Jameel, but some things are beyond words. They have to be discovered. Uncovered. Little pieces that cannot be given away.'

'So I'll never be as good as you. If you can't tell me everything you've learned, then something will always be missing.'

'True, but not true.'

Jameel remembered tearing some bread, bracing himself for another of Gulzar's riddles. 'True that I cannot teach you to be me. And why would you want to be me anyway? Not true because I can show you where to find what I cannot tell you.'

'Where?'

Gulzar pointed to his belly. 'In here, in your gut, Jameel, that's where the truth whispers to us.'

At the time, the idea repelled him. Now a wiser Jameel smiled.

'The heart is a poet's notion of things. A romantic falsehood used to wrap our emotions and sell them to us. Feeling is in our core.'

His explanation sounded hollow, inadequate, and he realised it. 'What I'm trying to say is simply this. Most often – almost always in my experience – if something feels wrong, it is wrong. If I begin to suspect a manager of stealing from me, even though I have no proof, I know that man is a thief. And how do I know? My gut tells me. Then I only have to watch and wait until the proof arrives, and it always does. It always does.'

His conviction was absolute.

Jameel stayed silent. A lifetime of experience and wisdom sat across from him eating a chicken leg, fresh from the tandoor.

'Instinct, intuition, feel, the name doesn't matter. I'm getting old, and old men are allowed to be vulgar once in a while, it's expected of us, so I call it my gut. The part that cannot be taught is what your gut tells you. Learn to listen to it, hear what it says and believe it. When all else fails, when the best advice has been sought and weighed, give an ear to your inner voice, wiser than any expert, more reliable than the closest friend.'

Jameel had heard him struggle to pass on the best of himself, willing his words to find their mark. And they had. Whenever his gut spoke, he listened. Nothing would be gained by the boss taking his ego for a stroll, frightening the managers, casting a perfunctory eye across his empire; deaf to the voice.

Over the years, Jameel hadn't wasted his time at his father's feet. He'd learned. Become a man. And not just any man: tall and handsome, confident and assured, Jameel Akhtar Hafeez, adopted son of Gulzar, was the managing director of Ravi Restaurants. His education, begun with Pir, was completed in the workplace. Gulzar had given him more, handed him pegs to hang a philosophy on, bit by bit, and, in conversations too many to count, had helped him fashion the pieces for hanging.

Jameel had fallen on it, devoured it whole, hungry for more. The love between them grew until Gulzar *was* his father, though not because it said so on a piece of paper buried in a filing cabinet somewhere.

Their relationship was no one-sided affair. Neither would have wished for that. His nephew's unexpected arrival brought a new purpose to the older man's life. The zest that had fuelled his success in business returned, rekindled, burning brightly to help the boy from Mundhi. But which one? They were both that boy.

Each presented the other with an opportunity, and each had maximised the chance. Mundhi was where they'd come from and no trace remained, in the father or his son, except in the deepest part of them.

Jameel was to be recognised by the Chamber of Commerce as the newest and youngest star in the sky. Gulzar was proud and silly with it. He had done his work well.

Tonight, as usual, his son walked through the cascade of bodies, unfazed. "Why don't you let me drive you?" How many times had Ali asked? He didn't want to be driven, he wanted to walk, like the first night when Ali led the way and he'd followed with no idea where he was going. Walking put him in touch with the feeling of adventure he'd felt, and reawakened his gratitude.

There had been other outcomes for Jameel Akhtar's life, very different from how it was, so he stopped and started, changing his path every few strides, dodging right then left, on through the masses. As complete in himself as anyone on the street.

Mazur, the lorry driver who had given him a lift, had told him to walk straight and tall and he did, so long as thoughts of Afra stayed away. Jameel still saw her face and heard her voice. She was always with him. There was no escape and he wanted none.

wherever you are I am. And wherever I am, you are too

***

'Good-evening Mr Hafeez.'

'Good-evening to you, Tariq.'

Jameel allowed himself to be led to a table set for four far from the main dining area. He wouldn't see much from there and suspected that was the hope. The manager interrupted a waiter on his way into the kitchen. 'Coffee for Mr Hafeez.'

Jameel frowned. Lateef was new to this level of dining and it showed. The man had done well in other places where the approach was more casual, in Jahan's things worked differently; the customer came first, even before the boss.

The coffee arrived. Lateef moved off. Jameel hoped he wasn't hiding in the kitchen. He made a note to have a chat with him, one-to-one. The assistant manager had promise that required nurturing. And that was his job: his and Ali's. He sipped the coffee – a prop to justify taking up table space while he studied the operation.

Lateef was back at the centre of things. Perhaps he was being hard on the man. Jameel lived in a black and white world. Gulzar had tried to persuade him there was plenty of grey in between.

The laugh cut through the hum of conversation like a cry in a library, harsh and unexpected. He followed the sound to a man sitting across from a female, and froze.

The customer clicked his fingers – a waiter hurried to respond – asking for his bill, no doubt. His companion was young, seventeen maybe, and very good-looking. They gazed at each other, heads bent close in the language of the intimate. When the waiter brought the bill, the man barely glanced at the amount and laid money on the table. Jameel saw him and remembered the sleek German car stranded on the baked earth. Eight years earlier their eyes had locked across the dusty compound. It could have been yesterday

Unforgettable – the face of an enemy.

The couple rose to go. He let the woman leave first, his delicate manners at odds with bawdy laughter and clicking fingers. They passed within feet of Jameel and he saw the girl was a fresh-faced beauty. In contrast, her companion was lined, a hooked nose hanging above a sensual mouth, thick and definite like sculpted clay. Time had added threads of white to the hair and moustache, but the eyes remained the same; hooded and cold.

They swept out, unaware of Jameel's scrutiny, impervious to his shock. He asked a waiter if the assistant manager was available and tried to make sense of what had just happened. 'You wished to see me before you go, Mr Hafeez?'

'Yes, Lateef. I have a question for you. Tell me, the man who just left, who is he? He was at table four.'

'Table four,' Lateef looked back into the restaurant. 'Table four. That would be Mr Dilawar Hussein.'

'Dilawar Hussein. Does he eat here often?'

'Oh yes, sir, Mr Dilawar Hussein's a regular customer of ours.'

'And the woman?'

'The woman I don't know.'

'Have you seen her before?'

'No, never, she's one of many.'

'Many?'

'Mr Dilawar Hussein always has glamorous company. He's a very lucky man.'

Lateef disappeared, happy to escape before the questions became more difficult. Jameel felt light-headed. He joined the tide of people out on the street and headed for home, drifting at the speed of the slowest pedestrian.

A regular customer, usually accompanied by a glamorous woman. One of many.

The core his uncle called his gut told him to be careful. Dilawar Hussein liked good food and good-looking women. Nothing wrong with that. Nothing at all except he was Afra's husband. Perhaps they were divorced or separated. Muslim men were allowed more than one wife, then again maybe he was an unfaithful spouse, or maybe Jameel's lost love was back in Mundhi.

Maybe? Maybe? Maybe?

Questions without answers. Tonight he'd seen the man who had taken his childhood sweetheart looking prosperous and well. He'd been with a woman. But the woman wasn't her.

The past was in the present and he was her protector again. Voices whispered to him, one louder than the rest. Over and over asking, where was Afra?

Chapter 19

Staff moved between tables, refilling glasses, mostly soft drinks or water. I thought about The Dorchester: my night. The comparison was easy to make though this hotel was in Lahore and I was a spectator instead of the star.

Today someone else had landed that role.

Seven foreign journalists shared two translators, one into English the other into German. Without them, I wouldn't have lasted ten minutes. My attention span, indeed my ability to stay interested in anything or anyone for very long, had diminished in inverse proportion to my drinking: the more I drank the less able I was to concentrate. I had little to say to the others who probably assumed I was a snooty bastard. The truth was something else. My silence wasn't assurance, it was the opposite. High flying, can-do, award-winning Ralph Buchanan had become an insecure actor playing the part of himself to an audience who couldn't care less.

Of course, once the alcohol started to work, that changed – for a while anyway. The cocksure guy who travelled on his own opinion and trammelled others into the ground in manic pursuit of 'the story' returned. Anyone who came near me wished for the taciturn aloof Buchanan, or better still, neither.

Today was a sober day. Not stone cold – no day was quite that. At the main table, the end of the chairman's introduction signalled sustained applause. I scanned the assembly, no different from any collection of businessmen anywhere. Apart from a scattering of tunics and turbans worn with one end starched and sticking up like a fan, most were dressed in Western-style suits, shirts and ties. Clouds of smoke hung in the air from after-lunch cigars and cigarettes. It seemed that every man in Pakistan smoked. Hands beating in acclaim made the wispy air drift as all eyes went to the figure standing at the microphone: Businessman of the Year, Jameel Akhtar Hafeez.

Jameel nodded as the clapping rolled around the room. If he was nervous, it didn't show.

His story was legend. He'd arrived penniless from the country and found his only living relative. Gulzar Hafeez took him in, adopted him and fitted him to run his businesses. The transformation was remarkable, and the boy had talent. Six restaurants had grown to fourteen. In Karachi, Islamabad and here in Lahore; a rags to riches tale, and not over yet. Rumour said the Hafeez family was looking for a suitable partner to take a stake in several hotel projects they were planning. The father was getting old; the driving force was his adopted son. I might be able to write something interesting about Jameel Akhtar Hafeez.

He smiled at the people who'd voted for him. 'Mr Chairman, fellow LCOC members, thank you for this award. It hardly seems real to be standing in front of so many friends today. It's one of the proudest moments of my life.'

I caught a waiter's attention, pointed to my empty glass and considered what I might say about this guy.

'When I came to the city, I had no idea what lay ahead. I believed everyone kept money in their shoes.'

He waited for the sophisticated group to laugh. They did, of course.

'Since then I've had worse ideas than that.'

The lunch guests laughed again. Jameel glanced at his prompt cards, looked out across the cream of the Lahore business community and said, 'I had three pieces of great luck in those early years. First, to have found my uncle Gulzar and my friend, Ali Kamal, my right hand in business.'

He pointed to a table where a man older than his years sat next to another in his early thirties and began to applaud. 'Gulzar Hafeez and Ali Kamal, gentlemen.'

The room took its cue from the speaker and clapped. 'The second was who my uncle turned out to be. Not just a well-respected man, a great man; kind and wise with a vision for himself, and for me. He became my teacher and my guide. What I am today is because of him.

'And last, the third piece of luck was something I didn't recognise at the time. I'm from a village to the south. Mundhi village. I was born there and would have stayed. I left because I could find no place for myself.'

He placed his hands on the table, palms and leaned back.

'So here I am. Fortunate, blessed and proud. Thank you again for the honour. I accept it for myself, my father, and Mundhi, because without the last two, the first doesn't exist.'

He sat down to more applause. Ali grinned. Gulzar Hafeez let a tear slip into his moustache. It had been a polished performance from a successful man. I could already see the headline.

***

The lunch improved my mood and the beautiful doctor came into my head. My ego wouldn't allow me to apologise, no matter what. Saying you're sorry was announcing a weakness. It hadn't occurred that it also revealed a fundamental flaw. So, why was I ready to do just that? The answer was that since our first meeting I'd thought about her all the time and wanted to see her again. That wouldn't happen unless I was prepared to concede I hadn't been at my best. Not a full-blown 'I'm sorry' but as close to an apology as I would come. In truth, I was more wounded by her closing comment than I would have believed possible.

I was told you used to be good

That hurt. Because that was my opinion too.

I made the call before the booze took me to another place. She seemed surprised to hear from me. Within seconds her memory marshalled her defences. When I suggested we meet, she said, 'I don't think that's a good idea.'

Silence on both ends of the line.

133

This was my last opportunity to connect with this woman.

'Look, Simone, we got off to a bad start, my fault, but we can do better. I want to hear what you've got to say. I'll help if I can.'

And here she was striding towards me. Gliding towards me.

Today's outfit was black and gold; everything else about her was the same. She could have been one of those "Bollywood" stars I'd heard about – cool in the heat, chic amid squalor.

But I wasn't the same. For a start I was sober. Almost. The dark-blue blazer, tan slacks and sky-blue shirt open at the neck spoke of a more considered approach to the day. On the table, a bottle of water, half-poured, completed the reincarnation. Simone Jasnin took it all in. Her expression showed nothing. Of course, she was pleased I was capable of raising my game. Pleased she might be, but flattered only a little, she was used to men making an effort to impress her, it had been like that her whole life.

'Simone!' I kissed her on the cheek.

'Mr Buchanan.' She wasn't ready to forgive.

'I'm glad you could come.'

I was struck again by how beautiful she was. 'Sparkling water, no ice no lemon, isn't it?'

'Yes.'

I ordered from a cruising waiter, for her, nothing for myself.

'Cheers.' I raised my glass. 'Let's pretend this is our first meeting. Best forget the other time. No excuses, my fault. Deal?'

'Deal.'

We sipped our drinks allowing the truce to settle round us. I leaned back in my chair. 'What do I know about you? French mother, Pakistani father. You love this country. You're interested in women's rights. How am I doing?'

'Well.'

'You'd like my help, and, oh yes, you heard I *used* to be good. Anything missed?'

'Not that I can think of.'

Despite her fermenting resentment, she laughed, and we were back at the beginning.

'So why here, why Pakistan?'

'This is my home, my father's home, I love it here. It's a wonderful country. And this is where I'm needed, where I can make the most difference. France has many problems and the resources to solve them. Pakistan doesn't, not yet. It's up to those with commitment and belief to lend their weight to cure the ills.'

'And what are those ills, Doctor?'

I used her title and lifted the conversation to the level she wanted, for the moment at least. 'Too many to list. The one that concerns me is the treatment of women in this country.'

'Not health issues? I'm surprised.'

'I'm engaged with health issues every day. I'm already doing what I can in that area. I believe I'm in Pakistan to make my contribution as a professional, and to work for change as a woman.'

Her beauty heightened when she was serious. Her mouth turned down and her skin took on the smoothness of alabaster. I already knew I'd help her in anything.

In everything.

'How long have you been here, Mr Buchanan?'

'Ralph, please call me Ralph. Three years.'

'And in that time who have you talked with, socialised with, done business with? Men or women?'

'Both.'

'Really? Both? Are you sure?'

I sipped from my glass. The ice had melted. I looked over the rim. 'No, you're right, my contact is with men.'

'Have you wondered why that is?'

'Because that's the way here, isn't it?'

'Wrong. You have few contacts with women because that's how men want it.'

I was listening now.

'The history of women in Pakistan is the history of oppression. All about power and inexcusable excess.'

'Go on.'

'In this country, women are the property of men. Let me do something shocking for a female here. Let me buy you a drink and tell you the everyday circumstances of life that exist in this country, the world outside refuses to believe. And when I finish, if you don't see it as I do, I won't ask for your help. You're not in a hurry, I hope?'

I was a newspaperman and she was a lovely woman with a tale to tell with her hand in her pocket to buy me a drink.

No, I wasn't in a hurry.

***

She told me her truth, truth it had taken her whole life to see. A reality I hadn't noticed though it had been in front of me every day. When the drink arrived – Chivas this time – a feeling of peace settled round me.

The gorgeous creature opposite spoke in a soft, confident voice while the whisky, dark and potent, waited for me. I relaxed in the over-stuffed armchair; it was going to be a very pleasant day. Her hands went to her head, adjusting the black and gold *chador*.

'What do you know about this country?'

'I haven't given it much thought.'

A sad half-smile darkened her face and she gave me a history lesson for the best part of an hour, while I listened and tried to make the whisky last. There was no doubting the doctor's sincerity, but she hadn't convinced me she wasn't just another kind of extremist – a man-hating feminist zealot. I hoped not.

When she finally stopped speaking, I reluctantly challenged her. 'Examples?'

'Examples! The entire life of a woman here is an example.'

'Specific examples.' I was a reporter now.

The doctor wasn't fazed by my sudden professionalism. Her charm, the offer of a drink and perhaps more had taken her this far. This was the end of that road, from now on her argument needed to persuade on its merits.

'While the birth of a boy is celebrated, the birth of a girl is a time for mourning. The father feels shame, the mother feels guilt.'

She shifted in her seat and moved closer, speaking quietly, conscious of being overheard. 'In 1985 the president of Pakistan set up a commission to look at the status of women in this country. The commission's conclusion is written on my brain. It said, "The average woman is born into slavery, leads a life of drudgery, and dies invariably in oblivion. This grim condition is the stark reality of half of our population simply because they happen to be female."'

She studied my face for a reaction and found none.

'Of course, the government suppressed the report.'

I waved a familiar instruction to the waiter. The gesture deflated her. She continued, sounding more confident than she felt. 'You need facts. In Pakistan women have a shorter life expectancy than men. We have the lowest female/male ratio in the world because of the poor health of women. In most families females eat after the males, causing girls to have a much higher malnutrition rate than boys. A girl will eat half what her brother eats but do twice the work. Anaemia is widespread, 97.4 percent of all women in Pakistan are anaemic.'

The doctor fired off the damning figures. The waiter arrived with the drink. She tried to keep her annoyance in check. She was losing me.

'Do you know the Hudood Ordinances?'

'No, what're they?'

'A set of laws applied to the crime of zina, sex outside of wedlock. Adultery, fornication and rape. Offences of rape are called zina bil jabr, literally it means 'forced adultery'.'

She played her big cards. 'According to the Human Rights Commission of Pakistan, every two hours a woman is raped in this country and every eight hours a woman is gang-raped. These figures are based on reported incidents. The real figures are much higher.'

'Shocking.' It sounded like a programmed response.

'Under this law women who've been raped can be charged with adultery or fornication. The way the law is applied the victim has to be able to produce four adult males of impeccable character as witnesses to the crime. If she cannot, and none ever can, the woman is prosecuted and the rapist goes free.'

Her voice had a bitter edge, her lips drawn thin and tight. 'This farce,' she almost spat the word, 'isn't treated the same as any other crime where DNA is accepted as proof. The courts prefer the literal four adult male witnesses however unlikely it may be to provide such proof.'

Something over her left shoulder caught my attention. Her tone lost its vigour. 'Rape is used as a weapon of punishment and revenge. It's rare for the police to make an arrest. Often, they're part of it. No one is ever convicted. And that's only the start of it.'

Her words trailed off; she was close to defeat. When she agreed to meet me again she'd been confident she could persuade me to join her. She'd been mistaken. When I spoke I wasn't unkind, or harsh, but negative just the same. 'Simone, what you've told me is truly awful, despicable and wrong. It's a national wrong, a cultural thing. You want me to write about it, tell the world. If I do, I guarantee two responses. It'll pass most people by because it's too much, too big, and too far away. Those left will see it as an attack on Pakistan. They'll be angry, all right, but not at the laws, not at the conditions of women in this country. And nothing will change.'

Her expression was impassive, the way little girls look when they're scolded. I said,

'"One death is a tragedy, a million is a statistic". Do you understand?'

'Joseph Stalin.'

'Was it?'

'Yes, and yes, I understand.'

'People can't relate to inhumanity on a grand scale, it's too impersonal.'

She said, 'Too impersonal? All right. Another Chivas, I think. Forget the many. Let me tell you the story of Afra.'

Chapter 20

Most mornings started with a drink, a reviver, something to help me feel human.

Not today.

A telephone call sorted it. I told Jameel Akhtar what I had in mind. No fuss, no problem. When did I want to come?

I thought of Simone Jasnin. Meeting her had left me with mixed feelings. She was accomplished, passionate, exciting. The stuff about gender inequality and abuse of women was difficult to relate to, but the tale she'd told was packed with human interest, with a horrendous crime at its heart. An unpunished crime. Even better.

Except it was old. News usually meant new. I wanted to help the doctor for reasons of my own but I needed a way in and couldn't see it.

In the taxi, I marshalled what I knew about Jameel Hafeez, most of it was already well-known. He was from the Punjab and had come to the city to find his only relative. Now he was managing director of his father's company and Businessman of the Year. No details. Nothing about who he was. Or who he had been: a mystery man.

The car nosed through the traffic. At times, Lahore's infrastructure groaned under the weight of its residents, tumbling over itself in its eagerness to grow. Spreading like spilled paint, fast following the disaster Karachi had become: a hellhole of squalor and crime. I could have relocated to Islamabad. I'd chosen Lahore, the cultural centre of the country, the seat of the Mogul Empire, the Sikh Empire and the one-time capital of Punjab – not for its rich history or because it was a city of academics and dreamers. But because here, I'd be left alone.

When the shit hit the fan for the last time in the UK, the foreign correspondent job was the last resort. If it had been possible to send me to Outer Mongolia I'd have been there. Only my reputation – fading memories of past victories – kept me in the game at all. I realised I was lucky, though I didn't feel it.

The car that brought me disappeared into the never-ending river of vehicles. I pressed the intercom and waited. A brass plate said Ravi Restaurants Ltd, no doubt after the nearby Ravi River, and when the door buzzed open, an alert woman greeted me.

'Take a seat, Mr Buchanan.' Her efficiency impressed. A man appeared: late twenties, dressed in a business suit, his hand outstretched in welcome. He said something to the receptionist and turned his attention to me. 'Thank you for coming. This way please.'

I followed. He knocked and we entered a stylishly-furnished room. Jameel Akhtar Hafeez, Lahore Chamber of Commerce's Businessman of the Year, sat behind a desk. He rose to shake my hand. 'Mr Buchanan, good to meet you. Thank you, Ali. This afternoon at two.'

Close up, the new star seemed boyish, too young to be running a growing group of businesses. 'So, you want to interview me. How very flattering.'

'Not really, you're a man of some achievement. My aim is to find out about Lahore's latest success story.'

'Is that what I am? I hadn't noticed.'

I didn't believe him.

'Can I offer you, coffee? Tea?'

I hesitated. 'Tea's fine. No milk, no sugar.'

He pressed a button and spoke. Quicker than I thought possible, tea arrived. The receptionist left the tray on the desk between us. Hafeez thanked her and poured two cups. 'Cheers.' He grinned. 'Isn't that what you say?'

'Yes, cheers.'

It tasted like tea ought to taste and seldom did.

'You're Scottish. I've never been to Scotland. I'd like to go. Do you miss it much? Pakistan must seem very backward to you, very dull.'

Before Simone Jasnin I would've agreed, especially with the last part. 'Not at all. Pakistan is an absorbing country. Fascinating. In some ways better than home, in other ways not as good. You know, the same as anywhere.'

'True. Now, how can I help you today?'

I took a notebook and pen from an inside pocket. 'I intend to write about you. I think you'll be interesting when I know more.'

'Okay, shoot.' Hafeez smiled at his phraseology. 'I watch a lot of television.'

'I've heard so many stories it's difficult to find a starting-point. Why don't you talk about yourself and if something occurs to me, I'll ask.'

For the next half hour he told me about his journey to the city, the search for his uncle, and the education Gulzar had insisted he have. At the end, he spread his arms. 'So now I'm Jameel Akhtar Hafeez. The luckiest man in Lahore.'

I scribbled as he spoke. 'When was this?'

'Eight years ago. I was twenty, unworldly and naïve with no idea where I was going in life. I shudder to think what might have become of that boy. Where would he be now?'

The irony of his question didn't escape me: he'd been on his way to a glorious future as I was leaving a glorious past. He poured more tea for himself. I placed a palm over my cup. One was enough. 'And since then?'

'Since then I've continued what my father began, and we've been blessed. We live in a time of change and opportunity. We've been able to harness some of that opportunity with the result our businesses have flourished. Ravi Restaurants has many avenues opening up in front of it. Exciting times, Mr Buchanan, we live in exciting times.'

I studied the entrepreneur. With him success was not loud gesture and extravagant talk, but rather, a quiet attitude focused on a clear vision.

'And Jameel Hafeez, the man, what of him? How does he live in these exciting times? Hobbies? Interests? A woman perhaps?'

Jameel shook his head. 'Business leaves little time for much else.'

Common knowledge. Maybe he was a workaholic who preferred business life to distractions like women. My instincts told me that wasn't so. Chic Logan had described it.

the same story as everybody else, the one that sits on top, the obvious stuff

'So, you arrived in Lahore, where did you come from?'

'From a village in the Punjab.'

'What's its name?'

'Mundhi.'

A bell went off in my brain. I didn't believe in coincidence. Mundhi village. Afra's village. And this man's name was Jameel. *The Jameel?* Hafeez had mentioned the village in his speech. 'Tell me about it.'

'It is much like any other in the Punjab.'

'Who were your friends?'

'The usual ones. Boys I played with after a day in the fields.'

'No females to catch a young man's eye?'

The question seemed to irritate Hafeez. 'None that I recall. Can we move on?'

'Of course, but our origins tell a lot about us. "The child is father to the man". Do you know that expression, Mr Hafeez?'

'No.'

'What about family?'

'My mother died. There was only me.'

'Were you lonely?'

'I don't remember being lonely. No, I was never lonely.'

'So life in Mundhi was good. You were happy. You liked the village.'

'I thought it was the best place on earth. The only place. My whole world.'

The self-deprecating hero, the award-winner, was in the room. I pretended to make notes. 'Why did you leave?'

Jameel Hafeez considered his reply. 'Things changed. It was the right thing to do.'

I believed I knew what had driven the young Jameel from his home. 'A friend of mine met someone from there, a woman called Afra. Did you know her?'

His voice faltered. '...No, I don't remember the name. Perhaps your friend was mistaken?'

I let it go.

'Have you ever gone back, back to Mundhi, I mean?'

'Never.' The reply was terse, hostile. I'd crossed a line. 'What would be there for me now? Life has moved on. The past is where it needs to be. I saw that village through the only eyes I had, the eyes of a boy. It would look very different to me now.'

He stood, the interview was over. 'Sorry. I have a busy day ahead.'

'Thank you for your time, it's appreciated.'

'Not at all. I told you, I'm flattered by your interest in me.'

The handshake was firm. I started to go when something caught my eye: wooden circles piled one on top of another. They'd been there all the time. In the old days, I would have spotted them earlier. Ali appeared to see me out. I picked one up. Jameel Hafeez hurried to shepherd me.

'These are interesting.' I counted in my head.

One, two, three...six.

The wood felt heavy. I was being rude and didn't care. My host put his body between me and the jewellery. 'They were my mother's and very special to her. I keep them close, they help me remember.'

I tried to imagine him as a boy.

'It's good to remember, isn't it?'

Jameel Hafeez didn't say if he agreed.

***

Ali came in and sat down. Jameel let the tips of his fingers touch as if he was about to pray and thought about what he wanted to say. 'How many times have we talked into the night, telling each other who we really are and what we really feel?'

'Many times, Jameel.'

Jameel ran his tongue over his lips. 'Of all the millions of people in Lahore, only two know what brought me to the city. My father and you.'

Ali relaxed. Jameel and Gulzar were more alike than they knew, neither was ever in a hurry to get to the point, and he loved them for it.

'From the moment we met I knew we would be friends. It's the friend I'm speaking to now. I need your help, Ali, and your silence, because I have no idea what I'm expecting, no notion of where the road is going.'

Jameel could be a serious man, never as serious as now.

'I'm confusing you because I'm confused myself.'

'What's happened, Jameel? Is everything all right?'

'Perhaps you can answer that question for us both. I told you about the car that stopped in my village and the man I saw across the compound. The man with the hooked nose and the cruel stare. I disliked that man, though I knew nothing about him, not even his name. Later, when I saw him outside Afra's house, I knew my time in Mundhi was at an end. He was there to take her away and that her mother would see in him what she couldn't see in me. I knew he'd come to marry Afra.'

'I remember.'

'He wasn't just my rival that day, he was my enemy.' Jameel paced the room. 'A few nights ago, I saw him again. In Jahan's, with a woman. The woman wasn't Afra.'

'She may have been a relation. Perhaps he had every right to be with her. Another wife, maybe.'

'That's not how it seemed. This was a girl. They played like lovers. And that's what I want you to find out.'

'Who the woman was?'

'No, I've no interest in her. If this man – his name is Dilawar Hussein – has another woman, even a wife, what has become of Afra?'

Ali understood: the village girl. Always the village girl.

'Maybe they're divorced. Maybe she's back in Mundhi with her family. Maybe he's deceiving her. A lot of maybes. I want the truth. Will you help me, Ali?'

'Of course.'

'I need to be sure she's all right.'

'Okay. When did you see him? Are you sure it was the same man?'

'Yes, absolutely. I'm absolutely sure. The face of an enemy is even more familiar than the face of a friend. If he's wronged Afra….'

'Where do I begin?'

'Watch. Watch and find everything there is to know about him.'

'What was the name?'

'Dilawar Hussein. If he's harmed her in any way….'

'I know,' Ali said. 'I know.'

'And the reporter asked about Afra. He said a friend knew her. Who could that be?'

***

'I've found him, Simone, I've found Jameel.'

'Are you sure? I mean, so fast?'

'I'm sure.'

'Who is he?'

'Have dinner with me and I'll tell you. Pick you up around eight?'

'No, I'll cook. Come to my place.' She gave me the address.

I put the phone down.

I was told you used to be good

Her flat was modern, spacious, and not overly feminine. A copy of *Vogue* lay on the coffee table, the only clue to who might live there. From the window, I could see the city lights blinking, giving way to the sprawl of the Lahore Garrison Golf and Country Club. Simone wore black slacks and a white v-neck. She mixed vinaigrette while I watched, intrigued by her grace, and the passion of her commitment to her beliefs. She produced a bottle of wine. I'd decided to limit myself to two glasses. Anyway, wine wasn't my poison. The meal was excellent: braised lamb shanks, Provencal vegetables and salad.

I said, 'This is wonderful.'

'Thank you.'

'Do all French women cook this good?'

'Only the ones who can.'

'You must miss France?'

'Sometimes I miss the shopping, but less and less.' Simone wasn't ready to talk about herself. 'So you've found Jameel. Who is he?'

'Someone you may know.'

'And you're certain? Jameel's a common enough name.'

'I'm certain.' I emptied my glass.

'You've spoken to him?'

'Yes.'

'And what makes you so sure?'

'He's from Mundhi.'

'Mmmm,' she pushed food around her plate, 'that doesn't make him *the* Jameel. There could be a dozen men with that name in the village.'

I teased it out, my fingers stroking the stem of the wine-glass. 'Yes, I suppose there could. Except he has the bangles. I saw them.'

Simone dropped her fork.

'You saw them? Where?'

'He keeps them on his desk. My interest wasn't appreciated.'

'Did you ask him about Afra?'

'Of course. He says it was too long ago. He couldn't remember anyone called Afra. I didn't believe him.'

'So why would he still have the bangles?'

'Why, indeed?'

I topped up our glasses. Simone brought the dessert – crème caramel, smooth and sweet. She toyed with hers and told me again about the woman in the Punjab and her love for a boy called Jameel. I studied the curve of Simone's neck, the perfect skin and her eyes, deep and clear. On the surface, a confident, assured professional, underneath a woman of passions.

'Will you ever go back, to Paris I mean?'

She lit a cigarette. 'My father taught me to love Pakistan the way he did. He was privileged, and as his daughter, so was I. His experience became my experience, a cosseted view that saw the best in everything, blinded to reality by money and education. I don't blame him – things were different then – though the glorious past he celebrated only existed in history books. Unfortunately, my father was too busy dreaming to notice that this place was returning to the dark ages. Dreaming is fine. I dream, too. But not of palaces and dynasties.

'In the Punjab, surrounded by so much need, it wasn't difficult to fool myself into thinking my contribution had value. Afra changed all that. When I saw what they'd done to her, I knew how misguided I'd been.'

'And came to Lahore?'

'Eventually. I've taken this flat and told the hospital I need extended leave. They're not expecting to see me for a while. Maybe never. The world has to understand. I was looking for a way to tell it, and found you.'

'Too bad you've missed the best of me.'

She laughed. 'Do you intend to hold on to that forever?'

'Not forever. Just for a while.'

'And that's my story. If I ran away how could I live with myself? So no, not to Paris. Not yet. What about you? Why are you here? Why Pakistan?'

'It wasn't my first choice, believe me.'

'So why?'

'Things went bad. I made mistakes.'

I emptied the bottle; she brought another and I told her, in a strange way hearing it for the first time. Not just Jo-Jo, all of it: Germany, where I'd lost respect for myself and the friendship of my colleague, Stanley Dow. A young reporter, Lonnie Harper, had died because I wouldn't listen. Simone didn't interrupt. We'd uncovered a racket involving the theft of armaments – a big-bucks scam. Nobody dared guess how high up it went. When it got too dangerous we were told to pack the tent and head for home. I hadn't passed on the instruction; nothing mattered more than another glittering prize to sit alongside the others. As the senior man, the responsibility was mine. And I'd blown it. They killed Lonnie. Back in London, the drinking really took over and my behaviour became more and more unpredictable, until the paper had no choice. The golden reputation hadn't saved me.

When I finished, Simone said, 'This is where they sent you?'

'My punishment.'

She put her palm across her glass. I poured for myself. The bottle was two-thirds empty. 'So. I'm not the only one with a tale to tell.'

***

The sun was already high when I woke. Memories of the previous night coaxed me into the day. Simone filled my head. I found her everywhere and in everything.

I'd slipped away in the early dawn, mindful that this was Pakistan and she needed to be protected. Back at the flat, I poured myself a drink. Part of me was afraid. She was a woman of ideals and high expectation, to be with her meant embracing her crusade. I hoped I wouldn't disappoint her. A story of lost love had brought us together. I wanted a happier ending. The beautiful doctor deserved no less. And I was beginning to understand what really went on in this country. But I hadn't left my demons in England.

Chapter 21

The house was impressive on a street of impressive houses. Towering above the high wall surrounding it and set back from the road, it was a world away from life on the street outside. The garden was grassed and planted with fruit trees. Tall black gates ensured privacy. In the shadows, its outline blurred, making it look larger.

Ali sat across the street in his car. This was his second time watching, no not watching – *spying* – on the Dilawar Hussein family.

Finding where they lived had been easy, learning more might be difficult. The street was well-lit. In this neighbourhood, how could it be any other way when the people who lived here had money and money bought security?

He yawned. It would have been no trouble to get an off-duty employee to cover the house. He hadn't considered it; he'd made a promise. If that meant spending night after night in his car, well….that's what a friend would do.

Ali had been in position since late afternoon. Three men arrived, then a taxi dropped a female at the gates. No sign of the woman he'd heard Jameel describe so often.

It was late, past midnight; the house seemed closed up for the night. The sky showed neither moon nor stars and now and then a car passed. Other than that, this tranquil suburb of Lahore had gone to sleep. He stretched against the beginnings of cramp in his thigh and thought about Jameel: how they'd met, how their friendship had grown, and how the success and recognition he'd achieved was nothing to him beside the girl from the Punjab. In the beginning, Jameel talked about her often. When he did his eyes filled with tears.

Though Ali hadn't heard him mention her in years, his friend hadn't forgotten. He'd found a way to live with what was. Until he saw Dilawar Hussein.

Ali had his own memories. At that moment, his comfortable bed was one of them. He checked his watch – twelve twenty-five – and slid further down into the upholstery. A man appeared from behind the gates, looked up and down the street, and started towards the city. Ali sat forward. Who was it? Not a servant. One of the men who had arrived earlier, though not the Dilawar Hussein he was interested in.

He waited, for over two hours he waited, no longer bored or tired. Around two-thirty the figure returned, keeping to the shadows wherever he could. The next night nothing happened. Nor the next.

Each evening, the same people came to the house. The man with a secret was with them. He might be having an affair with someone's wife which would explain the suspicious behaviour. Pakistan was not the place to get caught for that crime. Ali would find out about the family in due course; for now, he wanted to know what made one of them sneak around in the middle of the night.

During the day, street traffic was light, and by eleven at night it dwindled to the occasional car. Hours passed. Ali was alert and ready, poised to solve the mystery of where the man went when everyone slept. At one in the morning, he thought he saw movement behind the gates, and he was right. A figure slid from the shadows and set off in the same direction as before.

Ali eased out of the car and followed; another moonless night helped him stay hidden. For close to an hour he weaved behind his target, walking on his toes at times to avoid making a noise. Away from his own street, the man behaved like an ordinary person, no longer disguising his progress. As he got closer to the centre the man quickened his step. Jameel's friend trailed him past restaurants, noisy and fragrant. So late at night, the lights, the babble of diners, the sound of glass and metal and the fires of the tandoors glimpsed in passing made him feel he was moving between worlds; from the quiet of the middle-class suburb to the energy of a city.

The streets were crowded now and still he held back. Discovery might jeopardise his chances of finding Afra. Soon he was in an alley that narrowed and twisted, never straight or flat for long, a snaking tendril that ended as the moon showed itself and drowned the ancient houses in pale light.

Suddenly, he realised where the man was going and why.

To Heera Mandi, Lahore's oldest red-light district: to the prostitutes. Ali began the long walk to the car. He'd seen enough.

***

'So?' The question came out with more force than intended. Ali wasn't intimidated or offended. He knew Jameel. No doubt he'd thought of little else since he saw Dilawar Hussein and the past had come rushing back.

'The man in the restaurant was Quasim Dilawar Hussein, the eldest son. There are two more, Zamir and Firdos, and a sister, Chandra. The mother lives there as well. The brothers all work in the business, selling farming machinery and agricultural products. They have a warehouse in an industrial estate on the way to the airport. It's a big market, plenty of demand and they do very well.'

'How do you know all this?'

'Simple, I asked.'

'Asked who?'

Ali tapped the side of his nose with his finger. Jameel was too serious for jokes, so he told him. 'When I worked for Mohamed Abdul Quadir, one of our best customers was making his way in the world, a man who ate in the restaurant three times a week. In those days, he was slim and quiet and couldn't cook. Why we saw so much of him. He liked our food, and our prices. I still run into him from time to time though I've never been able to persuade him to come and dine with us. He prefers to give Mr Quadir his custom. But things change. My friend is no longer slim and has a lot more to say for himself these days. I don't know if he ever learned to cook. I do know he became the assistant chief of police, the youngest in the history of the force. You should meet him. He distrusts everyone, especially policemen. You'll like him, Jameel.'

'And he told you what?'

'That the Dilawar Husseins are respectable business people. As the eldest son, Quasim is the head of the house. He has a wife but nothing is known about her. Like most wives she stays at home and rarely goes out, even with her husband. The other two sons haven't married yet. Chandra works as a secretary in the city. She isn't married.'

Jameel was disappointed, he'd hoped for more.

'They keep themselves to themselves. There is one thing.'

Ali told him about Heera Mandi.

'Interesting. What does it prove?'

'About Afra, nothing yet. But where one secret exists there may be others.'

Jameel didn't disguise his feelings in front of his friend; they were too close for that. 'Perhaps, perhaps.'

His expression said he didn't think so.

***

Two days later, Ali thought their luck had changed. He'd abandoned night surveillance to discover what went on during the day, and when the brothers left, he was in position. Soon after, the daughter got into a taxi. Every hour or so, Ali got out of the car and walked down the street, crossed over then came back up again on the other side. At the entrance, he glanced through the gates, trying not to appear suspicious. Around mid-afternoon a car drove to the front of the house and Ali resumed his up and down patrol. He passed on the opposite side of the street, seeing nothing except the vehicle parked at the door. On his return, the driver was helping an overweight lady into the back seat. The woman was old and fat and needed assistance: the mother.

The man assisting her was the midnight rover.

Ali wondered what the matriarch's reaction might be if she knew her son used prostitutes. He considered what he'd seen. If it was his duty to drive his mother around, he must be Firdos, the youngest son.

Around five, with the heat slipping from the day, he tried again. A figure was in the garden. He crossed the street, level with the gate and peered through the iron railings and saw a woman strolling on the grass. Ali pressed his face to the bars and whispered. 'Afra.'

She didn't hear. He tried again. 'Afra.'

Her chador was pushed back. She sang to herself. Ali lost his head and called out. 'Afra. Afra! Here! Over here!'

The city was full of madmen, shuffling through a parallel universe, arguing with people who weren't there, shouting, talking to themselves. Maybe she thought he was one of them. He shook the gate. She turned and his excitement died. This could never be her.

She wasn't a woman, not yet, she was young, very young; a sad-eyed child, gazing in benign confusion. Ali said, 'Who are you?'

'Nobody.'

Ali edged away from the gate and stumbled to the car. He didn't look back.

Chapter 22

Jahan's was Simone's idea. Female curiosity. She wanted a glimpse of the man Afra called to through her pain; the one she insisted must never know. 'I must see what he looks like.' How could I resist?

In the shortest time we'd become inseparable. Every moment was shared, and as she revealed herself to me, my defences dropped. We sat in a corner of the restaurant on M M Alam Road, holding hands and whispering. Whenever the door opened, Simone held her breath and squeezed my fingers.

'Is that him?'

Eventually, she got tired of watching, returned to me, and it was just the two of us. The meal might have been superb – in our hurry to get to her flat we didn't finish it. A perfect evening in every respect, save one: Jameel Hafeez didn't show.

***

The sound of clapping and shouting was deafening. I weaved round the chanting crowd, imagining how ferocious it would seem further in, trying to keep Simone in sight. Thousands of women acknowledged their heroes on the stage. It reminded me of a Rolling Stones concert, yet the comparison could hardly have been less apt.

Simone looked back, wild-eyed and smiling, encouraging me to follow, edging through line after line of saris and chadors and faces burning with excitement. Twice I lost her. She found me again, touched my hand and continued her crazy progress. No one noticed me even when I pushed or pulled them to make space for myself. It wasn't possible to get to the platform; wooden barriers twenty yards from an open-backed truck prevented it. The police were here in numbers in a line of khaki uniforms in front of the barricade. To the side, many more, wary and tense, standing in groups to reinforce their fragile authority.

Two nights earlier, over coffee in her flat, the question had been asked so innocently and I'd fallen for it. 'Why don't you come?'

'Tell me about it.'

Simone had curled her legs underneath her on the chair. In her eyes, I saw someone complete in her beliefs. 'I've spoken about the injustice women suffer in this country. It's a bleak picture, but it's not a hopeless one. Some day the balance will be restored and women and men will be the partners in life they were intended to be.'

She looked irresistible. 'Until then, we struggle, building on small triumphs. Womens' movements here have a hard time yet they grow stronger, furnishing us with the most powerful tool, the one we'll use to bring about change. Information: the enemy of the oppressor.'

When Simone talked her passion overwhelmed her. I liked it.

'Which organisations? I assumed there wouldn't be any, that they'd be outlawed.'

'No, a few survive. Women Against Rape is one. Every obstacle that can be found is placed in their path. Still they live and campaign, thorns in the flesh of the government.'

'And what is it you're inviting me to?'

'A rally. Education for Us, it's called. You may learn something.'

'You think I need educating?'

She kissed me. 'You're a man, of course you do.'

***

The moment my eyes opened I was back in the crowd. There was no period of grace, no honeymoon; my brain started the awful pictures rolling within a second of being awake. I was thirsty and my body ached. Even lying in bed hurt. I pushed back the covers and swung my legs over the side. The tiled floor felt cold on the soles of my feet, at least there was a part of me that wasn't in pain. I padded into the kitchen and filled a glass with water from a bottle in the fridge. On my way back I picked up a bottle of J & B. The whisky had been trying to attract my attention for days. I took a sip of water. The liquid slewed round my mouth, a cool, healing sensation. My arms were bruised blue, black, and yellow. My chest was the same.

Lucky, so very lucky.

The day before was too frightening to forget, and too painful to remember.

I unscrewed the top off the bottle, poured three fingers into the glass and had my first drink of alcohol in days. The clock on the bedside table told me it was seven-twenty in the morning. So what?

Threads of fire ran down my throat. Yesterday played in my head.

***

'Stay with me, Ralph! Nearly there!'

Simone cut through the mass of women who'd stood for hours. A space opened in front, one final push and we were pressed against the barricades. A banner with red lettering, hung from the side of a truck, read Education! Education! Education!

A woman walked to the microphone and spoke in Urdu. 'One, two! One, two!'

The crowd cheered, the woman smiled, reassured about the sound quality. She picked her way over black lengths of cable and disappeared. Now we were at the front I saw police on the roof of almost every building, ready to act.

Authority is an illusion that exists as long as it's agreed and accepted otherwise it becomes coercion, held in place by force and fear. If the crowd acted together they could smash the illusion and take control. Weight of numbers would overcome any opposing force in the end. Gatherings like this were prohibited because they promoted belief; faith ignited in these conditions.

Dangerous stuff.

Simone stood beside me but her spirit was with her sisters. Her mouth was drawn in an unconscious grin, she smiled, happy to be a part of it. Her brown eyes glowed; the colour, the noise, the crush of bodies and their solidarity reflected in her flushed face. She was high, freedom was her drug. 'Can you believe it?' she said.

It was impossible not to feel the power generated by the crowd. The energy was tangible. I might as well have been waiting for Charlie and Keith to kick into *Honky Tonk Women* – that was a buzz I could understand.

Sun broke through an overcast sky. The platform party climbed the wooden steps at the back of the truck and filed along to their seats. All carried sheets of paper. The crowd gave up the second big cheer of the day. Many more would follow. Uniformed policemen straightened their shoulders, raising themselves to a higher level of alertness. It was beginning.

A woman in a sari crossed the stage, sorting through her notes. She called in Punjabi. 'Salam!'

The crowd clapped and called in reply. She said, 'I am Satta, Satta Wasim Akram!'

and pointed at the policemen on the rooftops. 'Shall I say it again for you?' The crowd roared their support of her defiance.

'Satta! Wasim! Akram!' Each word was cheered. 'Now you know who I am, remember me!'

Another cheer. Simone translated so I'd understand.

'We know why we're here today. The women of Pakistan are coming to the end of a dark night. It has been long and frightening, but morning is breaking over our country and the light of knowledge will show us the way forward, guide us to where we should be. The time of oppression is almost gone. In one thousand years people will say its end began on this day. With you! With me! With us!'

Some of the translation was lost in the noise. It didn't matter. I'd been to many rallies in the past, the phraseology didn't change. Short, uncomplicated sound bites. Communication through emotive one-liners. The technique of connecting with the masses. Nothing more was necessary, everyone knew the issues.

For ten minutes the woman set the tone, capturing the mood of the crowd, feeding it messages of courage and hope. After a while, Simone stopped translating, mesmerised by promises of a different tomorrow to pass them on. I was tall and white and male. And alone. A succession of speakers addressed the crowd, the atmosphere becoming louder and bolder with every optimistic generalisation. For some it was too much. Women who passed out were carried from the mass.

I was detached from the groundswell of passion racing through the thousands yet the energy was tangible and a little frightening. A glance at the policemen grouped together showed me my apprehension was shared, tension shone as clearly in their eyes as revolution did on the endless sea of female faces before them. I'd all but stopped drinking since the second meeting with the doctor, now I was overcome with creeping claustrophobia and an irrational need to get away.

I needed a drink; really needed.

The feeling grew. The speaker's voice came and went. I struggled to get back in control. Simone remembered I was with her. I faked it for her. She turned back to the speeches, my hands and arms began to tingle, a film of sweat broke on my brow. I inhaled and exhaled, slow and deep. A new speaker clutching a sheaf of paper, a woman of about thirty, dressed in the familiar tunic and baggy trousers made her way to the podium. I fought to stay in the moment.

She held her arms aloft. 'Women of Pakistan, the days of bondage are ending.'

Simone returned to translating, unaware she'd ever stopped. The woman organised her pages. 'Lies. We've been told lies, sisters.'

Her voice was strident and clear, her gaze strafed the crowd drawing each of them to her. From the first word I knew this was a performer. No introductions, it was what she had to say that was important.

'Those who keep us where we are do so with misconceptions, myths and barbaric traditions. These people will never set us free. We are the only ones who can do that, but first we must know the truth. When the women in this land know the truth, they'll rise against these liars who would steal our lives from us and walk out of the silence.'

The crowd cheered.

She shouted. 'Liars! All of them, liars!'

A young policeman fingered the gun at his side.

'And what have they lied about? Everything sisters! Everything!'

The speaker distracted me from my racing heart, the attack was passing.

The crowd was listening. 'Wife-beating! How many have not endured this indignity? According to the Human Rights Commission of Pakistan eighty percent of women suffer from some form of violence or abuse in the family. Beatings, mutilations, marital rape, are still not against the law. Why?

'And our friends the police, what do they do?' She waved a hand at the armed men around her. 'Nothing!' Her hands gripped the podium. 'Nothing at all!'

The speaker's face was a mask of anger mirrored by the crowd. The party atmosphere had been replaced by resentment. Everywhere I looked I saw sullen females, hardening against their oppressors. A time was coming when violence would be returned with violence.

'Acid burning increases, but no law to criminalise. Why? They tell us women cannot have education. Why? Every day we're told we cannot have jobs outside the home. Again, why?'

She scanned her audience. 'Read, sisters! Read and learn!'

Simone was transfixed.

'Rape is used for revenge or to humiliate a family. In Pakistan, a woman who is raped must supply impossible proof or be accused of fornication. So every woman here lives in terror. Who wants it this way? We know who!'

The speaker stopped to sip from a glass.

'I could go on. I could go on about the higher status of men, about inheritance, about divorce, female circumcision or polygamy. Only men could convince themselves that it's right. Because they have the power and they intend to keep it. They won't share it. Don't take my word for it. Don't take anyone's word. Learn to read, and read to learn. Lack of education holds us in chains, encouraging so-called honour killings. Honour killing isn't about morality or virtue. It has nothing to do with purity and everything to do with domination, power and the subjugation of women. Hatred of women considered to be less than human, things to be used, abused and disposed of when their usefulness is at an end.'

She raised her fist in a call to action. 'Woman of Pakistan, education will set us free! Education is the key to freedom!

'Education!

Education!

Education!'

The crowd followed where she led, taking up the slogan and the salute.

'Education!

Education!

Education!'

In the growing hysteria no one noticed the woman slip into the space at the front. She wore the outfit of the dominated; a black robe, a hood and a veil. She walked to the centre of the clear area. One hand held a beaker.

'Education!

Education!

Education!'

Thousands roared. On the stage the speaker paced, her fist punching the air. I was moved by her conviction. Next to me, Simone affirmed her sisterhood. Out of the corner of my vision I registered the woman from the crowd splashing liquid over her head and clothes. She turned her face to let it wet her skin and eyes.

'Education!

Education!

Education!'

From nowhere the lighter sparked alive between her fingers. The flame caressed her body.

Then everything changed.

Fire raced over her. She screamed and fell to her knees, a human torch blazing in the afternoon sun. I put my arms round Simone and turned her away. What happened next had been waiting to happen all day.

The police broke from the side of the stage and rushed towards the burning figure. The panic was instant. Many at the front thought it was a fight and swept the barriers away, eager to meet the attack. The terrified majority tried to escape. A few stumbled and were trampled. Others fell over them and shared their fate. The tide rolled through the crowd from the front to the back.

All around us police fought with females insane with injustice. Some of the blows found me. The burning body lay on the ground, ignored. I grabbed Simone and dragged her under the truck. No one would claim responsibility for the final piece of madness. At the first volley I ducked. The shooting continued, I could hardly believe it. The police fired from the roofs into the panicked crowd. Every shot found a mark. Simone twisted in my arms, we witnessed what happens when fear takes over.

Herd instinct. Stampede.

Tragedy.

***

Lucky, so very lucky.

The bottle by my bed was half-full. Soon, it would be empty. Walking through that street had been like crossing a battlefield. Mangled bodies lay everywhere. Police casualties swelled the numbers. The awful pointlessness of it was clear to me; the righteous lay just as dead as their oppressors.

There was little she could do, but the doctor in Simone wouldn't be denied, working tirelessly even after the emergency services arrived. Finally, she allowed me to lead her away. We walked in silence to the car parked streets from the rally. I drove with no idea where we were headed until a red traffic light halted our escape and Simone spoke. 'It really is a war. I thought it wasn't, but it is.'

'That was horrible, Simone –'

'I've been content to cheer while others did the fighting. No more.'

'Simone...' I couldn't reach her, she wasn't listening.

'I wanted to believe it was the long game my father talked about. That belief kept my hands clean, kept me a supporter. A spectator.'

She laughed a bitter laugh. 'But you can't get a little bit pregnant. I'm a doctor, you'd think I'd know that. Wars need deeds, not talk. And soldiers, not bystanders.'

She opened the door and disappeared into the crowd.

Hard to believe that had only been fifteen hours ago.

I poured another. I'd no plans for getting out of bed today.

Chapter 23

The angle-poise lamp threw a lemon-rimmed circle on the wall and over the stock sheets, itemised lists of where the business's money was hiding, disguised as earth-movers, tractors, pumps and hundreds of other things, big and small. Across from each was a number and a cost.

Zamir Dilawar Hussein bent over the papers. His concentration, absolute when he'd begun the wearying task, was fading. From his office window inside the warehouse light fell on the rough concrete floor. Pallets filled with drums and sacks rose like small buildings inside the corrugated shell. Row after row of industrial metal shelving held countless boxes of smaller goods. That was Zamir's job tonight, making sure they weren't countless.

His finger stabbed numbers into the calculator as his eyes moved up and down the columns. When he lost his way and had to start again; he cursed. Zamir had a system. He counted from the top to the bottom and wrote the total on the pad next to him then counted again, from the bottom. Incorrect figures were useless; Zamir was trying to establish the state of the business; accuracy was all. It was important work, and he hated it.

His mind drifted to his older brother. While he worked, Quasim was probably with one of his women.

Anger, the characteristic common to the Dilawar Hussein males, bubbled and died in him. The only son worth being was the first-born. How well he knew it. The business started by his father belonged to his older brother now. Zamir owned no share of it. He wasn't a partner, just an employee taking his instructions from Quasim; a stranger wouldn't guess they were related. The middle son had been eaten by resentment all his life. It never got better and never went away.

He drew himself to his task. Quasim would ask for the final figures tomorrow, better for him if he had them.

In the quiet, the noise seemed to dart past and disappear. Zamir looked out of the window to the semi-lit area beyond. Nothing moved. The floor was illuminated by safety lights, making mammoths of the towers of goods.

Zamir spent every day in the warehouse. It held no fear for him, even at night. The brother wasn't unhappy to have a reason to break from work. He went out to the cavernous space. Which direction had the sound come from? His memory flirted with him before giving an answer. It had been hollow, a drum or a can struck by something; a foot maybe. That meant he wasn't alone. If someone was snooping around they'd be in trouble. Zamir was in the mood for trouble.

Not far from the office, a pile of wooden shafts lay waiting to be attached to the metal that would change them into spades. Zamir considered lifting one and changed his mind; he wouldn't need any help, he was sure of that. He walked a few steps and stopped where he could see down the long walkways between the shelving, not expecting to discover the intruder at once, but he did. At the bottom of the warehouse, a figure stood in the middle of the aisle looking back at him. Zamir's face twisted in a smile. Arrogance prevented him questioning how easily he'd found the unwanted guest.

Thirty yards away, the trespasser returned his stare and disappeared to the left.

The stock-taker advanced past piping and sacks of seeds and broke into a run, determined not to lose the intruder. At the end of the row, Zamir's smile became a grin. The felon was close to where he himself had been a moment before, standing legs apart, hands on hips, shoulders back. Taunting him?

Zamir retraced his steps. Halfway down, the figure slipped out of sight again.

'So you want to play, do you? Fine. Zamir likes games.'

The middle brother guessed where his new friend had gone. Just as before, he stood at the bottom. Zamir was back where he started. A flicker of unease crossed his mind along with the memory of the rejected spade shaft.

'How can we have fun if you always run from me?' His question echoed in the store. 'Don't run, let's play.'

He edged nearer, his confidence restored by the sound of his own voice. Zamir was tiring of the sport, blood pounding in his brain demanded action.

The figure walked towards him and the distance between them closed. He'd assumed it was a man but suddenly, he wasn't so sure. A few more steps brought them almost face to face.

There was so much Zamir Dilawar Hussein didn't understand. Now it was too late.

***

In the morning air the smell hung on everything. Policemen keeping the small crowd of ghouls at bay outside the compound gate would return to their homes carrying it on their clothes, in their hair, even their skin. Yesterday the warehouse had risen above its neighbours on the industrial estate. Today all that remained was the twisted frame. Ribbons of black smoke wound their way to the sky. Around the perimeter, expensive machinery sat on melted rubber, their working lives over before they'd begun.

The heat had been unimaginable, fierce enough to weld rivets, pop screws, buckle and bend the corrugated panels that clothed the skeleton turning the warehouse into a deformed parody of what had been.

A car pulled up at the gate. The officer in charge spoke to one of the men inside and ordered his people to clear the crowd and let it through. The vehicle edged forward past curious spectators. Inside, the driver and his passenger kept their eyes fixed and ignored the gawking melee.

'Keep going.' Quasim's lips hardly moved.

The crowd and the gates parted, the car drove into the compound and the brothers saw what was left of their livelihood. Firdos stared, open-mouthed. Quasim Dilawar Hussein gazed at the charred shell; all that remained of his inheritance. His eyes narrowed, assessing the damage, weighing the consequences. Where others saw wreckage he saw ruin – bank loans that wouldn't be serviced, lines of credit that had become unpayable debt.

Detective Jan Asmet Rana had witnessed more than enough ugliness for one life, he was sick of violence and death. Scenes like this made him long to be done with it. Only a few months and he would be. His plans were made. He'd sit on his veranda with the books he'd been too busy to read, maybe once or twice a week take a trip, leave the city to bird-watch in the Punjab. Long days filled with nothing very much. And the world could go to hell – it was going there anyway in spite of his best efforts. He introduced himself and said, 'Mr Dilawar Hussein, it's your warehouse, I believe. I'm sorry to tell you it looks deliberate. Arson, almost certainly.'

Quasim eyed him with contempt; a fool could have come to that conclusion. Rana paused, there was more to say. 'Have you had any threats made against you? Any warning something like this was planned?'

Quasim shook his head.

'The machinery round the outside was set ablaze in a different attack. I apologise, but I have some questions.'

Dilawar Hussein dismissed the policeman. 'Ask my brother.'

'With respect, he isn't the owner.'

'He'll answer your questions.'

Rana had given bad news to many people in his time and appreciated that reactions were unpredictable. He closed his coat against the morning chill and smoothed the pencil moustache above thin lips, a tactic he used the way others counted to ten. He wasn't here to score points.

'You're the one who's suffered the loss, so you're the one I must speak to.'

Quasim turned to go.

'Sir! This isn't it all. Come with me, please, over here.'

The policeman forced civility into his voice and walked to a group standing apart from the smoldering warehouse. Quasim followed, Firdos behind just as the first ray of sunlight fell across a figure on the ground covered by a blanket.

'I'm sorry to have to do this, Mr Dilawar Hussein.'

Someone removed the blanket and the brothers stared at Zamir. Firdos gasped.

'Even out here the heat would've been tremendous but the fire didn't kill him.'

'What do you mean?'

'He was stabbed. The one through the heart caused his death.'

'When?'

'Around midnight we think.'

Rana spoke with authority, confident when dealing with facts and probabilities. He answered what hadn't been asked. 'Your brother was stabbed – as far as we can count without a complete medical examination – around thirty times. Thirty times is a frenzied attack.'

Quasim had had no love for Zamir, but still. Perhaps he'd been up to something, something that went wrong and brought this. He dismissed the notion. His brother was stupid. Zamir had no talent for duplicity. Or anything else.

'Was he murdered here?'

'We think inside then dragged out. The marks on the ground support that theory.'

Quasim exhaled, deep and heavy. 'So, what now?'

'We'll take the body to the morgue. There will be a post-mortem examination. At some point, I'll need to interview the family. I'll also need a list of everyone Zamir was in contact with. You'll have to come to the morgue, Mr Dilawar Hussein.'

'Is that necessary?'

'Sir, I'm afraid it is.'

'Why?'

The policeman chose his words. Despite this man's arrogance he had no desire to hurt him. 'I haven't told you all of it, and don't want to do that here.'

Quasim glared, impatient. His life had been destroyed. Didn't this idiot understand?

'Otherwise I wouldn't insist.'

***

Ali didn't bother to knock or ask if it was a convenient time to interrupt. He took a seat across from his boss. Jameel looked up, surprised to see him. 'What's wrong? Are you unwell?'

'I'm fine, Jameel, I've had a call I think you should know about from Shakil.'

'Who?'

'Shakil – my policeman friend. Yesterday was a bad day in Lahore.'

'The riot. What's the latest?'

Ali stroked his chin, wondering how to tell his friend. 'Fifty-three dead, seven of them police officers.'

'Do they have any idea how it started?'

'It was peaceful until a woman set herself on fire.'

Jameel screwed up his face. What a terrible death.

'That panicked the crowd. Someone fired a gun and then it got out of hand. Shakil says the police returned gunfire. That's when it became a stampede. Most of the dead were crushed or suffocated.'

'Mmmm.' Jameel was less than convinced. As usual in Pakistan, the establishment forces were never at fault. The police claimed to have returned gunfire. Of course they did. 'Most of the dead, what about the rest?'

'It's world news. CNN and the BBC have cameras down there and are asking questions, speculating, making the city look bad. Shakil doesn't know if he'll have a job this time tomorrow.'

'I'm only surprised they allowed the protest in the first place. All those people, agitated and angry. It was an accident waiting to happen.'

He turned his attention to the papers he'd been working through. 'And that's what you came to tell me, is it?'

'No. I came to tell you what you won't see on TV or read in your newspaper.'

Jameel put the pen down. Ali was a level-headed man who left cheap dramatics to others. He was calm, dependable. He'd played a big part in the success the business had enjoyed. Jameel listened to him, 'What would that be?'

'Shakil didn't call to tell me about the riot, he wanted to give me news about something else. Considering the trouble he was in this morning, he was the very last person I expected to hear from. There was a fire last night. A warehouse north of the city. Completely destroyed. Definitely arson.'

'Connected to the rally? A reprisal?'

'Perhaps. That's not why Shakil thought I should know. The warehouse was owned by Quasim Dilawar Hussein.'

Jameel rested his elbows on the desk, his palms pressing against his forehead. Dilawar Hussein. Even the name brought a reaction from him. 'Why did your friend think you should know about this?'

'Because I asked about the owner. Now that man has lost everything. He may never recover. Shakil doesn't know about insurance, the chances are he's ruined.'

'Interesting.'

'Interesting it may be, though not as interesting as the circumstances that go with it. One of his brothers was killed. Not in the blaze.'

'Which brother?'

'The middle one, Zamir. The one we know nothing about.'

'Killed how?'

'Murdered. The body was dragged from the warehouse into the open. Shakil tells me – all off the record, of course – it looks like the work of a madman. He was knifed again and again. A preliminary examination revealed thirty entry wounds, which suggests a couple of things.'

'What?'

'The violence of the attack probably means the victim was known to the assailant. Could be the motive was revenge.'

'You said a couple, what else?'

'Well, revenge is one possibility. A business dispute would explain the arson. Maybe the brother was the random victim of a crazy person.' Ali paused. 'Or a woman. Shakil says they've ruled that in. Women prefer to poison or stab their victims. Poison is the favourite. The violence might be pointing to someone who snapped, someone out of control. The thinking is that maybe they should to be looking for a woman.'

'A madman or a rival seems likely. I'd need more before I started looking in that direction.'

'They have more. The body was mutilated.'

'How?'

'Zamir Dilawar Hussein's clothing had been removed. Acid was thrown over his genitalia.'

They sat in silence, Jameel imagining the horror of what he'd been told, Ali searching for words to tell the rest.

'Sound like a woman to you?'

Jameel didn't answer. His throat was dry.

'One more thing – and nobody knows this yet – they're keeping it quiet. The killer left a clue. Under the body they found a wooden bangle. Very unusual, Shakil says.'

Jameel blanched.

Ali looked at the desk seeing everything he would expect to see. Everything except what had sat there since the day Jameel hired him. He wondered where they'd gone, and if the six were still together.

Chapter 24

The sound pulled me towards it.

'Ralph! Ralph!' Boom! Boom! Boom!

Against my will I dragged myself to the surface where the noise was louder.

Boom! Boom! Boom!

'Ralph! Ralph!'

I opened my eyes and regretted it. Light stabbed them closed again.

'Ralph!' Boom! Boom! 'Ralph!'

I groaned, rolled off the couch and staggered to the door. It was locked.

'A minute. Just a minute.'

The key was on the floor for some reason. I picked it up, stuck it in the keyhole and turned. The door opened and Simone glared at me. Her eyes assessed my ruined clothes, the same ones I'd worn to the rally. She wore jeans and a jacket over an orange shirt. Her hair was scraped back by a bandana the same colour as the shirt. She looked stunning, and angry. She strode past and opened the window as far as it would go. I closed the door and faced her. 'Do you know how long I've been pounding on that door?'

'I'm sorry.'

She looked round. 'How can you live like this?'

My head hurt. 'I'm sorry. I didn't know where we stood. You left in a hurry yesterday. I assumed you wanted to be on your own.'

'Two things. First – I did need time, so thank you for your consideration. And second – the rally was two days ago, not yesterday. You've lost a day. A whole precious day of your life.' She aimed contempt at the state of the flat. 'Easily done.'

The news drained me. I felt sick, physically, emotionally, and something beyond even that. I felt alone. 'Can I get you anything?'

'How about a man I can depend on? Got one of those?'

I pushed the crumpled shirt into the waistband of my crumpled trousers. I needed a drink but was wise enough to settle for bottled water. When I came out of the kitchen, she hadn't moved. I sat on the edge of the couch – my bed for the last thirty-odd hours. The glass shook in my hand. 'When you got out of the car, where did you go?'

'I walked. I had to think.'

'We were lucky.'

She neither agreed nor disagreed and sighed. Resignation or defeat, I couldn't tell. 'I had decisions to make. Decisions I wanted to share with you. That was a mistake. My mistake.'

'No, no. No it wasn't. Tell me, I want to know.'

She looked away.

'Tell me. Please. I want to know.'

I was standing on the edge and knew it. One false step, one wrong word and she would be lost to me forever.

'I've left the hospital, I won't be going back.'

She had my attention; the nausea and the ache in my head would wait.

'I have money so that's not a problem.'

'What do you intend to do?'

Possibilities flashed through my mind. The mayhem at the rally had persuaded her to return to France. She was about to tell me her love affair with the sub-continent was over and she was leaving. She'd seen enough.

'Work, here, in the city. If a woman finds the strength to break away from the oppression she lives under there's almost nowhere for her to run. Even her own family would send her back.'

She laughed. 'It's about honour. Her husband's honour, her family's honour, society's idea of honour. Everybody's honour but hers. They can quarrel and fight and maim and kill 'til their twisted notions are satisfied, but if the woman stands up for herself, she's an outcast. A few places exist, without government support, of course. I can help. That's one decision.'

She took my hand in hers. 'Ralph, in just a day the stories I've heard, the things I've seen, are scarcely to be believed, yet they're true. What goes on here is beyond reason. It's Afra – a million Afras – desperate, looking for someone to stand up for them and say what needs to be said. Shout it.'

She let go, her fingers tracing mine, gently severing her connection with me. I knew what she was doing. 'These women have no one. I don't know if I can be that one, but what's going on must stop. Someone must stop it. I'd hoped that you and I, that we….that'll never be.'

'Simone.' I tried to interrupt. She put a finger to my lips.

'Where I'm going, you can't follow. If you were stronger, maybe you could find a way. But I must. No more spectating. Faith without works, Ralph.'

The quotation was left unfinished. I watched her go, powerless to offer a word of protest or a promise of hope. Most of my words I'd sold for money, the rest had been squandered on excuses.

***

'Why does Quasim want to see me? What would I know about anything?'

Bilal's questions showed more than curiosity. The call from his cousin Firdos to tell him Quasim wanted to meet wasn't good news. The head of the Dilawar Hussein family never spoke to him, never recognised his existence. All of a sudden he'd been summoned – for that's what it was – and he didn't know why. They'd sent Firdos to collect him to make sure he turned up.

An uncomfortable thought came into his head. Firdos would have to drive him back, unless, of course, he wasn't coming back. A crazy idea. He'd be back at his own place in an hour or two. Quasim wanted to discuss some work with him that was all. From time to time, Bilal performed small services for the family, usually something they didn't want to do themselves, like frighten a supplier into reviewing his prices, or discourage a competitor. Strong-arm stuff. This would be one of those.

'But why does he want to see me?'

Firdos didn't answer. He knew better. His brother Quasim wanted to speak to Bilal, his job was to take him. And his cousin was right to feel afraid. Bilal's fingers pulled at the tahmat wrapped round his waist and legs. The driver wasn't unhappy to see his cousin's agitation; he didn't like him much and offered no reassurance.

'Tell me, what he said again?'

'"I need to speak to Bilal. Go and get him."'

'Only that?'

'Only that.'

'But why? Why does he want to see me?'

Firdos kept his eyes on the road, unable to resist a smile. Someone else's discomfort was always enjoyable, especially when it was Bilal. The car stopped and both men got out. Firdos went ahead. Bilal wanted to go to the lavatory. Instead, Firdos took him to the dining-room and told him to wait.

Bilal drew his hand along the polished wood table. They lived well, his cousins. Approaching footsteps told him they were coming. The thug tried to pull himself together. Quasim mustn't see his fear. The eldest brother was unpredictable, no knowing what he might be capable of. Life was sweeter without the Quasims of the world.

They arrived together, Firdos tucked in behind his brother, out of the spotlight, the way he liked it. Bilal spoke first. 'Quasim, cousin. I wish we were meeting in happier times. Please give my condolences to your mother. All of you must be – '

Quasim cut through the grovelling sympathy. 'Sit down, Bilal. And shut up.'

Bilal's fear wouldn't allow him. 'I know nothing.'

'That's interesting. What is it you know nothing about, exactly?'

'About the fire. About Zamir. I was at home.'

'Oh please, cousin, you judge yourself too harshly. You must know something. Everybody knows something.'

The mock compliment chilled Bilal.

'Just what Firdos told me.'

'And what was that?'

'That there was a fire and Zamir was dead.'

Quasim looked across at his loose-lipped brother. Another idiot. 'Well cousin, let me bring you up to date. You deserve to know, you're family after all.'

He rested his elbows on the table, getting comfortable, as though preparing to tell a story to a child. 'Last night, when you were at home fast asleep, someone set my warehouse on fire and murdered my brother.'

Bilal stared wild-eyed, his thin face drawn thinner with dread. 'Again, my regrets to you and your mother. She's too good a woman to lose a son this way.'

Quasim's eyes were empty. 'Bilal, I can't accept we're cut from the same cloth. How could my father's brother produce something like you?'

The insult was spoken softly. 'You're a weak, pathetic coward. I despise you, I've always despised you. What you should be asking is why you're here. Well, I'll tell you.' Quasim rose from the table and paced the room. 'Some time ago, you were given a woman by Zamir and Firdos, do you remember?'

'Yes. Yes, I remember.'

'And do you remember what you were told to do with her?'

'Yes. Yes.' Bilal seized on something he could understand. 'Yes, I remember.'

Quasim's walk had taken him behind his cousin's chair. 'Good. Now think carefully. This is very important. Don't lie, tell me the truth.' He bent and whispered in Bilal's ear. 'What did you do with her?'

A weight lifted from the frightened man. At last, something he could answer. The sweat on his neck started to dry. 'I did as I was told, Quasim. Just as I was told.'

'Good, very good, Bilal. That's what I wanted to hear.'

Quasim strolled to where he'd been. Bilal saw him nodding. 'Just as you were told. What was that, *exactly*?'

'Get rid of her. Zamir told me to dispose of her.'

'And what did you think he was asking you to do, *exactly*?' Quasim rephrased his question. 'No. What did you do, *exactly*?'

'I met your brothers at the warehouse. We put the woman in the back of my car. Firdos was there, he'll tell you.'

'Then? What then?'

'I drove south, deep into the Punjab, for almost two hundred miles. On a road in the middle of nowhere, I pulled her out of the car – '

'And drove back?'

Quasim imagined the scene.

'No.' Bilal refuted his cousin's lack of faith in him. 'No, I needed to be sure she was dead. I strangled her. When I left she was dead.'

Quasim stroked the side of his hooked nose. 'You did well, cousin.'

Relief surged through the assassin. Whatever was going on had nothing to do with him. Resentment pricked him. These superior people supposed they had a monopoly on hate. Not so, not so. Bilal hated them as much as they did him. And he should've asked for more money. 'Is that all? Can I go?'

'Almost, almost.'

Quasim put a hand in his pocket, pulled out a dark brown circle and tossed it on the table. The jewellery rattled and vibrated in a drum roll before coming to rest in front of Bilal. It meant nothing to him.

'Recognise this? She wore it. Recognise it, Bilal?'

The cousin dragged his eyes away. Fear was back. His voice cracked. 'I don't understand.'

'Neither do I. That's why you're here. I wanted you to see it before I return it to the police.'

Quasim lifted the polished wooden round he'd bribed a policeman into giving him. In Pakistan, such things were possible.

'I apologise, cousin. I haven't been completely honest with you. It's all been such a shock. But as you're family, let me tell you the whole story. Our mother knows only that one of her sons perished in the warehouse blaze. That's all she'll ever know. She's old. The truth would be too much for her. And what is the truth? The truth is that yes, my warehouse, my business, was deliberately destroyed last night. And yes, my brother was killed. But not in the fire. Zamir was knifed by a maniac who threw acid over him. Our mother couldn't survive that knowledge.'

'Of course, Quasim.'

'You see, there's something I'm trying to understand. This.' He shook the bangle in the air. 'This was under Zamir. Left where it was certain to be found.'

He'd made his point; the police could have their evidence back.

The room closed in on Bilal. 'How? Who?'

'By her. By Afra. She's alive!'

***

I could see lights inside the hall; it had been easy to find. Two men stood by the door, the nearest one put out his hand. 'John.'

His friend, a tall guy, stabbed an arm at me. 'Frank.'

Both were white and sounded English. I went inside. I was late, it had started. The room smelled musty, swirls of blue cigarette smoke circled overhead. I took a seat at the back and looked round. An overweight guy wearing a shirt and cardigan under a grey suit turned towards me. Another handshake. He whispered. 'Colin.'

I whispered back. 'Ralph.'

Three dozen chairs faced a table at the end of the room: two men were behind it. One of them, casual in jeans, T-shirt and an open denim jacket, was speaking. The other, an older man with cropped grey hair wearing a suit and a shirt without a tie, sat beside him. Slogans printed on laminated sheets were pinned to the walls. Simple messages: Easy Does It. Give Time Time. Think Think Think. Twenty people listened to the younger guy. Nobody looked down and out.

'Our primary purpose is to stay sober and help other alcoholics achieve sobriety.'

So it had come to this. Ralph Buchanan, the great I Am.

The trembling in my hands reminded me why I was here. Everyone else seemed relaxed and at home, happy to sit back. I found it difficult to settle. I hadn't felt well all day. A guy near the front read from a book. I switched off, and for the fiftieth time reconsidered my decision to come.

The man in the denim jacket introduced the person next to him. It had taken until late into the night to come to terms with what I suspected. Ironically, a couple of drinks helped me have the discussion I'd put off for years – the discussion with myself about my life and my drinking.

Simone's reaction to the tragic way the rally had ended and how distraught she'd been at the flat, allowed a shaft of clarity to find me. Behind the passionate professional, Simone Jasnin was a fragile woman who needed a strong man to lean on. I wanted the job but didn't qualify. In truth, I hadn't been able to meet the criteria since leaving Scotland. Until now, it hadn't bothered me.

The older man said, 'My name's Gert and I'm an alcoholic.'

He spoke English with an accent – Dutch, or Swiss perhaps. Everyone replied 'Hi, Gert.'

Spooky.

But what did I have to lose? Calling the number I got online was my own idea. A woman answered and told me what I wanted to know. Sometime in the last forty- eight hours I'd arrived at a place I'd never been before: the bottom. And it hadn't been my worst moment, not even close. That was in Germany when young Lonnie was murdered. This was the first time I'd faced the truth instead of running from it.

I was tired of running.

Gert took a sip from a Coke bottle in front of him. 'When I came here I was sure my life was over. Thanks to my Higher Power and the fellowship of Alcoholics Anonymous that was wrong. I'm sorry, my English is very bad. I'll try to tell you something about me. My name is Gert, and one day at a time I've stayed sober for thirty-eight years.'

I did the math and reckoned this guy must've stopped drinking in his thirties. Thirty-eight years, my lifetime ago. Over the next forty minutes, Gert talked about where alcohol had taken him, and what had happened to enable him to walk away from the drug. I didn't know what to make of it. Impressive, no doubt about it. Did it apply to me, that was the question? When Gert stopped speaking everybody clapped.

A woman and a man appeared carrying a catering-size kettle. Coffee time. The audience milled around, most of them with a cup in one hand and a sandwich in the other. They seemed to know each other, chatting and joking with an easy familiarity. Regular attendees, I assumed. A guy in a sleeveless safari jacket, all zips and flaps, ambled over and sat down. He laid his cup on the ground, wiped crumbs from his lips and offered his hand.

'Jack.' I hadn't had my hand shaken so often since the night at The Dorchester when people thought I was a hero, most of them anyway.

'You new?'

'Yes, first time.'

'It's odd at first, but it works.'

'Where are you sitting, I didn't see you?'

'First row. Don't want to miss anything. My life depends on it.'

'What do you mean?'

'I can sit at the back and catch every third word, or I can hear everything. Don't come because I've nothing better to do. It makes sense to take as much of it home with me as possible. Just for the record, I don't... have anything better to do, there isn't anything better. My condition needs to be treated on a daily basis.'

He waved a hand at the humble room with its damp smell and peeling paint. 'This is a big part of it.'

We talked until the guy in denim rang a bell. Jack said, 'Why don't you sit with me?'

I followed him to the front row. The young guy said, 'This is your part of the meeting, and Tom we'll start with you.'

Tom, a stocky, ruddy-faced, forty-something in a tweed jacket was three places along. 'Thanks, Alec for taking the meeting, and thanks Gert for sharing your experience, strength and hope with us. I got plenty of identification. Different drinking pattern but the same results. Alcohol and trouble. When I lost my wife, I didn't stop. When I lost the job, I didn't stop. When I lost my kids and my licence and, on a couple of occasions when I almost lost my life, I didn't stop. One day I saw what I'd become. Then I decided to stop. And I couldn't. It wasn't my decision anymore. It hadn't been my decision for a while.'

He cleared his throat. 'Finally, I got here. Started doing what was suggested and was able to stop and stay stopped. That's the way it's been since. I joined a group and come to meetings. I've got a sponsor and I work the programme every day to the best of my ability. I'm not the big shot I used to be, but I'm not the unhappy egomaniac I used to be either. It's good, really good.'

A powerful admission from an ordinary man. Whatever else it was honest.

'I wanted what was on offer and I was "prepared to go to any lengths" to get it, as it says in the Big Book. Thanks for keeping me sane for another day. I'm glad to be here and glad to be sober.'

The chairman asked the next person if they'd like to say something and I had a frightening realisation. It would be my turn soon. Sweat broke over me, my heart beat faster, my face flushed. I didn't want to speak. I had nothing to say, certainly not to a room full of strangers. When it came to me, I shook my head and the threat moved past. Jack talked without anxiety, similar stuff to the first guy. My heart returned to normal, and in a way I couldn't explain, I felt foolish. I'd missed an opportunity. The chairman invited Gert to have the final word.

Gert gazed round the smoke-filled room. 'Every day I shave.' He stroked his chin. 'I run hot water, take my razor and my shaving cream and get ready to start. I look in the glass. Aaaaghhh!' He pointed. 'In the mirror, there is the problem.'

The room rocked with laughter, then the regulars joined in a prayer. At the door, Jack said, 'What did you think?'

'Not sure. It was certainly very interesting,'

He handed me a scrap of paper. 'Take my phone number. If you want to talk or feel like having a drink, give me a call. What did you say your name was?'

'Ralph.'

'Keep coming back, Ralph, just keep coming back.'

Chapter 25

They were walking down the dusty path, just as they always did. He tried to appear casual and kicked a stone; a cloud of dust rose and fell to the red earth path. She waited for the familiar question, ready with the well-worn reply. He pretended to be interested in where the stone had gone, following its progress through the short grass. He shuffled, tense, prepared for rejection. She frowned, bemused by his performance. How long had this been going on? How many times had they walked home in a group laughing and joking, or together in the straggling line of heavy-eyed, weary villagers? The answer was years, since they were children. And it would continue like this maybe all their lives.

He spoke, as she knew he would. 'Will I see you tomorrow?'

They lived in Mundhi village where each day was like the one before, no different from the one after.

'You're a good boy,' she said, 'but you are nothing in the world, so no, not tomorrow, not ever.'

His jaw dropped. His heart stopped. His life was over. His eyes opened.

He was lying against the headrest staring at the roof of the car. It took a moment to realise what was happening. Then it came to him. Where he was and why. Across the street the big house held its secrets just as it had for the last three nights. Three nights of waiting and watching and seeing nothing. But it had to be done. If she was out there he had to find her.

The torched warehouse and the body were dramatic events. Dramatic, but someone else's trouble, surely? Nothing to interest him – except the warehouse belonged to Quasim Dilawar Hussein, the man who had taken the woman he loved. Now, she was nowhere to be found. Jameel needed to be certain she was safe. Any wrong done her was his concern.

The work of a madman, Shakil told Ali; or a rival. Or a woman.

Violence was an everyday occurrence in the world, often beyond explanation. Jameel resisted the notion of a woman assassin, and he knew why. The fire and the viciousness of the attack on the brother had unsettled him. When Ali discovered no sign of Afra, Jameel's imagination travelled a path he didn't want to take. True, Dilawar Hussein might be divorced or separated and Afra may be back in Mundhi with no idea where he had gone. The murder and the destruction of the warehouse could have nothing to do with Quasim.

Mutilation was a different story. A jealous lover, a business rival, an unpaid debt, could have provoked it. The victim might have been the random choice of some maniac. Everything was a possibility.

Except Ali's description of the bangle left under the body told another tale. Jewellery carved from wood was common enough, though not like that. There were only two sets. He had one, Afra had the other. She was married to the dead man's brother and she was missing, the reason he'd been here for the last three nights.

Jameel stretched and sighed. In the great city of Lahore he'd worked and grown and learned to forget. Seeing Dilawar Hussein in the restaurant brought it back. What Jameel Akhtar Hafeez had achieved was nothing set against the memory of what he'd lost.

There were few cars parked on the street. The big house stood dark and silent, nothing stirred. He looked at his watch and settled down to wait.

***

Firdos opened the gate and closed it behind him. The street was empty, not surprising at this time. The family was unaware of his nocturnal forays; he wanted it to stay that way. Quasim had warned him and Chandra to be careful where they went and who they met. For days, Firdos looked over his shoulder, expecting to see his brother's wife. Bilal's account of how it ended made it impossible to believe she could have survived.

So what about the bangle?

It may have slipped from the assassin's wrist during the murderous act. That would mean the killer was a woman, or someone trying to convince them it was a woman. Bilal was the last to see her alive, he might have taken the bangles and was using them to scare the family. Bilal was capable of anything. And Zamir had been an unpleasant man, not hard to believe he had an enemy.

Hiding inside the house for the rest of his life wasn't possible, and anyway, as the youngest he was the junior partner in everything his brothers did. No one had a grudge against him. Quasim, Zamir, yes, but him? No, he couldn't see it.

And he wanted a woman.

On the street, he kept to the shadows. When he judged he was far enough from the neighbourhood he hurried along the deserted streets, now and then glancing back. Jameel saw him close the gate and leave the house. He'd follow the brother and find out where he was going in Heera Mandi. His mind abandoned logic. Crazy thoughts tumbled out - Afra had run away and was hiding in the red-light district. This man was helping her and was on his way to meet her.

Jameel had been joined by a new enemy: himself.

***

The decision was the right one. Alone in the shadows she wasn't so sure. The first time had been so easy, it ought to get easier. Instead, she was paralysed with fear, sweat running in rivulets down her arms while the sounds of the city were unknown terrors.

Ralph Buchanan had been her great hope – before the rally, the point of no return. What happened forced her to do something she had avoided. Making a real commitment. Nothing changed until someone changed it. Until the riot, the responsibility wasn't hers.

She could still picture the smiling faces before the woman set herself on fire. What hellish demons had driven her? After that, firing into the crowd crossed a line; the injustice of it overwhelmed Simone. In the car with Ralph, her silence was a mixture of shock and anger, and something else: a realisation of why she'd returned to Pakistan.

She pulled the hood over her head, black to blend with the night. An image of a little girl walking with her father – holding his hand – carried her to a simpler time. Simone loved her father, he'd been a good man, but she'd outgrown him and his ideas.

Footsteps. Someone was coming.

The doctor screwed up her courage. Tonight had nothing to do with gardens or towers or golden yesterdays. The steps grew louder. Her heart beat faster.

Time to be ready. And she was.

***

The brother followed the route taken the night Ali saw him. Jameel trailed at a distance, gradually closing the gap between them. Ali had let him go, he wouldn't. Firdos relaxed the further he got from the house; his shoulders opened, his back straightened. He began to enjoy himself.

On and on through the shifting landscape of Lahore at play. Touts outside restaurants called to him, assuring the best seat, the best price, the best food; his if he would stop. Jameel ran the same gauntlet of promises. One look at his face was enough to persuade the most indefatigable barker this customer was beyond reach. He lost sight of Firdos, sometimes for a few minutes. Panic took hold, washed away when he spotted the brother striding ahead, as focused on his objective as Jameel was on him.

The streets narrowed, winding canyons of semi-darkness between some of the oldest buildings in the city. The sound of late-night diners and excited conversation were left behind and the labyrinth ended. Carts selling food and flowers lined up under the night sky as people went about their business. Quasim's younger brother disappeared into an alley.

Firdos had no destination, only his lust was fixed. He'd know what he was looking for when he found it; it was always the way. Two women talking in hushed voices glanced as he passed and returned to their conspiracy. Deeper into Heera Mandi, he took a turn to the left and saw a figure in the shadows, clothed from head to foot in black.

Firdos smiled. 'I've been searching for you.'

They embraced.

'And I you.'

The blade plunged into his neck, releasing a jet of warm blood that sprayed the ancient cobble stones. Like his brother Zamir, Firdos Dilawar Hussein met death with confusion in his eyes. The last thing he saw was a surprise to him.

Jameel almost fell over the body. Moments ago this had been a living, breathing man. Now, it was a cooling carcass on a grubby street, surrounded by garbage and the smell of cats.

He forced himself not to run, dreading someone would come. His fingers scraped the earth, worn smooth by countless pilgrims to the shrine of pleasure, and touched something wet and sticky. Bile gurgled bitter in his throat.

It was lying next to the head. Even in the poor light Jameel knew what it was, he'd caressed the others too many times to be mistaken.

***

There were days when the Lahore detective hated his job. This was one of those days. At the warehouse fire Rana had found it difficult to sympathise with Quasim Dilawar Hussein despite his loss. He set his opinions aside; this man's family were victims. First Zamir now Firdos. To have lost two brothers as well as your business was an awful thing. He'd expected to see the head of the household stricken with grief, distraught beyond words. Not so. In the main room, Quasim held himself straight. Rana offered his hand. Quasim ignored it and the detective felt his expression tighten.

Quasim was brusque. 'Do you think you'll have more success in the search for Firdos' killer than you did with Zamir's? Perhaps someone else would be more effective? Maybe you're not the right man for the job?'

It was impossible to like this person.

'We're piecing together your brother's movements last night. Have you any idea what he was doing in Heera Mandi?'

Quasim sniffed. 'I should have thought that was obvious.'

'As to my fitness to conduct this investigation, that's for others to decide.'

'And have you discovered anything?'

'So far not much, there are no witnesses and few clues.'

'Few? So you have something?'

Quasim Dilawar Hussein wasn't struggling to come to terms with the deaths. Even in these tragic circumstances, the role of interrogator belonged to him. Rana walked to the window and bent to look at the bird in the cage. 'An unusual pet if you don't mind me saying so.'

'At last! A subject you know. And unusual, how so? There must be millions in Pakistan.'

Rana let the insult go. 'Birds are a hobby of mine. This is a Blue Rock.'

Quasim's reply was sarcastic and terse. 'Is it really?'

'A thrush. A wild bird not meant to live in captivity. How does it survive?'

'It adapts. It has no choice. Now can we concentrate on the case in hand instead of talking nonsense? Tell me what you've found out.'

Rana was reluctant to share the discovery of the bangle, Quasim pressed him. 'Otherwise I'll speak to your superior. Surely you don't want that?'

The threat failed to impress the detective. A few more months and he wouldn't have to put up with arrogant bastards like this.

'I insist on knowing.'

Rana was blunt. He'd had enough of this man's bullying. 'Very well. Firdos died from a single stab wound to the throat. We found a wooden bangle similar to the one underneath Zamir. What does that mean to you?'

Quasim's arrogance evaporated. His voice faltered. 'Nothing.'

Chapter 26

'I never took drugs. All my life I avoided that shit. It scared me. And I didn't like the types they attracted – hippie-losers, drop-outs, talentless dreamers. Weak people.'

He held up two fingers in a peace sign and put on a faraway face. 'Yeah, colours, man. I hated all that crap.'

It got the laugh he expected. He took a deep drag on his cigarette and tapped the ash from the end. 'So none of that came my way. I stuck to something I understood and started small: a couple of beers before I went to a dance. Didn't think it was a drug. Now I know different. Not just any drug, the world's favourite drug. I bought into the clever marketing: beautiful people drifting over the Nile in a balloon, or running along a Caribbean beach. Completely acceptable socially, unless you're addicted to it, and that's okay as long as everyone you're with is addicted too. But when you start to stand out from the crowd, all of a sudden it's not acceptable anymore. You're not acceptable. When it starts to really work. Works so well you can't get through the day without the fucking stuff, then…

'Then it's a different story. I started drinking so I could be on the inside looking out. By the end no one wanted to know me. I was on the outside looking in. Always.'

He paused to let his words get through.

'I couldn't stop. Alcohol, the drug I'd trusted, had me as hooked as any junkie. And for years, I didn't know it.'

He pulled another lungful of smoke out of the cigarette. 'Cunning, baffling, powerful. Today I see that. Back then, all I saw was the next glass, the next bottle.'

In the first row, I listened, unsure exactly why I'd come back to my third meeting in eight days. But I had. Talking to people during the coffee break and hearing them speak about their experiences told me things I hadn't known. Everybody I met was from outside the country. Some had had well paid jobs, some still did. They shared a common problem and a common solution. I was no longer alone.

One or two faces were familiar, Jack wasn't one of them. Back at the flat the first night I'd done a strange thing. Made a cup of tea. Without milk. There wasn't any milk. It tasted all right. Something Jack had said at the end of the first meeting stayed with me.

'Keep coming back, Ralph, just keep coming back.'

I'd taken his advice.

***

Two nights later I took it again. This time the man at the table – the top table they called it – was Australian, at least his accent sounded Australian. He was somewhere in his mid-thirties, five o'clock shadow colouring his lantern jaw in charcoal. He wore a checked shirt and smoked all the time, lighting a new one off the smoldering tip of the last. That wasn't the addiction he was fighting.

I sat in the front row again. The shakes were gone and I hadn't had a panic attack since the rally. That had been the alcohol; pulling away too fast, from excess to zero. There had been a few shaky times but each day it got better. I'd started to eat and had managed to write a belated overview piece on the riot. It even crossed my mind to earn my money for a change.

There was no word from Simone; she hadn't returned my calls and I worried about her. In the meetings, I'd heard "the most important person you meet in A.A. is yourself." That made sense in a way I couldn't explain. The proof was on too many faces to be denied. "It works if you work it." It was already working for me. Someone shared they were glad to be alcoholic. I didn't know about that. I did know I didn't want to drink. More than enough for now. I felt better. My head was clearer. I saw life in a new light. One question wouldn't let go. What part had I played in it all?

Little by little, I was uncovering the truth about myself. I'd let Jo-Jo's name slip to force an early capitulation from those carrion at MEDICAL. What kind of man would do that? The answer was the kind of man I no longer wanted to be.

In the toilet at The Dorchester, Stanley Dow had been right to blame me. The order from my editor was to get out of harm's way. I'd ignored it and Lonnie Harper had paid the price: ego, pride, the great I Am. Yet, I was changing. At least, I was willing to change.

It had been a long painful journey to the bottom but now I was striking out for the surface, taking the first unsteady strokes towards clean air.

I tried Simone again and didn't leave a message.

***

After the meeting, I didn't feel like going home. The hotel bar was exactly as I remembered. 'George' was on. I hadn't seen him in a while though any thoughts he might have about my absence, he kept to himself. 'Good evening, sir.'

'Good evening yourself. Coke and ice, please.'

He poured the drink, condensation frosting the bottle. I'd been coming here almost from the beginning and I didn't know this man's name. I asked and he told me it was Ibraheem.

Five men sat at the back, western faces above western clothes. I didn't rate these guys and usually avoided them. Tonight, I needed to touch base with people in the business because, despite my best efforts, I was still a journalist. I took my drink over to the group. One said, 'Long time no see. Where've you been hiding?' Layers of fat rippled under his chin. I sat down. 'Been ill. I'm recovering. What's going on?'

'Apart from the rally, not a lot. See the pictures of the woman?'
I was there
right at the front,

I saw her burn
could smell it
'Doesn't do much for Pakistan's image. And the warehouse fire was definitely arson.'

'What warehouse fire?'

'Same night. Somebody killed one of the owners and torched the place. They're certain it was murder – the body was found outside. Speculation it might not be a coincidence.'

'What's the connection?'

'It's just talk.'

'Who was the victim?'

'Somebody called Dilawar Hussein.'

Suddenly he had my attention.

'How did he die?'

'Knifed. A couple of dozen times.'

'Have they got anybody for it?'

'Not so far. Police issued a statement then closed down.'

'Which Dilawar Hussein?'

'Middle son, Zamir.'

'What about motive?'

'Nobody knows. Sounds like your kind of thing.'

you used to be good

I lifted my drink and went back to the bar. What I'd heard had shaken me. On a stool at the end was a familiar face. Dan Meiklejohn. We hadn't spoken in years. He raised his head from a Punjabi newspaper and smiled. 'Hello Ralph. Still fooling some of the people all of the time?'

Meiklejohn was a lifer who had worked in just about every war zone in the past couple of decades. Three divorces and crippling alimony persuaded him to bury himself in Pakistan. He was a bear of a man, fifty-five with a fleshy face and a loner's disposition. Our paths crossed in the good old days. We weren't friends but we weren't enemies, either. We appreciated each other. 'Tipple?'

'No thanks, Dan. Coke.'

'Good idea. Wish I could do it.' He signalled the barman for a refill. 'Still here, then?'

'Nowhere else to go.'

The drink arrived with the coaster and the bowl of nuts. Standards.

'Cheers.' Meiklejohn took a healthy pull. 'Watched you mingling with our brain-dead colleagues at the back. Learn anything interesting?'

'They were telling me about the warehouse murder.'

Meiklejohn snorted in the direction of Bob and the others. 'Those guys.'

'They're happy.'

'Happy idiots. Don't believe a word they say.'

'They reckon it might be linked to the rally.'

'Based on what exactly? The body in the fire was stabbed thirty-three times and mutilated. The dead man had acid poured on him. They mention that?'

Acid and the Dilawar Hussein family.

'On his genitals.'

'Fucking hell!'

'Looks like revenge. The police are keeping quiet about it. And here's the thing. Last night there was another one, in Heera Mandi. Same family.'

My throat felt dry. I lifted the Coke and drank.

'Firdos Dilawar Hussein, found in an alley.'

'Mutilated?'

'No, nothing like that.'

'How do you know all this, Dan?'

'Because, although I'm hiding from a shit-storm back home, I'm still working, still got my ear to the ground.'

Meiklejohn finished his drink in one swallow. 'Last night might just be bad timing. A boy goes where he shouldn't and ends up dead. But two sons gone and the business up in smoke in less than a couple of weeks...'

He let me draw my own conclusions.

'The first was a savage out-of-control attack that suggests the killer and the victim knew each other. Genital mutilation is sexual. Could mean the attacker's female. Women move freely in Heera Mandi. Ever been? Don't answer that.'

'You're saying the killer's a woman?'

'I'm not saying anything, Ralph.'

'Thanks for bringing me up to speed. Appreciate it.'

I had to think, had to get out of here. Meiklejohn caught my arm and I realised he was drunk. 'Whoa boy, not so fast. Under the body at the warehouse the police found something.'

'What?'

'Found another one in Heera Mandi.'

'Another what?'

'The killer left a signature. A bangle. Now who wears stuff like that?'

My heart stopped and started again. 'Got to go.'

I hadn't spoken to Simone in over a week. What I was thinking was ridiculous.

wars need deeds not talk
and soldiers not bystanders

Meiklejohn said, 'Give me your number.'

I wrote on a napkin, he did the same.

'Wondering why I told you?' He tapped the side of my glass. 'You're drinking Coke. Whisky you'd have got nada. Loose lips and all that. Then again, three divorces say my judgement's flawed.' Meiklejohn grinned. 'But only with wives, Ralph, only with them.'

Chapter 27

Still no answer from Simone. I left a message and replaced the receiver.

The time for games had passed. I needed to talk to her and find out what was going on. Already I was stronger than when we'd last met. Strong enough not to get involved in something bad? Yes, I believed I was. Strong enough to stand in the way of a woman bent on changing the world? I doubted it. The conversation with Dan Meiklejohn had come out of the blue, his information called up more possibilities than I could handle. And I didn't kid myself: I was in love with the dark-haired doctor. Loved her commitment, her passion, her refusal of the easier options she might have chosen for her life; her eyes, her smile, all of her.

But, if underneath was a cold-hearted murderer bringing an awful kind of justice to those she believed deserved it, what then? What if that was the real Simone? A whisky thought crossed my mind. I resisted it and tried to find some clarity. I was still a journalist, what were the facts? Not theories or suspicions – the facts. What did I actually know? That question underlined a sad truth; avoiding ex-wives hadn't prevented Dan Meiklejohn from keeping his oar in the water. He had contacts. I had none. The police would refer me to a statement, and I'd have...

the same story as everybody else

The reporter reappeared, a lifetime of experience standing at my shoulder. I fished paper from a drawer and drew up a Q and A. All I could lay my hands on was a pencil that needed sharpening; it would do.

Question: What crimes had been committed?

Answer: Two members of the Dilawar Hussein family, Zamir and Firdos, had been brutally murdered and the warehouse destroyed.

Question: Why?

Answer: Not known.

Question: What was unusual about the crimes?

Answer: The violence. Thirty-three stab wounds and castration by acid, and a carved ebony bangle found beside each body.

Question: Why was so much rage involved, especially in the first murder?

Answer: Because the murders weren't random slayings? They were personal? The motive was revenge?

Question: Revenge for what?

Answer: Not known.

Question: Why had the killer left a bangle at each crime scene?

Answer: A warning. They said you know who I am.

Question: What was the significance?

Answer: Afra had been married to the eldest son, Quasim, for seven years and had often worn the jewellery. The family would recognise it.

Question: And?

I paused. So far there was nothing to connect Simone to anything.

But?

The 'buts' were easy to find.

Question: What connection did Simone have with that family?

Answer: Afra told Simone about her life with them.

Question: So how did that involve Simone?

Answer: Maybe it didn't, but she knew Afra's story, and was the only one apart from her to have access to the bangles.

Question: So what?

Answer: She was disturbed by the scenes at the rally, talked wild talk about not being a spectator and wars needing soldiers. I had been unable to contact her in almost two weeks, during the time the murders were committed.

faith without works

If only I could speak to her, find out where she'd been and what she'd been doing. I'd made mistakes in my life but I'd called it right plenty of times. I ran through the Q and A again. Something was off. On the third read through I saw it right in front of me. So often the Q and A showed up a discrepancy in the evidence or the timeline or, in this case, an assumption.

And there it was, plain as day. The answer to number ten wasn't correct. I read it again.

Question: So how did that involve Simone?

Answer: Maybe it didn't, but she knew Afra's story and was the only one apart from her to have access to the bangles.

Wrong! So wrong it made him gasp.

the only one apart from her

Two sets: Afra had one; the other was on the desk of the businessman of the year. Jameel Akhtar Hafeez.

***

Detective Rana smoothed a hand through his thinning hair and scribbled on a sheet of paper. In his youth, he'd dreamed of becoming a lawyer, but years of studying when his family needed him to earn made the decision and he'd joined the police force. Until his wife died it hadn't been a bad life, he'd had his share of success. Now and then he failed of course. All in all, he wasn't unhappy with his humble contribution to make Lahore safer.

This case was probably his last and it was a strange one, violent and disturbing. It would be good to go out on a high.

The fire could have been started by the owner, though with the level of insurance it seemed unlikely. And why destroy a successful business? Perhaps it was the work of a rival, a jealous competitor or a dissatisfied creditor. That would make Quasim the target and Quasim Dilawar Hussein was an easy man to dislike. At the warehouse, with his brother dead on the ground, he'd shown a callous disregard he hadn't bothered to disguise. So why attack anyone else? Why not come for him?

Zamir may have discovered the arsonist and paid with his life. His mutilated body ruled that out; the killer had been prepared. Bad enough if it had ended there. Events in Heera Mandi said otherwise. One brother detested enough to have his corpse defiled was possible; two murdered from the same tribe suggested a vendetta.

Then there were the bangles, the killer's calling-card. Bangles meant a female. Or something the detective shuddered to contemplate: a madman rampaging through the city. He dismissed the thought. Instinct told him Quasim was lying about having no idea who was behind the crimes.

Rana spoke to his assistant. 'Rafee, find out everything you can about the Dilawar Husseins. Who they are and what they do. I want to know what about them could inspire such hatred.'

'But sir, they're the victims, aren't they?'

'Maybe somebody doesn't think so.'

***

The woman made no sound.

Her grey ghagra hung on her underfed body as she moved towards the man seated at the end of the table. In the candle's half-light she saw the fleshy jowls and the hooked nose; a face very different from hers.

Once she'd been beautiful, now her own mother wouldn't recognise her. Her hair, long and lustrous, was dull and patchy. Beneath its tangled confusion, the sharp contours of a face poked through skin stretched taut around sad eyes.

Daliya had stopped caring about such things, the constant grind of life in the house and months of malnourishment had taken her beyond vanity. There was no grace period for her, no Chandra pretending to be a friend, the family had done with that. From the beginning, her station had been well-defined. She'd slept in Quasim's bed just twice, the rest of the time she dragged herself to the cupboard room high in the house at the end of every weary day.

Quasim massaged his temple and opened his eyes. 'Go away.'

Only ten months and already he was tired of her. She'd produced no son. She was unnecessary. Just like the other one.

He clenched and unclenched his fists when he thought of Afra and Bilal's claim to have finished her on a lonely road somewhere. His cousin was a fool who'd say anything to keep trouble away from his door. The last weeks told a different story. His brothers were dead. His business was destroyed. He was ruined, and the insurance wouldn't cover half of what was lost.

Quasim Dilawar Hussein blamed others for any misfortune. His opinion of himself left little room for negative conclusions. Still, under-insuring the warehouse and the stock had been his decision. He'd judged the premiums excessive, seen the risk as low. A bad call.

He wanted to speak to Bilal again. Make the coward change his story. Then at least he'd know the truth. It had been a mistake to trust anything important to that idiot. Zamir's choice. And he'd paid for it with his life. Quasim recalled the atrocities done to his brother, by comparison Firdos met an easy death. When he allowed himself to be persuaded about the woman and the dishonour she'd brought him, he'd known what his brothers would do, and didn't care. The error was in trusting Bilal to dispose of her. Now, a year later, Zamir's miscalculation had caught up with him, with Firdos, and more important, the business. Quasim would have to start again.

That was one thing. Except it wasn't the only problem. The killer was still out there; the police had nothing. When they'd asked about the bangles found beside his brothers, he'd told them they meant nothing to him.

Not the truth.

Why would they be next to the bodies?

The answer was clear.

Bilal had lied. The woman was alive, and, unbelievable as it was, she was here in Lahore. Quasim found the idea of the cringing waif who'd once warmed his bed returning to attack anyone difficult to believe. The evidence was the bangles.

The candle guttered, its light growing thin. Quasim got up. For a second he thought of Daliya, of her body, then brushed the want away. He'd decide what to do with her later. A deranged killer was stalking him and his family. Quasim hadn't told his mother the details of how her sons had met their end. She grieved of course, she was a mother. He cared little about his brothers. Quasim hadn't loved them in life and didn't miss them in death. He was more upset about his business. If the woman came for him, he'd do what the others had failed to do. There would be no wooden ornaments found next to Quasim Dilawar Hussein. He'd end her life as easily as he blew the candle out.

The jewellery was part of a plan to scare him. An image of the woman he'd taken from a village in the Punjab rose behind his hooded eyes. He smiled in the dark: let her come.

How little she knew him.

Chapter 28

Ali said, 'I have to ask something. Please know your answer alters nothing between us.'

Jameel knew his question.

'Shakil tells me there's been another murder, a brother from the same family. Stabbed in Heera Mandi two nights ago. He says the murderer left his fingerprints at the scene.'

'Fingerprints?' Jameel was certain he'd removed every trace of himself.

'His words not mine. He meant the killer left another bangle with the body. It's the same as the first. A match.'

The men stared at each other, realising they'd come to a point only the strongest friendship could hope to survive. Whatever Ali said, Jameel doubted he could travel where he must go. If Afra was the murderer she had to be ill, unbalanced. His duty was clear – find her and save her from herself. Take her somewhere safe. Love her and protect her, just as he'd intended in Mundhi. As for the awful crimes, there had to be a reason, some explanation. Jameel resolved to discover what that reason was. If there was any chance to save the girl he'd lost his heart to he'd seize it and hold on.

In Heera Mandi, he almost caught her. Firdos Dilawar Hussein was dead less than a minute when he stumbled over him and found the bangle. Afra was close that night; he felt her presence on the air. For an hour he prowled the dark alleys, softly calling her name. Women for sale smiled his way; Jameel didn't notice. At one point, a figure dressed in black coming towards him down a narrow passage, suddenly turned and hurried away. He followed, quickening his step, whispering 'Afra? Afra is that you? It's Jameel.'

The female broke into a run, ducked into a gap between two ancient stone buildings and disappeared.

It had been her, he was sure of it. And she'd recognised him, yet she'd fled. Sadness like he'd never felt washed through him. Poor Afra, ashamed of what she'd become, afraid, even of him. Didn't she remember how much he cared for her? That hadn't changed and never would. He'd die for her. But would he lie for her? Would he let her crimes go unpunished? Absolutely. No question. For Afra, anything.

'Shakil says they're beginning to piece together a motive, that they'll find this lunatic and bring them to justice.'

'Shakil has a lot to say. Ask your question, Ali.'

'Jameel, we've known each other since you arrived in Lahore. I can still see the awestruck boy following me through the crowds. Since then we've been friends, you and Gulzar have – '

'Ask me, Ali.'

'Are you involved in these crimes? You have reason to hate Dilawar Hussein, and we haven't found Afra.'

'Involved? Yes I am. Until Afra is beyond harm or beyond doing harm I'm involved.'

'That doesn't answer me.'

'Am I a murderer?' Jameel paused. 'No Ali, I've killed no one.'

Ali studied him. 'I look at your desk, my friend, and something is missing.'

'There were six and you suspect only four remain, am I right?'

'No, I see they no longer sit where they did, that's all.'

'Your powers of observation are remarkable, one of your many gifts. But I'm no murderer.'

Ali nodded. 'I believe you, Jameel.'

***

It was late when she got back to her flat. She kicked off her shoes, pulled off her clothes and stepped into a hot shower. Twenty minutes later she made coffee, lit a cigarette and pressed the button on her phone. Two messages – both from Ralph. He sounded different, agitated, but in charge.

'Simone, it's Ralph. I'm worried about you, please call.'

'Simone, where are you? Are you alright? Something's happened. I want to talk to you. Please, Simone, please call.'

Call him? She'd have to think about that. Coffee was fine – a drink would be better. There was a half-finished bottle of wine in the fridge, Simone poured a glass and sipped it on her way to the main room. It was cold, tasteless. Still, it would do.

Her clothes lay where they'd fallen. She collected them, repelled by the dull colours and coarse fabric. Looking at them depressed her. She was young, French for God's sake, what was she doing wearing this? She knew the answer. She'd made a choice, a difficult choice. The clothes were a means to an end, nothing more. They didn't define her – that wasn't correct – they did. The dark tent coat with the hood defined her perfectly.

Simone sat in the chair and picked the coffee up. He wasn't making it easy. She wanted to see him, wanted him to know and longed for his approval, although he'd never give it.

How could he? He hadn't seen what she'd seen. It was unrealistic to expect him to feel the way she felt. Simone had been moving towards this since the night in the Punjab: the rally finished her. Ralph was a man – how could he understand? That was unfair. Ralph Buchanan had championed more than one lost cause.

Not in Pakistan.

She opened a window, finished the coffee and quickly fell asleep until the recording of the Imam woke her, one of many booming out across the city. It reminded her of the country her father had believed in, the one in his dreams, and hers.

It was dark. Her head felt thick and her joints ached. If she'd met Ralph in another time they could have saved each other. With him it was alcohol. With her it was…. What? How would she describe what she'd been doing? Righting wrongs? Questing after justice? She wouldn't call him although she wanted to, not while the fire raged in her. Questing for justice. A fancy phrase, nice-sounding words, but obsession just the same.

***

Bilal wasn't surprised to see the two men standing at the gates. He'd expected Quasim to tighten security and would have done the same himself. He slowed the car. One of the guards checked the licence number and talked into a two-way radio. The gates opened, the vehicle passed through.

As he began making his report to Quasim he noticed the strain on his cousin's face. The guards had been the first indication. Quasim had never showed fear. Now his eyes blinked, his fingers trembled and he looked like he hadn't slept in days. The man was fighting to stay in control and losing.

Bilal sensed the other's weakness. It gave him strength.

'She's not in the village. The family's gone. Somewhere further south.'

Quasim heard the news in silence. He bit his lip. 'Then she must be in the city. She must be here in Lahore. But where, Bilal?'

Quasim never asked Bilal's opinion on anything. The last time they met he'd been his usual self; superior and intimidating, afraid of nothing. This was not the Quasim he'd known: this man was on the edge. The vulture in Bilal soared and circled, pleased and emboldened. Throughout his life, he'd been despised. From today all that was ended. He'd help, of course. First, he'd have a little fun.

'She's dead, Quasim. She left this world a year ago. The killer isn't her.'

'Then who?'

'Someone close. Close enough to slit your brother's throat. Close enough to mutilate Zamir. Too close.'

He watched Quasim blanch. 'What can we do?'

Bilal wanted to laugh out loud. We do? What can *we* do? When had he become part of it? Whatever this family had done, they were paying for it. It was nothing to him. They left him to his poverty while they lived in their big house. Only asking him to do things no one else would do. Even with the woman, Afra, they'd forgotten how little they'd paid him to dispose of her. Bilal hadn't forgotten. It hadn't been enough, not nearly enough.

'First of all, be strong. Remember you are Quasim Dilawar Hussein, and depend on me. Whoever is responsible is insane. They'll push too far and we'll have them. For now, we stay calm. Your guards will keep everyone away. I'll stay with you. You'll be safe, I'll see to it. When it's over, we'll rebuild the business, you and I, as cousins and partners.'

A flicker of hope lit Quasim's face. 'Yes, cousin, yes.'

'I'll come every night until the danger has passed. During the day I'll search the city for this dervish. Meanwhile, tell the guards to look to me for their instructions. Your security will be my responsibility, Quasim. We'll catch this mad dog and put it out of its misery. No one need know, not the police, not anyone.'

A week earlier Quasim would have laughed.

'We'll keep it to ourselves. Family business, eh, Quasim?'

'Family, yes, family, Bilal. Family business.'

Outside, Bilal waited for the guards to part the gates before letting his impatience show. From now on, these men would answer to him. That thought made him smile. He eased the car out on to the road.

Family business. He liked the sound of it.

***

Ali said, 'She's not there, hasn't been since she left to be married according to the old woman I spoke to.'

He looked tired. He'd driven all the way to Mundhi and back; his eyes were bloodshot and he needed a shave. No one asked him, it was his own idea. Jameel should have thought of it himself. Any awkwardness between them from their last conversation had disappeared, their friendship equal to the test. Jameel nodded and waited for the rest of it. 'The woman remembered her all right, remembered you too.'

'Okay. So, who is there?'

'No one. At least, no one from that family.'

'Where are they?'

'The mother died the woman says, and the children moved away. South she thinks, to stay with a relative – a cousin, an uncle, she wasn't sure. None of them live there now and haven't done in a while. She showed me the house, it was empty.'

Jameel pictured it: Afra, fresh and lovely, young Fatima, and little Shafi. Even Uncu the donkey. And their mother, terrified of an old age she would never know. People spent their lives longing for moments in the past so rarely appreciated at the time. Jameel had realised he was with a special person. His mistake had been to think it would never end. And one day, without warning, it had, leaving him alone and unsure of his worth. But it was *his* worth he questioned, never Afra's.

He ached for her. 'She's here, Ali. I know she's here in Lahore.'

'Maybe, but where? Not in that house.'

And it was true. For days, Jameel had watched from the street and saw no sign of her. 'Somewhere in this city. Heera Mandi, maybe.'

'Heera Mandi; a bazaar of diamonds.' Ali dismissed the description with a snort. 'Heera Mandi is for fools and lost souls. Do you really believe she could be there, Jameel? Can you really see Afra in that place? Where would she hide?'

'I don't know.'

'You think she's the killer because of the bangles. She may have been forced to sell them.'

'No, Afra would never sell them, I'm certain of that.'

'I'm suggesting they could have had many owners by now.'

'And what about the murders?'

'Who can say? The violence speaks of more than a common crime. Two from the same family. Except what do we know of these people? How they lived, who they crossed, what enemies they made? We don't know them at all.'

Jameel wanted to be persuaded, he wasn't. 'So where is she?'

'Divorced or separated. Or maybe she ran away.'

'And why leave a bangle at each scene? It's her, Ali, it's Afra,'

'Why does it need to be her?' His friend didn't reply. 'You think of Heera Mandi because of what happened there, where's the proof? Afra probably ran off, perhaps she wouldn't go to her village for fear of being rejected, or worse, forced to return to her unhappy life.'

Jameel looked away. 'I can't explain why.'

His voice was small and far away. Ali was wise enough to let him speak. 'These crimes are horrific. The Afra I knew was gentle and kind, the most gentle person I've ever met. If she's at the heart of this she must be ill. I shudder to imagine what she endured with those people. Her mind must be broken to have any part in these hellish acts. And the bangles? They're a sign, all right. But not to the Dilawar Husseins. She's telling me she's out there and is calling on me to save her.'

'How could she think you'd know anything about them? The police haven't released that information. If it weren't for Shakil, we'd read what's in the newspapers and be no wiser about the bangles.'

Jameel smiled. 'You don't understand, my friend. She trusted in their power to bring us together. They've been left for me. You're forgetting, they reunite people in love.'

Ali ran his fingers across his brow. 'Jameel, that's only a story, a romantic tale. To believe some force, some mystic power is at work …'

He didn't finish, there was nothing more to say.

'Do you have something better for me to believe in?'

They were as far from the truth as they had ever been and there was one more thing to tell. Ali pursed his lips. 'The woman I spoke to in Mundhi told me something else.'

'What?'

'The day before, a man asked about Afra.'

'Who? What did he look like?'

'Just a man'

Jameel's fears were written on his face. 'That means the Dilawar Husseins think she's involved. They think Afra's the murderer and, God help me, so do I.'

Chapter 29

Bilal eyed the guards with all the suspicion he could raise, his expression saying he wasn't fooled for a moment. They were uncertain how to respond to their new boss. He barked questions, enjoying his power. 'Why are both of you here? Does it take two to open the gate? What if an intruder decides to use the back door? Who'd be there to stop him?'

Bullying others was his special gift, honed to perfection on a succession of scrawny women lifted from the streets of Lahore. Easy prey.

'You! Make a circuit of the garden every half-hour. Stay at the rear of the building and keep to the shadows. Who would approach through the front gate?' He scowled at their incompetence. 'Think man, think.'

The guard hurried away. Bilal loved it. At last he'd found his place in the world and it felt good. He strolled, watching for movement in the trees edging the compound. Tonight he was superior to his fellow man and it showed in his posture, the way he pulled back his shoulders, the measured purpose in his step and the set of his jaw. He knew now why Quasim had acted as he had; a leader was a man apart. Before he allowed himself to be devoured by fear. Bilal suffered no such fear. When the killer came, he'd end it once and for all, whoever it was. Simple as that.

Everything was quiet, nothing stirred. His cheap watch told him it was ten minutes to one. If the murderer was coming, it would be soon. And something else. Out on that lonely road he'd strangled her, he was sure of it. She may have already been dead. Bilal flexed his fingers, remembering his hands round the unresisting neck. Yes, she was dead all right.

Inside the house, Quasim slumped on one of the big couches. Above the fireplace, an ornate gold clock ticked its way through the hours and every few minutes he checked the time. Night was passing, though not quickly enough for him. Bilal coughed to announce his arrival. Quasim jumped. Bilal collapsed into a chair. 'No sign of her.'

'Nothing?'

'Not yet.' The cousin's new station sat well with him. 'Where are the women?'

'Upstairs in their rooms.'

'Good, keep them there.'

With every hour terror grew in Quasim, leaving him paralysed. He was appalled at the change. Only days ago, he'd relished the confrontation. With each night, his confidence ebbed away a little more until he welcomed having even vermin like Bilal around. Incredible, but true. The danger he imagined lurking in every shadow revealed him to himself. Shame warmed his face: Quasim realised he was a coward.

Bilal spoke with authority. 'From now on no one leaves the house after dark.'

He saw his cousin in a new light and wondered how he could have been afraid of him. Bilal was enjoying the drama, Quasim was petrified by it. Dread lay on him like unwashed linen. Bilal reassessed the future. Fifty/fifty was too generous, sixty/forty was nearer, or maybe seventy/thirty. He'd think about it when this was over; it was a delicious prospect. He wouldn't be just a player, he'd make the rules. The slights and insults Quasim had dealt him jostled in his head. He dismissed them. For now.

'The police were here again trying to find a connection between Zamir and Firdos. Questions, questions. Who did they both know? Could I think of a common enemy?'

'What did you tell them?'

'What could I tell them? They left no wiser than they arrived.'

'Well done, cousin. We'll handle this, you and I. You're protected, and tonight, tomorrow, whenever, she'll show herself. I'll finish it and life can begin again.'

He spoke of 'she' because his cousin was convinced it was the woman. Let him.

It was impossible to tell if Quasim heard Bilal's encouraging words. A girl came into the room. Quasim dismissed her with a weary hand. Bilal said, 'I must go, the men you hired are useless without me.'

He followed the woman to the kitchen. She didn't hear him approach. His hand closed round her bony wrist. She cried out. There was no one to hear. 'What's your name?' Bilal tightened his hold, twisting her round to face him. The woman smelled his breath and recoiled. 'Daliya.' Her voice was a monotone.

'Daliya.' He savoured his power a moment longer and pushed her away. She stumbled and fell to the floor. Bilal lived alone now – something else that would change. Maybe he'd take this woman with him. Quasim was done with her. Soon, he'd take whatever he wanted whether Quasim was done with it or not.

***

Chandra stared at herself in the mirror. She was bored.

The fire and Zamir's murder had upset her life, more so since Firdos was killed. Before, she'd come and gone as she pleased. Now she was afraid to go out, especially at night. The first death left her unmoved. Brother or no brother, Zamir had been a strange one. Chandra didn't like him and he'd had no interest in her. She was a woman. Zamir was afraid of women.

There had been nothing that might exist between a brother and sister, even as children. They received no guidance from their mother and grew up strangers under the same roof. Not so Firdos, he'd had his good side but he'd been stupid. To have your life-blood washing the gutter trash in Heera Mandi was a fool's death.

She lay on the bed and drew her legs up tight. Like her cousin, Bilal, Chandra judged the tragedies that had befallen her family the way she judged everything: by how she would be affected. Quasim didn't discuss things with anyone, least of all his sister.

His order not to leave the house was as close as he got to brotherly concern.

She turned on to her stomach and leaned on her elbows. She should've left when she'd had the chance. There had been opportunities – she'd turned away more than one suitor. Quasim could have insisted she marry someone of his choosing; he never had. Though it meant she was a burden on her family, Chandra had no intention of marrying. She'd witnessed the lives of too many married women in Pakistan to want any part of it. She preferred things as they were. This way she stayed in control. Her decision – one she hadn't regretted – was to use men, rather than be used by them.

And the sister hadn't been short of company or sex. All it required was discretion and ruthlessness. Discovery wasn't an option, not in this country. In the garden, it had been easy to put the blame on Quasim's wife. Chandra's lover, a married man older than her, foolishly loitered too long at the gate. Chandra blurted out her denials without malice, concerned only in escaping her brother's wrath. The consequences didn't occur, and if anything came of the lie, what was that to her?

The servant left the house. Chandra hadn't seen her from that day. No one mentioned her. She was only a wife; nothing really.

She sighed, turned on to her back and stared at the ceiling. Her mother slept next door. The deaths had aged her, the fire in her dimmed to an ember. She had even lost weight. Most days, Mrs Dilawar Hussein stayed in bed while Quasim visited her, at first every day. Then he stopped and she was alone with her memories. The past: vivid and alive – her husband and her life when the children were young. Good times. Happy times. The car journey through the night with Quasim's wife-to-be came to her in dreams. Too late the matriarch realised bringing the girl to Lahore had been a mistake.

***

Since the rally, every hour was filled with the fear of capture and punishment. Weeks ago, she'd been Doctor – a far cry from the path she was on now. Ralph Buchanan had called and called, finally he'd given up. Not how she wanted it. In his voice she heard something different, something not there before: strength.

Simone wished he would come and get her, talk her out of what she was doing and take her from the hellish mess. More than once, she found herself day-dreaming about them together, living a life away from here. But if he asked her to go with him tomorrow she'd refuse.

She didn't dwell on it. It was difficult enough without taking on more doubt. However strong her faith in what she was doing, she'd be glad when it was done. Buchanan would oppose her actions with good reason. For the moment, there was nothing else. Simone pulled the hood over her head and stepped into the night.

***

'Stop!'

They were outside Bilal's house. Quasim hadn't been here in years. It looked exactly as he expected; rundown, ramshackle, the exterior a warning of what to expect inside. 'Come with me.'

Last night had been the worst of his life. Despite his promises, Bilal hadn't shown up. Quasim spent the entire time sitting in his chair, dying a little at every sound. Around dawn, he'd fallen asleep. Now, he was angry enough to kill, furious with himself for believing anything Bilal said. Talking big talk was all he was good for, doing was a different matter. In all his worthless life, he'd done nothing, achieved nothing. He wasn't dependable. How much simpler things would be if people delivered on their words instead of impressing themselves with what they were going to do. The bodyguard knocked on the door. No one answered. Quasim barked an order. 'Again, harder this time.'

The fist beating on the door went unanswered.

'Break it down.'

The man threw his weight against the frame. The door cracked, the wood was weak and old and resisted hardly at all. A final contact with the bodyguard's meaty shoulder was enough to make it splinter in jagged pieces. The hinges collapsed and the door flew open. A fetid stench rushed out. Quasim paused before going inside. A few steps were enough for him to see the evidence of his cousin's detestable life. Peeling paint and patches of damp made him wonder whether anyone could really stay in this place. He moved cautiously down the passage into the first room on his right. A scene of dereliction greeted him.

Cardboard boxes and old newspapers covered the uncarpeted floor, dark brown marks stained the floorboards. Quasim didn't stop to guess what might have caused them; his disgust was stretched to the limit. There were no curtains or blinds on the windows, and the glass was covered in grime. Bilal lived alone, that was obvious. Quasim was careful not to touch anything. 'Bilal. Bilal. Are you there?'

His question echoed in the dank interior. While he checked the other rooms on the ground floor, the bodyguard remained silent; he wasn't paid to speak. Quasim looked at the narrow staircase and started to climb. 'Follow me.'

The bare wood boards creaked under every step and the smell was worse. Only an animal could live like this. Quasim screwed up his face against the foul odours. This wasn't a house, it was a lair. He stopped on a landing at the top and waited for the guard to join him. Hard to believe that outside the sun was shining and the sky was blue. Three doors offered themselves to him. He turned the handle on the first and pushed. Nothing apart from an unmade bed and a cheap cabinet marked with cigarette burns. The second door was ajar. He pushed. It swung open. For a moment, he'd been the Quasim of old – in command and unafraid. What he witnessed ended that.

Bilal hung from the ceiling, the rope round his neck secured to a cast-iron radiator against the wall and threaded over a hook above the centre of the room. One of his hands was trapped inside the noose; a futile attempt to escape the pressure crushing his throat.

A chair lay on the floor. Bilal had been forced to put the rope round his own neck. How he would have cried and begged and pleaded. Pitiful. The killer had kicked the chair away and sent him into a death dance.

On the floor under Bilal lay a polished wooden circle, clean and new against the dirty boards. Quasim almost fell down the staircase in his haste to get away. His stomach emptied, bile burned his throat as he staggered to the car, bathed in sweat.

He was going to die and there was nothing he could do about it.

Chapter 30

I followed the figure cutting through the crowds, holding back for the right moment to interrupt the businessman and speak to him face to face. Jameel Hafeez and his weekly tours were famous. Every article written about the man mentioned how his father had taught him to stay close to what was going on. Catching up with him hadn't been difficult.

Ridiculous but it needed to be done. The receptionist had been immoveable. 'I'm sorry, Mr Hafeez is unavailable today.'

I'd heard that so many times it might have been a recorded message. Mr Hafeez was very definitely out to Ralph Buchanan.

Hafeez stopped at two small restaurants and stayed twenty minutes at each. Then it was back to the street. Once upon a time I'd been a patient man able to wait for things to break. Patience – one of my lost talents – was coming back. What was worthwhile in me was returning and it was like meeting an old friend. Hafeez went into another restaurant. I crossed the busy road, through slow-moving traffic. The doorman smiled and pushed it open for me. 'Good evening, sir, have you a reservation?'

'No, no I haven't. I'm meeting someone. Ah! There he is.'

I breezed past. Jameel Hafeez was alone at a table towards the rear. I made straight for him. 'Mr Hafeez, may I join you?'

His face showed his displeasure. I didn't care, I needed to talk to him; there was something I had to know. 'You're a difficult guy to get hold of, Lord knows I've tried. That receptionist's as good as a guard dog. Keep her.'

'I intend to. What can I do for you Mr...?'

That made me smile. This man made it his business to remember names.

'Buchanan, Ralph Buchanan. I need a little more background for my piece. We hardly touched on your early life at all. Things changed, you told me, you didn't say how or what. That part of your story could use some expansion.'

'Mr Buchanan, now isn't a good time. I'm working.'

'Oh, sorry! Okay, what about later, when you've finished?'

'No, that isn't possible. I'm too busy.'

'All night?'

'All night.'

I considered the rejection. 'Mr Hafeez, I can't get past your frontline defence. I don't need much time, just a few questions.

'Not tonight, I'm sorry.' Hafeez was resolute.

'Tomorrow then? Twenty minutes, tops.'

tomorrow then?

Hafeez looked away. 'All right, eleven at my office. Twenty minutes, no more.'

'Eleven, I'll be there and thank you.'

Hafeez didn't shake my hand.

***

Through the thinnest smile the receptionist asked me to take a seat; she didn't use my name, unlike my previous visit. That time was over. A clock said ten fifty-five. Minutes later Ali appeared. I followed him just as before.

'Mr Buchanan.' Jameel Hafeez didn't get up. He'd been coerced into this meeting. He needn't pretend to enjoy it. There were better things to do than answer more questions. Hafeez looked at his watch. 'Twenty minutes, Mr Buchanan. Starting now.'

I was dealing with a very different animal. Hafeez could be warm and charming, but there was steel in him, too, he wasn't successful by chance, although being the adopted son of Gulzar Hafeez had hardly been a handicap. I made a show of bringing out my notebook. The man across the desk was fine-featured, well-built – and poker-faced.

'I apologise for intruding last night, I'm sorry. I hope I didn't spoil your evening.'

'Nineteen minutes.'

I pretended to recap from my notes. 'Mundhi village. "Things changed," you said. What did you mean?'

'I really don't recall.'

'Let me read what you told me, maybe it'll help.' I turned to the page. '"I thought it was the best place on earth. Things changed. I was young, I left. It was the right thing to do."'

I closed the notebook. 'Your words, Mr Hafeez. What changed, and why was it the right thing?'

a woman told me I was nothing in the world

'Mmmm, I really don't know what I was thinking.'

'Were you in some sort of trouble? Did something go wrong back there? To come to Lahore hoping to find a relative you'd never met was a daring step, don't you think? I mean, whatever drove you to leave must've been traumatic.'

Hafeez considered his reply. 'I'm sure you're right but I really can't imagine what it might have been. I probably came to a fork in the road. It happens.'

I let it go. 'Were you happy in that village?'

'Yes.'

'You weren't unhappy yet you left to take your chances in an unknown place?'

'I always had ambition, Mr Buchanan, perhaps that was it.'

'Ambition to do what?'

His expression softened. 'I wanted to be something in the world. Coming from England – '

'Scotland.'

'Of course. Coming from Scotland you may not understand that quite as I did. It was important to make something of myself.'

'Why?'

'It just was.'

'So you left the only home you'd ever known and, eight years later, can't remember why, have I got that right? You left a peaceful village to come to Lahore, to strangers and noise and crime. A place where there's no safety, even in our homes. Where lunatic killers walk the streets.' My disbelief was unguarded. 'I'm working on the Dilawar Hussein murders. Do you know the family? Quasim perhaps?'

Hafeez didn't rise to it. He stared past me. 'I can't say that I do.'

'Terrible business.'

I closed the notebook. 'Well, thank you for your time if nothing else, Mr Hafeez.'

'Goodbye, Mr Buchanan.'

No offer to shake hands. I pointed to the desk. 'Those wooden bangles you had here, they're gone, I see.'

'I'm having them cleaned.'

'Really? They looked to be in excellent condition.'

'I like them to stay that way.'

'They belonged to your mother, I remember.'

The man reappeared at the door. 'Please show Mr Buchanan out, Ali.'

'You owe me eleven minutes,' I said. Hafeez didn't smile.

I held it together until I left the building. I wanted to shout for joy. They weren't there, the bangles weren't there. Where Hafeez kept them was anybody's guess, but thanks to an early-morning call from Dan Meiklejohn, I was certain he'd left one under the mutilated body of Zamir Dilawar Hussein, dropped another in the younger brother's blood in Heera Mandi, and last night, placed a third on bare floorboards beneath the kicking legs of their cousin, Bilal.

For all his outward show, Jameel Akhtar Hafeez was a killer.

***

The curtains were drawn; it was difficult to see. Jameel closed the door, not wanting to disturb the figure in the bed. His father wasn't asleep. These days that was rare even with strong medication. He lay with his eyes shut, the covers pulled up to his chin.

He was dying. But he wasn't afraid. During his life, Gulzar nurtured a philosophy that sustained him now. Ceasing to exist held no terror for him. People resisted change, few embraced it without reservation and there was no bigger change than no longer taking part in life, yet everyone came to it, there was no way of avoiding it. Dying was the difficult part, the actual process; the pain, the suffering. And after? Well, he'd know soon enough.

In the half-light, he was an island in a sea of white. Gulzar heard the door and opened his eyes. Jameel was beside him at the bed smiling an optimistic smile. What he got in return was smaller, less hopeful and more genuine. Jameel whispered. 'Father, I'm here. How are you today?'

Gulzar lied. 'Better. Much better.'

'Good, good.'

They had the same conversation every time, both men playing their parts. Gulzar raised himself in the bed with what strength he had left. 'Move these pillows, Jameel. Help me sit up.'

His son built the starched rectangles against the headboard and Gulzar leaned back. 'That's better, now we can talk.'

Even such little exertion came at a cost, his breathing laboured, he spoke through shallow breaths. 'So what's new in the world? What am I missing?'

'Nothing. Day to day, not much changes. Business is good. I'm all right, apart from worrying about you. Mohamed Abdul Quadir sends his regards. He wants to come and see you.'

'Why would you worry about me? I made peace with myself the day we met. I'm fine.'

This man had been the single guiding light of Jameel's adult life. Soon he'd be gone. Emotion engulfed the son. His father might be at peace; he was not.

'Sit, sit.' Gulzar pointed to the edge of the bed. 'Tell me what's wrong, and tell me the truth.'

'Two things are causing me more unhappiness than I've known since I arrived in Lahore. When I see you here it breaks my heart. If I could, I'd take your pain and bear it myself. The other is harder to explain.'

Gulzar listened; maybe there was one last service he could do this boy, this man he loved so well. Jameel said, 'You remember I told you about the girl from Mundhi, the one I wanted to marry?'

'Yes. Her mother rejected you and she married someone else.'

'Well, I think she's in the city.'

'The marriage is over?'

'I believe so.'

Jameel stopped short of telling him about the murders and the jewellery. It sounded ridiculous, even to him. Gulzar had lost weight: the skin on his face hung loose, his watery eyes stayed on his son. 'You want to find this woman. And then what?'

'Save her, Father. She needs my help. First I need to find her.'

'Helping another human being is always admirable. Taking action when action is required is the right thing. However, planning results is a mistake.'

He stopped, wracked by coughing. 'We become attached to them, Jameel, do you see?' Jameel didn't see. 'The solution to both your problems is the same. Detach yourself from the outcomes. Everything will be fine.'

'How can you say that? I see you lying here. We both know how sick you are, yet you tell me everything will be fine.' Tears rose at the edges of his eyes, his voice choked. 'So, I should do nothing?'

Gulzar spoke softly, knowing this was difficult. 'Only when there's nothing to do. You must do whatever you feel, but distance yourself from the result. Look for this woman. Day and night if you have to. Just don't demand it turn out any particular way. You'll hope it does, of course. Let it be whatever it is.'

Another coughing spasm took over. Too involved, Jameel hadn't understood a word. Gulzar waved a bony hand for a cloth to wipe his mouth and Jameel was reminded of his mother.

'Pain, Jameel. We cause ourselves such pain. Why? Because we must have the world the way we wish it. And when we find it isn't, we're disappointed – afraid, like you are now.'

This was not what Jameel wanted to hear. 'Then I must learn to care about nothing. Not you. Not Afra. Is that it?'

'You must learn not to care over much.'

Gulzar adjusted himself against the pillows, his face tightening with the effort. 'It's quite simple, really. What has become of the girl you knew, what you see here with me, these things aren't happening to you. They won't be made better by adopting their hurt.'

Jameel was unconvinced.

'I'm the one who's dying, not you. You'll have your turn, depend on it. We've had our time together. That cannot be changed. And this girl, a woman now –'

'Afra.'

'Afra, yes. Perhaps you can help her, perhaps not. First help yourself. Don't let your happiness depend on some future event. You have a life to live and a business to run, so live in this day and trust. Things will be as they are meant to be.'

Talking was too much. Gulzar closed his eyes and fell silent.

Chapter 31

Chandra came downstairs to the dining-room where not so long ago they'd eaten breakfast together. It seemed like a dream now, everything was so different. The room was empty. Daliya appeared with plates of food and bread and laid them on the table. Chandra didn't acknowledge her. Quasim arrived red-eyed and haggard. Once her brother might have been considered attractive, handsome even, but the strain of the last few months had aged him beyond belief. She – on the other hand – was untouched. The fire, the murder of her brothers, and now her cousin Bilal, weren't real for her. In spite of Quasim's rules about curfews and his ranting at the guards, she didn't feel any sense of personal danger. Because she had harmed no one.

Chandra broke off a piece of bread.

'You can't go out today,' Quasim said.

His sister didn't lift her head. 'What do you mean?'

'You must stay here until this maniac is stopped.'

'But my work?'

'I've already spoken to them. They understand.'

'You've talked to my employers? I don't believe it.'

'They agree.'

'No. No, Quasim, I won't be a prisoner in this house. It's bad enough to spend every night here, but during the day?'

They shared the same genes, the same arrogance and contempt, and the same capacity for anger. 'There's nothing to discuss, it's decided.'

'Not by me.' Chandra stormed out, almost knocking over Daliya bringing breakfast to Quasim. Her brother made no move to stop her. The Quasim of before would have quelled any revolt against his actions with a look: his authority was depleted. Unable to save his business or his brothers and so afraid, he hardly registered his sister's outburst. Chandra could do as she pleased, he didn't care anymore.

Quasim wasn't hungry. He went to check on the guards; six men working twelve-hour shifts in teams of three, providing round-the-clock protection. But Quasim Dilawar Hussein didn't feel protected.

Chandra spoke to one of the security men at the gate; her brother watched them argue. The guard produced a key and let her through. Chandra strode into the world. Of course, the guard had been no match for his sister. He hadn't met a man who was – one of the reasons he hadn't insisted she marry. Chandra could be a fearsome creature. A real Dilawar Hussein. He went out to chastise the guard. He'd need to fare better against the real threat if it came, especially if it was woman.

***

I replaced the receiver in its cradle. I'd had my chance and blown it. The room was tidy, a symptom of my growing recovery and I no longer stayed out half the night or slept the day away. Earlier, I'd called my editor. That had taken courage.

'My, my, I don't believe it,' Andrew McArthur said. 'We thought you'd died. I was just about ready to contact HR to cancel your cheque and calculate an in-service payment, but you're still with us.'

'Andrew. Thank you for your patience.'

'Patience. Patience ran out a year ago, Ralph. What you've been getting is the sympathy vote. When was the last time you copied anything we could use, eh?'

I let it wash over me. I deserved it. McArthur had cut me more breaks than I deserved, he was allowed to chew me out. 'That's why I'm calling, Andrew.'

'Mr McArthur to you. Only productive employees call me Andrew.'

I ignored that one, he didn't mean it. McArthur was pissed at me. We'd worked together for more than a decade. The fiasco in Germany hadn't been the end of my fuck-ups. In the months following Lonnie Harper's death, my drinking had really taken off. Most days I spent in a pub until I was well-oiled and spoiling for a fight. On one memorable afternoon I returned to the office. A big mistake. I actually started to cry. My stunned colleagues stood helpless, watching their award-winning star unravel.

Embarrassing for them. Worse was to follow.

After an hour of raving self-pity and breast-beating, my mood changed. I was too good for them. I was a giant, they were pygmies. What had any of them achieved? Parasites clinging to my back. On and on it went. A crowd gathered to listen to my drunken ramblings and groundless accusations. Someone called security to escort me from the building, a call that was long overdue. Two uniformed guys struggled to move me to the door. I broke free, climbed on a desk and surveyed my friends and workmates as the guards closed in. No-More-Mr-Nice-Guys. Seconds before they got to me, I offered the entire staff a last critique.

'You're all cunts!'

Two days later, I crashed my car into a neighbour's garage when I was drunk. Nobody was injured but my licence was history. A week after that, McArthur told me the score. The final humiliation.

Pakistan.

That was then, now I said, 'Andrew, listen a minute, I'm sending a couple of pieces.'

'A couple?'

'A killer is loose over here. Three victims so far. It's a long story. I'm pretty sure a prominent figure in the business community is the murderer. Haven't got all the proof but I'm close. If it's who I think it is, I've interviewed him twice.'

Thousands of miles away, McArthur stopped taking his revenge.

'And I'm writing a series of articles called Behind the Veil. I expect to shock you, one way or another.'

'I'm already shocked just to hear from you. You sound different, Ralph.'

'I am different, Andrew. Tell you all about it next time we meet.'

'A killer? Behind the Veil? Sounds like the old Ralph Buchanan's back.'

I laughed. 'Not so, Andrew. Everybody can relax on that one.'

***

Detective Rana listened to the verbal assault. It was understandable; the man was terrified. Veins in his neck stood like cords, flecks of saliva gathered at the edges of his mouth. He didn't speak, he bellowed. 'Where are you? Where're any of you when my family's being murdered?' Quasim didn't wait for answers. Rana hadn't any.

'I assure you, Mr Dilawar Hussein, we're doing everything possible...'

'You assure me. You assure me. Better you assure my two dead brothers and my cousin. Perhaps you could call my creditors and assure them.'

The policeman didn't respond. Standing beside his boss, Rafee was angry. Asmet Rana was as good as any policeman in Pakistan and this crazy man was abusing him. He wanted to speak out. Instead, he followed his superior's example.

In two months, Quasim Dilawar Hussein had lost his business and three relatives, and they were no closer to catching the killer than they'd ever been. The senior officer took the full blast of this man's anger; it was part of the job. It wasn't personal.

Detective Jan Asmet Rana was on duty the night it began. It was his case and he wished it wasn't. Pressure from above piled higher every day. Unsolved killings reflected on the department and the city. There was a rumour the prime minister was following progress. Or, in this case, lack of it.

'The world is watching,' his boss kept telling him, as if that would speed an arrest.

'What did the chief say?'

Rana was philosophical. 'Apparently, the world is watching us, Rafee.'

Dilawar Hussein said, 'I've men guarding the house night and day, otherwise I might not be here to have this conversation with you.'

Quasim spat his contempt, his fingers playing with the tahmat wrapped round his waist. 'If there are no results soon, if you don't catch this madman…if you can't protect me in my own home, then I've no choice but to speak with your superiors. Do you understand?'

Detective Rana understood all right. More pressure. He saw his reputation evaporating before his eyes because he hadn't solved a case no one else would be able to solve. Everyone in the household had been interviewed and everyone in contact with the family. And no one recognised the bangles, or if they had, they hid it well.

'One final question Mr Dilawar Hussein, one I've asked already. Can you recall ever seeing the wooden jewellery before?'

'I told you the last time you asked. Never.'

***

I disliked Quasim Dilawar Hussein immediately and would've felt the same even if Simone hadn't told me the story Afra had begged her to write.

'I don't know why I'm talking to you,' he said. 'How can it possibly help?'

I didn't share his confusion. I wanted to meet this man, observe his reaction when Afra's name was mentioned, and find out if he knew Jameel Hafeez.

'I told you on the telephone, Mr Dilawar Hussein, I'm writing an article about the crimes. You're the head of the family targeted by the murderer. I hope highlighting your case might persuade an informant to come forward. Someone out there must know something, don't you agree? Have you any idea why this might be happening to you?'

Quasim watched me from beneath heavy eyelids.

'Your first reaction will be to say no. Perhaps if you look harder you'll find something, some circumstance that could provoke this level of violence?'

'No one deserves what's happened to me.'

I disagreed but then I'd been told how this man had treated his wife. 'As I say, only you could know that.'

Footsteps echoed in the house and a woman in her late twenties wearing a stylish maroon sari with matching earrings and make-up came into the room. The nose and eyes were the same as her brothers', her face frozen in the same imperious look.

'I'm going out.'

'I've told you already. No.'

'I'm not listening. I'm going.' She stormed away. Quasim sighed. Chandra would be sorry for humiliating her brother. He said, 'You see, Mr Buchanan, it isn't easy to protect those you love.'

'Indeed.'

A servant carrying a tea-tray appeared in the doorway, the air around her hardly stirring. Her arms suggested a skeletal frame beneath the shapeless clothes. It was impossible to guess her age, so little of her face was visible. I wondered how long this one had been in the house. How soon had this monster replaced his first wife? I pictured the poor undernourished soul climbing the stairs to the cold box every night, too tired to undress, too exhausted to cry: this was the new Afra.

'Your wife?'

'Yes.' The comparison with his sister shocked me; he saw it on my face. 'You were married before. Afra, wasn't it? Where is she now?'

'I divorced her. Ask your questions.'

Quasim didn't hide his antagonism. I'd shocked the brute and that pleased me. 'The crimes aren't random. I think we can agree on that. So where's the connection? What's the link?'

'The police ask the same. My answer remains unchanged. I have no idea. Some madman has singled out my family. Believe me, if I knew, the matter would be dealt with. It would end today. I'm a respected figure in my community, maybe my success is too much for someone to stomach?'

'Have the police made progress?'

'The police are imbeciles. They'll solve nothing.'

'Any warning or threat?'

Dilawar Hussein shook his head; he had little time for this.

'Did the killer leave any clue?'

'Like what?'

'Fingerprints, fibre, anything?'

The man dismissed the notion with his hand.

'Okay. I see security guards outside, so you must think you need them.'

'Mr Buchanan, if some maniac was attacking your family, wouldn't you do everything in your power? When this is over they'll be gone. For now, they stay. My mother lives here as well as my sister. Women need to be protected.'

The tea stayed in the pot. 'What surprises me is how similar this place is to where I'm from. Murders and success stories, side by side. I'm working on a piece about Lahore's Businessman of the Year, Jameel Akhtar Hafeez, do you know him?'

'Never heard of him.'

'Well, if you think of anything, anything at all.'

Quasim ignored me.

***

Simone wanted to call him, and he'd come, she was sure of that. But not yet. She'd taken on more than she could handle. Her conscience had backed her into a corner. To continue filled her with dread, yet stopping was unthinkable. Her behaviour worried her; she was becoming bolder. Reckless.

She'd made a deal with herself. When the morning came she'd end it. Contact Ralph and start again. If he'd have her. She turned the key in the ignition. The doctor's hands felt cold. And when he asked, what would she say?

Would she begin a new chapter of her life with a lie?

Yes, she'd lie.

Compared to other wrongs, lying was such a little thing.

Chapter 32

Slipping the guards and breaking the window at the rear of the house was a lot less difficult than it should have been. But the danger wasn't over. The floorboards cracked and groaned under the weight of slow footsteps. The noise boomed through the house. At this hour, the building was a living thing, breathing quietly, more at peace than those who slept here. As it cooled, it sighed, and when it did the intruder waited.

Progress was slow, not because the house was a stranger, but because capture was unthinkable. The figure found the staircase, measuring every tread on the bare wood, testing how far to trust the non-planed timber. It took fifteen minutes to complete the climb. Sweat ran down the face beneath the hood. Minor discomforts were filtered out, all that mattered was the next step, and the next, and the one after that.

There was no attempt at hurry. To act in haste was to lose. Will power governed every muscle, controlled sinews and held fear in check.

A vanilla beam passed across a downstairs window. Voices grumbled, torchlight played against the glass and disappeared, returning the house to darkness.

Three steps, two. One more.

At the top, the interloper listened. Nothing. Fingers caressed the night like the tendrils of a weed, searching for the door handle. It scratched against its fittings and released. Shapes formed. The figure knelt beside the iron bed-frame and let the hood fall back. The next moments decided their fate.

Under a single tangled sheet the girl slept, unaware she wasn't alone. Air rattled in her lungs, rasping to escape. A palm cupped her mouth. She writhed and turned, fighting against the surprise attack, and tried to scream. If she succeeded they were lost.

The rescuer bent close and whispered. 'I'm a friend.'

She stopped struggling. 'Don't make a sound, not a sound.'

The hand withdrew, reluctant to trust. 'Get up, and dress. Quick.'

Daliya hesitated. Who was this? What was happening? 'Now.'

The girl threw back the cover. 'Who are you?'

'Someone who knows. Here, take my hand.' Daliya did as she was told.

The stranger stepped to the door with the bewildered girl clinging to her and made the slow descent. They waited for the guards to pass, then they were over the wall and running, stopping when they reached the shadows. Daliya fell, retching and vomiting. Her rescuer rubbed her back.

'Who are you?' Daliya searched the face for an answer, found none and began to weep.

'Come on, a little further.'

Her saviour pointed across the street. 'Look. Over there. Go. You'll be safe. People are expecting you. I'll see you tomorrow. Go. Be a brave girl for me. Can you do that?'

Daliya replied through tears. 'I'll try.'

They embraced and started in different directions – one to freedom, the other back to the house.

***

Chandra woke with a start. She wasn't alone. Her heart beat against her chest. She cast round in the darkness, trying to locate the danger and heard a noise just before the blow struck. When she regained consciousness the room was pitch black.

The pain hit. Chandra roared against it, her mouth on fire. She passed out again and came to screaming. Suddenly, the room filled with light. Help had arrived. Rough hands lifted her from the soaked bedcovers; her nightdress was a crimson rag.

'Who was it? Did you see?'

The words wouldn't come. In their place, mangled grunts. Quasim appeared in the doorway, wild and dishevelled. The guard nearest Chandra stepped back.

'What?' Chandra tried to ask. 'What's wrong?'

Quasim didn't reply. He didn't understand the question.

'What! What!'

Chandra heard her voice. Her hands went to her mouth. She looked at Quasim, asking him to save her. His eyes told her it was too late.

It began as a low whine deep in her stomach and rose to an anguished cry that rooted everyone to where they stood. She threw herself on the bed and wailed. No one noticed the carved circle by the pillow.

Chandra Dilawar Hussein told a lie, she would never tell another.

Chandra had no tongue.

***

During his years as a policeman, Detective Asmet Rana had made his share of mistakes. He didn't chastise himself too much, his was a difficult job. Occasionally, his instincts let him down. The truth was hard to see when it laughed in your face. He could empathise with victims and think like a criminal, and his determination to see justice done never wavered. Now and then, he got it wrong.

Rana was unconcerned by his fallibility. What he couldn't tolerate was being made to look a fool, and Quasim Dilawar Hussein had made an ass of him. From their first meeting at the smoking warehouse, he'd lied. The policeman had put up with his arrogance because of the man's loss. His brothers had been brutally murdered and his business destroyed. Rana assumed he was in shock. People worked out grief in different ways. The elder brother had acted like a cold bastard. That was Rana's error. It wasn't an act. Dilawar Hussein was a cold bastard.

'Stay with it, Rafee. Don't let anyone in, understand?'

The detective went to look for Quasim. Time for some straight talking. In the main room, he found a very different man from the one who had snubbed him at the fire. 'Mr Dilawar Hussein, what happened tonight is as evil a thing as I've ever seen. I pray for your sister's recovery.'

Rana might have spoken in Japanese. Quasim leapt to his feet and pointed to the empty cage. 'The bird, it's gone. Can't you understand what that means?'

'No. What does it mean?'

Quasim roared. 'Daliya! Guards! Guards! Daliyaaa!'

No one answered. No one came. The guards had left before the police arrived. It was too much for them, more than they'd bargained for, and besides, they hadn't been paid.

Dilawar Hussein's eyes bulged, veins stood thick against his skin. The gold robe he was wearing fell open – he didn't notice – all he knew was his fear. The change in him took Rana by surprise. He'd witnessed every emotion under the sun, or thought he had, but never terror like this. The man was on the point of mental collapse. He fell back onto the couch, exhausted.

'Where's Daliya?' Rana was inured to his pain, unmoved by his distress. He smoothed his moustache. 'Check the house, Rafee. Find his wife. Bring her here.'

He turned to Quasim. 'Mr Dilawar Hussein, every time we meet some awful crime has been visited on your family. I ask the same questions and receive the same answers. You tell me you've no idea what's going on. You ask why me?' He paused. 'I'm only an underpaid public servant, but even someone as limited I am must wonder the same: why you? What would make your family the target of so many brutal acts? So I ask again, except this time I need to hear something I can believe.'

A trace of the old arrogance appeared in Quasim's eyes. Rana wasn't intimidated. 'Why you, Mr Dilawar Hussein? What have you done to deserve this?'

Quasim screamed. 'Daliyaaaaaaa!'

'Daliya? Where is she?'

'You don't understand. The bird – '

'Are you telling me Daliya has taken the Blue Rock?'

'Not Daliya.'

'Then who?'

Quasim slumped in his seat.

'Where should Daliya be?'

The reply was a long time coming. 'Upstairs.'

Rana met Rafee returning from the basement 'Wait here,' he said, and climbed the stairs. At the top he steadied himself, sensing a different horror from Chandra waited for him. The room was tiny, dank, ice-cold and empty: an iron bedstead filled the space, a tap dripped into a stained sink. This was where the wife slept. Animals were treated better.

Downstairs, Dilawar Hussein hadn't moved. He sat, staring at the floor with his gold robe carelessly gathered round him, his chin on his chest. The detective knelt beside him, inches from the stricken man's face. 'She's gone. Your wife's gone. I found this.'

Rana held up a bangle. 'Mr Dilawar Hussein, all that stands between you and your fate is me.'

Quasim shrank like a cornered beast, his eyelids fluttered, sweat washed his forehead. The disgust Rana felt for this *thing* was only just under control. 'No more games. I want the truth. How long have you been married? And don't lie. In the morning, I'll have that information without your help. How long?'

Quasim put his head in his hands and cried. Rana watched, unmoved. 'How long?'

'A year.'

'To Daliya?'

'Yes.'

'Your first wife?'

Quasim hands covered his face. Behind them a tale was being born. 'No, my second. My first wife is at the heart of this. She was from the Punjab. We married years ago. At first, we were happy – at least, I thought we were – until I caught her. Then I knew I'd been a fool.'

Rana couldn't picture this man caring for another. 'Caught her doing what?'

'With her lover.'

'You found your wife with another man?'

'One evening, I saw her at the gates with a man. He ran when he recognised my car. Afra – that was her name – fled to the house and locked herself in our bedroom. I pounded on the door for hours. She wouldn't open it, afraid of what I might do, but I wouldn't have hurt her. I loved her.'

His tears flowed. He wiped them away, embarrassed by his weakness. Rana wasn't convinced.

'For days she stayed there. I didn't know what to do. My wife was unfaithful. I was lost. Finally, my brothers persuaded me.'

'Persuaded you to do what?'

'That Afra had dishonoured the family. They said she had to leave our house. Even my sister Chandra spoke against her. I'd trusted this woman and she'd betrayed that trust. Reluctantly, I turned my heart against her. It was the saddest moment of my life.'

'What then?'

'Then? Then I made the error that has cost me everything. I called out three times 'I divorce you'. That was my mistake. My brothers broke down the door, took her away and I never saw her again. I tried to put her out of my mind. I remarried, in necessity this time, not love. My love left with Afra.'

'And how does this explain what has gone on here?'

'Detective, my brothers lied to me. They had no intention of taking her back to her village. They killed her, them and that reptile, Bilal.'

'How do you know this?'

'I know it.'

'So if your wife is dead who is responsible for these crimes?'

'Her lover, of course. The man I saw run away. Somehow he has discovered what they did and thinks I gave them my blessing. They're dead and I'm still here, Detective, doesn't that tell you something?'

'And the wooden jewellery?'

'The bangles belonged to Afra. She must have given them to him. He leaves them to mark his motive as well as his crime. He's the one you should be looking for.'

'And Daliya, what about her?'

'He's taken her to punish me. Maybe he'll demand money for her return. With the business gone, where would I find it? He's the one. He's the killer.'

'Why didn't you tell me this before?'

'I couldn't be sure. When I asked, they told me lies. Besides, how could I give up my flesh and blood? What they did, they did for me, for the family, for honour. Don't you see?'

The detective didn't see. Pakistan was a country of strange notions about all kinds of things. Rafee knocked on the open door. 'We're finished in the bedroom, sir.'

His boss nodded and spoke to Quasim. 'I want everything you've told me in writing. I need you to describe this man, this lover. Tomorrow, at the police station.'

Quasim bowed under the weight he had carried too long.

'Of course, Detective. Of course.'

***

In the car, Rafee said, 'Do you believe him, sir?'

'How much did you overhear?'

'Most of it.'

'Mmmm. And do you?'

'I don't know.'

'Rafee, if you saw where his second wife lived. Not lived,' he corrected himself, 'was kept. That man is a scorpion capable of sacrificing anyone to save himself.'

'But is he telling the truth, sir?'

'I wish I knew, Rafee, I wish I knew.'

Chapter 33

I sat my laptop on the table. People on airplanes, in taxis, everywhere, could balance them on their knees, not me. To work I needed quiet. I marvelled at war correspondents who managed to get their pieces together with bombs going off all around. Now that was award-winning stuff.

Onscreen was the beginning of something. I typed everything I could remember; facts, notions, suspicions, possibilities, and set up a three-file system, another trick Chic Logan taught me. The first was 'What do I know?' The next saved as 'What do I need to know?' and the final one, the all-important 'So what?' file.

The challenge was to make enough from the first two to have something to put in the last. It required a degree of creative thinking. And the story had to stand on its own. Everything needed to check out, but, as Chic had said, "Facts don't stop being true because you can't prove them."

What do I know?

The heading waited for me to bring it to life. I typed in a two-fingered tippy-tappy that filled the screen with statements in no time.

Jameel Akhtar Hafeez, 28yrs old.
Source – JAH.
Adopted son of Gulzar Hafeez.
Source – public record.
MD of Ravi Restaurants.
Source – ditto.
Businessman of the Year.
Source – ditto.

Originally from Mundhi village, Punjab. [Afra's village.]
Source – JAH/ Simone.
Afra was forced to marry Quasim Dilawar Hussein.
Source – Afra.
7 years later Afra called out 'Jameel'.
Source – Simone.
Quasim DH doesn't know JAH.
Source – QDH.
QDH has a new wife.
Source – QDH.
Bangles [6] no longer on JAH's desk.
Source – witnessed myself.
The Dilawar Hussein family members met mutilation and violent death.
Source – public record.
Afra had the bangles given to her by Jameel.
Source –Afra.
A wooden bangle is left at each crime scene.
Source – D Meiklejohn.

It was a start.

What do I need to know?
Why is this happening?
Bangles gone from JAH's desk [why?]
Does JAH have an alibi for the murders?
Is Jameel working alone?
What's Simone up to? Is she involved?
What's Quasim DH doing about it?

So what?
Someone is destroying the DHs
Bangles are symbolic of motive. [revenge?]
Murderer is ruthless, driven by passion.
Old boyfriend?

I looked at the evidence on the screen. Promising maybe but far from conclusive. This story would send me back to the top. McArthur would love it if I brought it home.

Jameel Akhtar Hafeez, Businessman of the Year and killer.

***

Ten o'clock in the morning and Simone was still in bed. Not asleep. Thinking. She lay on her back staring at the ceiling, more confused than she'd ever been. Ralph had stopped calling. No messages either. If she'd lost him she knew who to blame.

So far she hadn't been caught, though it hadn't brought the peace she imagined. Nevertheless, it was the right path. Her life had changed with the first words.

my name was Afra

The knock on the door crashed through her lethargy. She scrambled off the bed and dragged on jeans and a T-shirt. In the mirror, she saw herself. What a mess. The hammering came again, louder and more insistent. Somebody was short on patience. She opened the door and he was there. The grizzled face and slept-in clothes were no more. A reversal had taken place. She was the lost soul now.

'Simone.'

She froze.

'Ralph. Come in, come in. Sit down. Can I get you something to drink?'

'Nothing, thank you.'

They sat, as awkward as teenagers. 'You didn't call back.'

'I'm sorry, I meant to. I've been so busy. I meant to, really.'

'Busy doing what?'

She didn't reply.

'Simone, I'm here because I need to hear you say you don't want me in your life. If there's no future for us I'll go, but I want you to say it.'

'I could never tell you that. You look different, Ralph. You look good.'

It was a compliment, not an answer.

They met in the centre of the room and kissed. She said, 'Ralph, sit down, we need to talk. I want us to be together. No lies, no secrets. Do you understand?'

'No secrets.'

'I told you I'd been busy. I have to tell you why.'

None of it mattered. He listened because she wanted him to listen, fearing he'd be appalled, horrified when he knew.

'Ralph, Ralph, let me speak, please. It began that night in the Punjab but the rally tipped the scales. I was angry. At everyone: my father, this country. Even you. You see me as Simone, there's more. I wish there wasn't.'

'Nothing you can say will alter anything, Simone. I love you.'

'And I love you. Remember we've agreed. No secrets.'

'No secrets.' He repeated it to satisfy her.

'Well, I have a secret. One that may make you change your mind about me.'

He took her hand. 'Impossible.'

'We'll see.'

***

Quasim pulled the car into a space down a side street. It had taken an hour to find somewhere to park. In better days he would have had the vehicle stop outside wherever he was going and expect Firdos to be waiting for him when his business was complete.

Those days were gone.

He slammed the door without locking it. Why bother, what was left to steal? The western suit, shirt and tie had been replaced by a kurta and pyjamas. The other clothes were symbols, marking him as different, successful. He wouldn't wear them again.

Two boys played football in the busy street; one of them kicked the ball against the car. It struck the chassis with a dull thud. Quasim went wild. Another indignity. Even street urchins disrespected him. The children weren't more than eight or nine years old. He roared at them; they grabbed the ball and ran.

He was on his way to an important meeting, one he'd been putting off since the warehouse fire. At first, he'd refused to take the calls. Then the letters arrived. He'd opened the first few, after that they piled up on the floor by his bed.

Bad news. Every meeting was bad news.

In the end, his accountant had come to see him. He spoke frankly. 'It's no use, Mr Dilawar Hussein, these problems have to be faced and decisions made. In the long run, it will happen anyway, with or without you, it would be better if you were involved. That way perhaps you can influence what's left.'

'There will be nothing left.'

'Then maybe you can delay, buy yourself some time. Relocate your mother. Find a partner. Begin again.'

Quasim answered like a spoiled child. 'I don't want a partner.'

'Whatever.' The accountant's job was to give advice, the client could take it or not. At the end of the day, it wasn't his problem.

***

In a room across the city, there was no anger or fear, only regret. Jameel Akhtar Hafeez was saying goodbye to his father.

He had been at the bedside for six hours, listening to the laboured breaths, studying the wrinkled face. This was not the Gulzar he would remember. The one that would live in his heart was a strong, wise man who'd learned the lessons life had taught him and passed those truths to his son. Gulzar's eyes fluttered and opened. He turned his head and tried to smile.

Neither spoke, there was no need, they had made each other complete in their different ways. In another place that would be again. The dying man's lips were dry. Jameel poured water from a jug into a glass and held it to him, supporting his head. Gulzar took a sip. It was enough. He saw the pain Jameel was going through.

Gulzar's last words on earth were more important to him than any he had ever spoken. 'Jameel Akhtar Hafeez,' he said, and was gone. Hot tears rolled down Jameel's face.

"Death is always sad. Life must not be the same."

Thanks to his father, Jameel could meet life on life's terms and survive. What a gift.

He stayed, praying quietly, then placed the chair against the wall and walked into the sunny day.

***

Nurse Idris Phadkar hurried along the hospital corridor. Many of the staff were strangers. SHL was a teaching hospital; people came and went all the time. There was always so much going on. Six months since she'd moved to the city and it still excited her.

Working in the Punjab had served her well. She'd learned, come to terms with nursing in a way she wouldn't have anywhere else. Her colleagues had been the same age, had joined the profession at the same time. They'd struggled together and were bonded by common experiences: they were her friends. Her memories of them and the little medical outpost were good memories, but she'd always known she would move on. It thrilled her to have actually done it. The work was no different. Her day began at 7am. Now it was past midday. Nurse Phadkar filtered the sounds around her and concentrated on her duties. Often when someone called to her she wouldn't hear, a form of deafness which most of the staff developed.

She passed reception. For once her brain wasn't taken with other things. Even so, she would've missed it if she hadn't noticed the man talking to the woman at the admissions window and heard him say '….anyone called Afra?'

Nurse Phadkar stopped.

'From Lahore, or perhaps from a village called Mundhi?'

The receptionist stared at the screen, made a face and shook her head. He turned round and almost bumped into the pretty nurse. 'Oh, sorry!'

'That's all right. I was standing too close. I overheard. You're looking for a woman called Afra?'

'Yes. Admitted sometime in the last year. This is the fourth hospital I've tried today. No luck.'

'I met a woman in the Punjab. Her name was Afra.'
Ali held his breath.
'About a year ago. She'd come to the city.'
The hairs on his neck bristled.
'From a village called Mundhi.'
'Do you know where she is?'
'Yes, I know.'
He put his head in his hands. 'Thank God.'
The search was over.

Chapter 34

She forged a path through the crowded streets. I followed, just like the day of the rally. My destiny was to go where she led. In the car, Simone had been quiet, speaking only to give directions through a part of the city unfamiliar to me. I parked and we walked through empty streets. It was hot, the sky had clouded; a change in the weather was on the way. There was tension between us that wasn't coming from me.

no lies no secrets

She stopped in front of an old door with a metal ring attached and looked to make sure we hadn't been followed. I'd no idea what to expect. Simone put her hand on the ring and struck it four times against the door. The sound of someone on the other side loosening bolts filtered through the thick wood. It opened. An eye appeared and judged us. We hurried inside and the door was bolted.

It was clear Simone was no stranger here. A woman in her sixties, wearing white shalwar and kameez embraced her, delight in her eyes.

'Doctor Jasnin.'

Simone turned to include me. 'This is my friend from Scotland.'

The woman's hair was grey under her headscarf, her skin smooth and unlined except for a few wrinkles round the eyes and at the corners of her mouth. She was small, not more than five feet. Energy radiated from her and I guessed she'd been beautiful in her youth. Simone introduced her. 'This is Priya, my second mother.'

The women held hands.

'Salam,' Priya said.

They spoke in Urdu. Priya patted Simone's arm. 'Pareshan nahi hon, don't worry.'

The house was a warren of rooms with women everywhere. I was the only male. Our guide moved swiftly, Simone behind her. I trailed them, forgotten, wondering why I was there.

The woman stopped, embraced Simone again and disappeared. She faced me. No smiles now. 'This is what I've been doing. Working here. Helping.'

A female passed in the airless corridor, her hands were bandaged and her face was bruised. She drifted by without making a sound. Someone used to being invisible.

Simone knocked on the door and entered. A girl sat on a bed. When she saw Simone she rushed to her, threw her arms round her and started to cry.

'There, there. It's all right. I told you, you're safe now. They'll never find you.'

She held the terrified creature, whispering reassurance. Whenever she made to leave, panic returned that needed more hugs and more words to calm it.

Simone had those words.

And I began to understand.

***

Simone visited a dozen women, each time replacing fear with hope. There was no need to explain. After two hours, she said, 'Only one more.'

As a man, I had nothing to contribute. I stood in the narrow corridor; awkward and self-conscious while women hurried past, their eyes averted. Silent women who'd suffered more than I could imagine. Perhaps there was a way to help. Simone said the refuge and others like it survived without government assistance. Publicity was the key. The world was awash with money looking for a home. If I wrote about it, shone a spotlight, surely people would respond?

Across the corridor, a door was open. A female with her back to me held a sobbing girl, patiently wiping her tears.

'How long can I stay?'

'As long as you like.'

'Forever?'

'Forever is a long time, Daliya'

The name struck a chord and made me give her a second look. Quasim's wife huddled on the edge of the bed – the thinnest person I'd ever seen. Dead eyes in an emaciated face. Dangerously undernourished. Anaemic, like 97.4 percent of her sisters in Pakistan. She was frail and wasted, but the mute Chandra Dilawar Hussein would have traded places with her. This was the long game Simone's father had believed in and I'd discovered how true that sometimes was. At least Daliya could have a life.

The comforter gave her a hug and left, pausing to glance into the room where Simone knelt with yet another victim. She heard a frightened voice ask 'Why are you here?' and stopped to listen to the reply.

'To make certain you're all right.'

'And am I?'

'You will be. In time.'

'Are you a doctor?'

'Yes.'

'What's your name?'

'Just call me Simone.'

***

'So now you know, some of it anyway.'

'There's more?'

'A lot more.'

The car edged through the late-afternoon traffic. Lahore was like any city; it took patience to survive it. 'My first thought was to offer my services as a doctor to the refuge.' Simone pulled cigarettes from a pocket, lit one and exhaled a blue cloud into the air. 'That was the plan, but it wasn't enough. Not nearly enough. When Priya asked me, I didn't hesitate.'

'What did she ask?'

'To become more involved. To make a difference.'

'How?'

'By helping to free those who were in chains. Sometimes the chains actually existed. Sometimes they were psychological, though just as binding.'

I marvelled at her courage, awed by her commitment. 'What did you do?'

'What I've been doing for more than two months. Helping the fortunate few make their break for freedom. I've been a part of it.'

She stopped talking. Outside Lahore passed, gaudy and noisy. 'It's dangerous, very dangerous. If we're caught…'

Simone let the consequences stay unnamed.

'I'm afraid. Terrified. I can't do it anymore. I told Priya I can't go on. I feel I've let them down. All those women. There has to be another way to help.'

Tears welled in her eyes. 'I'm a coward, Ralph. I talk – oh yes, I can talk – but when it comes to really giving…' She looked away, ashamed.

I took her hands in mine. 'Simone, there are other ways. Let's find them together.'

***

The last months had aged Jameel. He was travelling early towards middle age. His friend saw the change. Gulzar's death had been a blow, and his fears and hopes for the girl he loved and lost were too much to bear. He conjured a welcome from nothing.

'Ali. Good to see you. How are you? How's everything?'

Ali hadn't seen his friend since the funeral and hid his surprise at the difference. Jameel's eyes were dull, his skin was lined and there was grey in the hair. Grief was a terrible thing. 'Fine, Jameel. And you?'

Jameel lied. 'Better.'

'Well,' Ali braced himself, 'I had an idea Afra may have been injured and asked at the hospitals in the city. A nurse overheard.' Jameel tensed. 'Her name is Idris Phadkar. She met a woman called Afra a year ago.'

'Afra's a common name. It may not have been the same one.'

Ali leaned closer: this was hard for him. 'Her name was Afra. From Mundhi village. Jameel. The woman she met was your Afra.'

we must have the world the way we wish it and when we find it isn't we're disappointed

afraid like you are now

'She was brought to Lahore. Her path was very different from yours.'

Jameel closed his eyes, his lips trembled. 'Tell me.'

***

No one noticed the woman walking towards the vehicle. Her dress was like many in the city, from head to foot in black. One hand held her niqab in place so even her eyes were veiled. In the other hand, a sack drawn together by string dangled from her fingers. She approached the car and opened the back door. It wasn't locked. She placed the sack on the floor behind the driver's seat and pulled the drawstrings apart, then swept a hand down her arm and tossed a bangle on the back seat.

In moments, she was swallowed by the crowd.

***

'Fucking accountants.' Quasim fumed. What did they know? What had they ever risked? Nothing.

'The house will need to be sold, Mr Dilawar Hussein. The insurance doesn't begin to cover the loss.'

'My mother lives in that house. She's old and ill.'

Quasim was ashamed to hear himself pleading with this fool.

The accountant was unmoved. 'No matter, you'll have to find alternative accommodation for her, your creditors will demand the property be released.'

The Dilawar Hussein family had dealt with this firm for years. Today, that counted for little. Quasim's frustration crystallised into hatred for this man, so calm, laying the unpleasant reality of his life before him. 'Mr Dilawar Hussein, do you have any idea how high your debts are?'

'No'

'Neither do I. That's how bad the situation is. Your creditors are baying like wolves.'

Quasim spat. 'Jackals!'

'You owe them money. In some cases, a lot of money. The property will be sold, sooner rather than later. I'm sorry.'

At the car, there was no sign of the young footballers. Quasim started the engine and pulled away, too preoccupied to notice the bangle on the back seat, or anything else.

***

The telephone rang. I was expecting the call. It was McArthur.

'Ralph?

'Hi, Andrew.'

'Hey Ralph, got the copy. Love it, really love it.'

'Thank you.'

In spite of everything, McArthur was a fan. He'd okayed most of my requests and backed my judgement when others wouldn't. Apart from the final few episodes, he'd rarely been disappointed. 'Behind the Veil. The truth's the truth. Right?'

'The piece – '

'Series.'

I compromised. 'What it'll highlight is barbaric behaviour.'

'Yeah, yeah, yeah. Just keep it coming, Ralph, that's all.'

'I intend to.'

'And what about the killings? How's that going?'

'A work in progress. Bit like myself.'

'Ok. Good. Maybe it's time you came back to London, eh?'

'I'll think about it, Andrew.'

Early evening in Pakistan is a beautiful time. In the kitchen, Simone cooked dinner wearing one of my shirts over blue jeans. She looked wonderful. I'd told McArthur I'd think about a move. Maybe I would. But not yet.

Chapter 35

Quasim sat in traffic trying to make some sense of what his life had become.

Things had never been better until that woman reappeared. He should have dealt with her himself instead of trusting his idiot cousin. An image of Bilal hanging from the ceiling got no sympathy from him, only a deepening disgust that their blood was in any way the same. And his brothers, Zamir and Firdos, could they really have been cut from the same staff? He needed a plan. A plan for Quasim.

To begin, his mother and sister required care. For certain, he wouldn't be involved, he'd find another Daliya – one of the first things he'd do.

Loneliness settled over him. But he wasn't alone.

The bangle stayed where it had been left, it didn't move.

The sack on the floor did.

***

The city crowded in on him. He had to get away, even for an hour or two. He needed to think. There was a way. Of course, there was a way. He reminded himself that he was the one who had taken the small business his father left and built it into an enterprise worth something.

do you have any idea how high your debts are?

Quasim smiled; his confidence grew. Traffic thinned. He had told the buffoon of a policeman he'd see him at the station – a waste of time – he couldn't be bothered. Soon he'd be in the country, away from his troubles.

Zamir had lived consumed with resentment. Quasim, on the other hand, had made his own opportunities, took risks, rode his luck and grown the business beyond anything his father ever dreamed. That was the part his jealous brother missed. Quasim had been given a chance. He was the one who'd capitalised the inheritance, manipulated the openings, worked long and hard, until he owned what his brother would never own.

And he could do it again.

When the car cleared the outskirts of Lahore, Quasim pointed it south, passing fields where families tended crops. The afternoon sun shone on them; they seemed content. Some were meant to toil. Others – like him – were fitted for better things. Quasim Dilawar Hussein started to feel better. He was enjoying himself.

The big vehicle hovered over the highway and glided across the rougher surfaces of the minor roads. Why hadn't he done more of this, just for the freedom of it? When fortune returned, as it surely would, he'd set aside time for Quasim.

He drove on, across the fertile plains. It was warm in the car, Quasim felt pleasantly tired: a good feeling. On the passenger seat something caught his eye. A minute later a movement on the edge of his vision made him look again. Nothing. He took his attention back to the road. What a peaceful scene, what a marvellous country to live in, and less than an hour from the city.

The snake appeared from behind the upholstery, as if it was playing hide and seek with the driver. A black tongue darted in its mouth. Cold eyes studied Dilawar Hussein.

Daboia. The Lurker.

The brake met the floor and the car slid on squealing rubber, painting a dark streak on the road. Quasim was frozen with fear. The snake slithered on the seat next to him and prepared to strike.

The BMW juddered to a halt. Quasim groped for the handle and jerked the door open. Before he could get out, the second snake rose between his legs, head weaving from side to side. He saw the three rows of dark brown patches bordered with yellow, the flickering tongue and the fangs.

He tried to scream. A strangled gurgle was all that came. His chest tightened. He couldn't breathe. His eyes bulged.

The Russell's Viper and the heart attack struck together. With lightning speed, the other snake added its venom. But Quasim Dilawar Hussein was already dead.

***

A fatality on a country road, miles from the city, couldn't be expected to concern detective Jan Asmet Rana in Lahore. It became his business when the identity of the driver was established. And when a policeman at the scene found the wooden bangle in the back of the vehicle, his involvement was guaranteed.

***

I looked at the writing on the screen in front of me. Words, lots of words, beginning with the eye-catching heading *Revenge in Lahore!* and the strapline *Someone Knows*. But words weren't the same as the truth and the proof, the absolute proof, was missing. What I had was enough to make trouble, to create a stir, though it wasn't enough to go with. It was also libellous, I was certain of that.

A work in progress, that's what I'd told McArthur, and I was right. Somewhere along the way, I'd traded my humanity for a place in the sun. Except that was the old Ralph. The new me treaded more carefully, the reason I hesitated signing off on the article. I read the text and the edits, thinking about Jo-Jo, and Tony Fascionni, Stanley Dow, Lonnie Harper and all the people I'd let down chasing "the story".

The article was in four parts. One and two majored on the crimes. Three and four suggested a prominent Lahore businessman was the killer. But Hafeez wasn't a bad man, and there was justice to the murders.

I hesitated. McArthur wanted me home, this was my ticket. Back in the game. Back in the black. Everybody's favourite guy. Would that be so wrong?

you must remember you were the star of the show

I could have it all. The same as before. Better than before. My finger hovered above the keyboard. The e-mail address was up, the attachment a little icon at the bottom.

Back in the black. How nice that would feel.

...the star of the show

My hand trembled. Decision time.

Simone called from the kitchen. 'Ralph! Dinner! Remember, we're going out!'

How would I react if she had been abused like Afra? I closed my eyes and stabbed delete.

***

Jameel was behind his desk when Ali knocked and entered. He looked better today, that pleased his friend. Still no wooden jewellery. 'Ali. Sit down.'

'No I won't. I just wanted you to know, Quasim Dilawar Hussein was found dead in his car sixty miles south of Lahore. They think it was a heart attack. A wooden bangle was found on the back seat.'

'Really?'

'Yes. Shakil called to tell me. He'll know more after the autopsy. Want me to call him back?'

Jameel played with the pen in his hand. 'No, leave it. We've got a business to run.'

***

The room was packed with people, most of them smoking.

'All I can tell you is what I know about myself. Nine years in the Fellowship and life is great. But I have to be careful and never forget. I may've got the monkey off my back' he tapped his temple 'but the circus is still in town. Know what I mean? Glad to be here.'

The crowd laughed. They knew exactly what he meant. I noticed a lone figure, unsure, holding back and introduced myself. 'Ralph.'

He hesitated before accepting the handshake and didn't tell me his name. 'First meeting?'

'Yes, it is.'

'What did you think?'

'Don't know,' the stranger said.

'Well, don't judge us on just this one. It worked for me.'

The newcomer eyed me up and down. 'I can see that.'

I took his hand again. 'Keep coming back. Just keep coming back.'

Chapter 36

It was cold in the bus station before sunrise. A dozen diesel engines growled in neutral under a dark sky, waiting to begin the daily exodus from the city. An old couple struggled with two overfilled bags; wherever they were going their world was going with them. The young woman made for the back by the window. Soon after a man got on and sat next to her. They didn't speak. No one did; it was too early for conversation. The burly driver dropped behind the wheel, closed the doors and the bus crept into what remained of the night.

A few drifted to sleep, heads lolling, mouths open, gently tossed by every bump in the road. The woman watched the shadowy landscape pass. The man said, 'Where is this bus going?'

'I don't know. South, I think. It doesn't matter, does it?' She squeezed his hand and whispered. 'Wherever you are I am.'

He whispered in return. 'And wherever I am, you are too.'

They silently watched daylight give form to the world outside. After a while, she reached into her coat pocket and brought out sheets of paper, split and cracked where the folds had been. The doctor's letter lay on top.

Doctor Simone Jasnin had been in the refuge – she'd heard someone ask her name. Strange their paths should cross so close to the end. Fatima wanted to speak, wanted to thank her, but the danger of discovery was too great, and Shafi needed to be protected.

Her eyes moved over the pages, reading words she knew by heart, savouring the contact with the past...

my name was Afra

...following the clean, clear writing through to the end, then, brushing tears away. There would be no more. She had no more.

Her companion was asleep. How good he'd been and how brave though the last months had been difficult for him.

When the letter arrived he'd agreed to everything she felt they must do. The idea had been hers, even the awful symmetry – the acid thrower burned, the strangler hanged, the liar made dumb, and all the gory rest. She'd been driven by revenge, his commitment had a different stamp: to her, always to her. At times, when she'd despaired and lost her nerve, it was his courage that kept them going. And, when there was something no sane person would do, he did it, not her. The day he returned holding the sack with the draw-string top she realised he'd die for her. That thought made her humble, and sad. At night, she heard the price he paid for the bloody violence she had conceived. What had she forced him to become?

But it was over. It had to be.

Yet it had almost ended too soon in Heera Mandi. Hearing Jameel's voice made her want to rush into his arms, beg him to protect her and her brother as he had when the rabid dog threatened them. Instead, she hid, and later, overwhelmed with the past, she'd cried.

Fatima opened the bus window and remembered the cage bird. Freeing it had been a good thing. Afra would have wanted that. Creeping through the Dilawar Hussein house had been frightening. Outside in the street, she imagined she heard it call; a beautiful sound on the midnight air. Perhaps her mind playing a trick.

Her trembling fingers held the pages. The paper, once so clean and fresh, was dirty and worn. Fatima folded the sheets and tore them into ragged squares. Beside her, her brother woke with a start from another bad dream. She stroked his hair to comfort him. He was her responsibility, just as he'd always been.

'I'm sorry. I fell asleep.'

'That's all right, that's okay.'

He shuddered. 'When I close my eyes, I see their faces.'

'I know.'

'What can we do?'

She touched his cheek, feeling him soothe because she was near. 'Accept. Accept, find the shade and live on. We live on, Shafi.'

Fatimah cupped her palm and held it up, opened her hand and released the little cloud of confetti. Fragments fluttered in the draught of the racing vehicle, rising at the beginning of their separate journeys to earth. Some floated longer than the others, riding the current, reaching back towards the city. Back to Lahore.

1998
National Press Awards,
The Dorchester, Mayfair

When the press finds a hero it doesn't hold back. The president's description had me somewhere between a warrior and a saint, praising my commitment to a difficult and dangerous job. I thought of the rally and the woman who set herself on fire; that was commitment. Next thing, I was headed for the stage and everyone was on their feet. Strangers shook my hand. One of them scolded me. 'Should've known you were up to something,' he said. It was the guy from the Pearl hotel, and I still couldn't remember his name.

you were the star of the show

I looked out at my peers and felt a lump in my throat. McArthur led the applause, grinning like the cat that got the cream. Simone clapped and smiled. Surely to Christ I wasn't going to cry?

If I'd learned anything from my last speech it was to keep it short. I thanked my editor for his faith and said I hoped Behind The Veil would raise awareness of the plight of women in Pakistan. No mention of Simone – I'd been warned – and a wise husband listens to his wife.

The next few days would be shopping, a West End show and back to work. McArthur was making noises about my future in London. He was going to be disappointed.

An old pro gave me good advice at the start of my career – the story is always underneath he told me – and he was right.

Sometimes at night, I wonder. Did Jameel's mother make up the tale to console her son? Or could the bangles really have the power to help lovers find each other?

Then Simone stirs in her sleep beside me, and I know.

Epilogue

Shakil handed his friend a brown paper package held with string.

'You do realise this could cost me my pension, Ali?'

'In another country perhaps, not here in Pakistan. The case is closed and won't be reopened. The detective who investigated it has retired.'

'Evidence is still evidence.'

'Are they all here?'

'Yes. The whole set.'

'Not quite the whole set. But you've done a good thing, tonight.'

***

The car drove through the open gate and up the hill towards the brow. When it stopped, a man got out and walked the few steps to a raised mound of earth no different from many others. He bent and placed a faded red and grey square tied in a parcel next to the simple headstone some unknown hand had etched with a word.

Afra.

Idris had been right, the cemetery behind the hospital was deserted; there were no flowers. Nobody came here. No one cared about this place, so far from Lahore.

He whispered his prayer and returned to the car. As the vehicle pulled away, from the back seat, Jameel spoke to the driver.

'Thank you, Ali. Thank you.'

Out Of The Silence arrived unexpected and unannounced in my life. We were in the Thar Desert, our comfortable bed in the castle at Jaisalmer, left behind. In the distance with the sun setting, nomads raced camels across the dunes like medieval raiders. Nearby, a woman dressed from head to toe in black, had set up a rickety wooden table on the sand. What on earth could she be selling in the middle of nowhere? As it turned out, salt. A veil covered her face making it impossible to tell her age, but she moved like a girl in her teens. Christine bought a small bag from her, carefully weighed against a grubby collection of old spark plugs in the other pan of a rusty scale. When she paid, the girl's almond eyes lit up; underneath her hijab she was smiling. That was the first time I met Afra. But it wouldn't be the last.

Back in Scotland with winter knocking on the door, we often remembered the galloping silhouettes against the never-ending sky and the lone salt-seller, quietly going about her business, asking ourselves what became of her. Had the camel race been a performance by some young man to impress her? Were they in love? Perhaps they were still there – poor but happy. Or was she destined to abandon her stall among the dunes for a different future? The idea for the book sprang from one such conversation.

Acknowledgements

Out Of The Silence arrived unexpected and unannounced in my life. We were in the Thar Desert, our comfortable bed in the castle at Jaisalmer, left behind. In the distance with the sun setting, nomads raced camels across the dunes like medieval raiders. Nearby, a woman dressed from head to toe in black had set up a rickety wooden table on the sand. What on earth could she be selling in the middle of nowhere? As it turned out, salt. A veil covered her face making it impossible to tell her age, but she moved like a girl in her teens. Christine bought a small bag from her, carefully weighed against a grubby collection of old spark plugs in the other pan of a rusty scale. When she paid, the girl's almond eyes lit up; underneath her hijab she was smiling. That was the first time I met Afra. But it wouldn't be the last.

Back in Scotland with winter knocking on the door, we often remembered the galloping silhouettes against the never-ending sky and the lone salt-seller, quietly going about her business, asking ourselves what became of her. Had the camel race been a performance by some young man to impress her? Were they in love? Perhaps they were still there – poor but happy. Or was she destined to abandon her stall among the dunes for a different future? The idea for the book sprang from one such conversation.

Out Of The Silence is unlike anything else I've written. The story came to me almost whole, how it would end as clear as the Rajasthan horizon that day: a harrowing account of twisted notions of honour answered with pitiless revenge delivered from the heart. Over time India became Pakistan, the Great Thar Desert morphed into rural Punjab and the city of Lahore, and I realised Out Of The Silence was more than just a murder mystery.

Along the way, many people – too many to mention – encouraged me. I'd like to acknowledge the team at Bloodhound Books, especially Alexina – she knows why. My editors John Hodgman and Ben Adam, and the many authors and experts whose insight helped me to better understand a culture which was and in large part remains, alien to me.

As ever, my wife played a huge part in creating, developing and shaping the final tale. Where would I be without her? Thanks, Christine.

Things may have improved in that part of the world since I came across the girl in the sands. For Afra and the millions of Afras I hope so, I really do. Today more than ever, it seems we are awash in iniquity to the point where reading the news is best avoided. But now and then, something restores our faith and allows us to believe the forces for good are still out there, fighting against the darkness threatening to engulf us. Although it is a work of fiction, my sincere wish is that this book is one of them.

Owen Mullen
Crete, November 2018